HEART OF ICE

H.M. MCKAIN

ISBN 978-1-3999-5737-3

Cover design & typesetting by Raspberry Creative Type

To my mum and dad
– always with me

CONTENTS

PROLOGUE

The car was just mangled metal, difficult to tell what make, its front embedded in a knarled old oak tree, sheltering in a dip from the harsh winds blowing in from the North Sea. It lay alone, its wheels spinning with nowhere to travel.

The silence broken only by the sound of the sea crashing on the deserted beach, the stretch of road heading out of Wick in the north of Scotland was empty in the minutes before sunrise. Then a vehicle stopped and a woman got out, dressed in a long black coat with her straggly brown hair done up in rough bun.

She saw a young woman, her head motionless against the steering wheel of the crashed car, her long blonde hair falling over her face.

CHAPTER ONE

17 years later.

It's funny how life can change in a minute.

It happened to Morgan Cooper as she was getting ready for work. Busy drying her hair and thinking what she could wear: was she in any meetings? Did she need a suit or a dress? Did she have clean tights? She really should plan what to wear the night before, hearing her mother's voice in her head admonishing her for not preparing.

While she was getting ready, her mind kept drifting to more pleasant things, like meeting her partner for dinner at the local Italian restaurant and getting a chance to talk about holidays and meeting up with friends.

Looking forward to getting away from Edinburgh to Galloway with Max next weekend. She hadn't seen much of him recently and he seemed to be out a lot more. Perhaps this break would be the time they needed together. They were both so busy all the time – she a communications director for a power company – rushing about trying to be important and cope with the stresses of life. It was not even the middle of the week yet and another difficult Wednesday lay ahead with meeting after meeting. Max was a professor at a university, always respectable and safe to be around.

It had been five years with Max, great to start with, the constant sex and touching and staring into each other's eyes, the finding out about each other. Then – she wasn't sure when – it started to get a bit less exciting. Perhaps that's what happens when you love someone, when you become comfortable with each other? Did she still love him?

This was all going round and round in her mind as she went through the motions of getting the work face ready and checking the clock. Yes: plenty of time. Max had been away early and hadn't even had breakfast. He'd shouted that he would grab a coffee on the way to the University.

At their last dinner together, things had seemed strained between them. They usually talked nine to the dozen. But at that last meal, Morgan had been a bit surprised when he'd started talking about how he loved Facebook and Instagram. She was more unsure of social media and it was part of her job and at home she preferred to keep in touch with friends by meeting them and talking to them. They seemed different people that night and Morgan wondered if she really knew him. Do you really know someone? She shrugged and took a last look in the mirror as she got ready to leave. Yes, she looked ready to face the public: her short blonde hair tidy and make up ok.

It was then she noticed Max had left his mobile on the kitchen table. Strange, that mobile was never out of his sight.

He'll come back to get it, she thought. Just when she was wondering whether to call his work to let him know he'd left it behind, the phone gave a ping. Morgan wasn't sure why she picked it up and looked at the message. But she did.

And in that moment her life as she knew it, changed.

It was a text with a picture of breasts and a message – 'thanks Max for an awesome night. These babies are waiting for you. Suz.'

Morgan threw the phone down as if it was contaminated. Her mind was racing: this couldn't be happening. Max was a quiet, loving man who never even looked at other women when they were out. After what seemed like a lifetime of being with unreliable men, it was what attracted her.

She felt dizzy and clutched the side of the kitchen island. She couldn't stop her thoughts from tumbling over each other. Max Fraser, respected professor of ancient history at one of Scotland's top universities. Boring, some of her friends said. A bit older than her, he was 37 and she thought more sensible.

She looked again. She had no idea who Suz was, but she felt bile rising in her throat as she thought – why has Max got involved in this kind of sleaze? It must be a mistake. She thought it strange the message had come by text.

Her first thought was *Run*. That was always her first thought. If it gets difficult get away. She'd run away from her family when her mum died and moved 300 miles north. You can cope on your own, she thought. Even although she had moved in with Max, she still had her old flat in Edinburgh, rented out, as security.

She seemed rooted to the spot staring at the phone. Then she heard the front door opening and saw Max standing there. Everything seemed to be happening in slow motion and when she looked at his face it was just like it must have been when he was a wee boy caught with his hand in the cookier jar- guilty.

He spoke first: 'Oh Morgan, you've seen it. I'm sorry.'

'Sorry? What's going on Max?' Morgan could hear her voice almost screeching. It didn't sound like her. Max made no move to come towards her.

'Give me a hug please and tell me this is just a dream,' she thought. But his face told her it was true.

'How long has this been going on Max?' she could hear the anger in her voice. 'How could you be so bloody stupid? I thought you loved me. How long have you been seeing this woman?'

He came over and picked up the phone.

'Listen it was just one mad night and I regret it, but I didn't mean for you to find out. It was stupid. I need to get to the university now. Can we talk about this tonight?'

'Talk about what? You obviously saw this message on your Ipad. I wasn't meant to see it and you don't seem surprised by it. How do you know her? This young girl,' she stressed.

'She's one of my students. Look I can explain but I need to get to work and think. Can we not talk tonight?'

Morgan struggled to speak: 'One of your students? God you are stupid. You can't ignore this. She could have told her friends, put it in social media, told your colleagues and the whole university will find out that you slept with one of your students. I assume this happened last Friday when you didn't seem to come home. You seem to have broken the cardinal sin of all university lecturers and broken my heart as well. Well done Max. I hope it was worth it.'

She looked him straight in the eye as she said: 'I'm not going to be here tonight, Max. I can't go to work now and concentrate. I need a few days by myself and perhaps then we can talk. I am not sure what you've got involved in but I don't want to deal with it just now.'

'Where are you going? What about your work?' Max was clearly in a bit of a state and the questions came one after another. Morgan was trying to stay calm.

'I'm going to go that place we were booked to go this weekend in Galloway. I will call work and take some holiday and ring the bed and breakfast and change our booking. We can talk but I think some miles between us would be good just now.'

Max sounded cold and had a look on his face, unlike anything Morgan had ever seen before, saying: 'Ok. You do what you think you need to do.' He turned and slammed the door behind him.

Morgan stood stunned for a few minutes and decided to go out for a coffee, make calls and plan what she could do.

It was only as she took a seat in a quiet corner of the café that she realised she was crying.

Perhaps it's a joke and he can explain it all. Do I trust him? Is this an affair or just a one night stand? He's been out a lot more recently and last Friday was a leaving do, the third one in the last four weeks.

She seemed incapable of doing anything but sit with a cold coffee in front of her.

Morgan lived with Max in the first floor flat in the west end of Edinburgh he'd owned for 10 years. As soon as she moved in three years ago, she'd fallen in love with the big rooms and the feeling of space. It felt like home and they hadn't talked of moving. She was in her mid-twenties when she'd met Max and he'd fallen in love with her, he said, because of how she made everything fun. She'd been a real party girl then.

She was 30 now and taking a mirror from her bag to check how she looked she saw her reflection: she looked just the same, short blonde hair, blue eyes, bit swollen with crying, but she looked just like she always did: confident and bright. Perhaps he just didn't find her fun any more?

Pushing the untouched coffee aside, she glanced at her watch. Grabbing her bag, she pushed her way through the knot of people queuing for drinks and went back up to the flat. As she opened the door, she half expected to find Max there ready to hug her and tell her he loved her and that everything was going to be ok. But the flat was empty and the rooms silent.

It must have been an hour later she pulled her forehead gently from the pane of the window where she'd been standing, waiting for his car to pull up. It had been sixty minutes of rehearsing what she'd say, rewriting it over and over in her head. But now, she'd had her fill of waiting. Full of sudden and unexpected energy she went into the kitchen to get herself a glass of water. *Enough. I need to get right away to think.* Back in the living room she returned to her place at the window, phone in hand. Ironically, now she was checking to make sure he wasn't about to return. It only took a moment to call work and explain that she needed a week off to attend to some family issues. Carol, the chief executive's right-hand woman, had been sympathetic.

'Of course, that's no problem, Morgan, I'll let the boss know and he'll call you if there is any problem,' she'd said warmly. 'Just call us if you need more time.'

That, she thought, would give her space to think and get some perspective. At the moment she wasn't even sure if there was a relationship to return to. But she would have to face Max at some point, and there might be a simple explanation. *Yeah right.*

Next call was to the bed and breakfast they'd booked to change the reservation from two to just one. She also booked it from that night and said she would stay up to five days. They were busy but her booking was good. Something was going right.

She opened her wardrobe and looked with a critical eye at what she could take with her. Not her usual work clothes, obviously. It was the end of March but it was also Scotland. She'd better take clothes for any eventuality. In the end she grabbed a black cashmere polo neck that went well with her short hair and a bright red wool jumper she'd invested in from a boutique in the West End.

Some thermal vests with some casual jeans, and she

decided to pack her new red tartan trousers. Just in case she got lucky with the weather she also put in a new green silk shirt. She had bought it for a meal out with Max. *Not needed now*, she thought.

Although it was nearly Spring it still felt cold. She grabbed a warm padded jacket. She also had a fleece and a warm hat in the boot of her car for emergencies.

Dropping her bag by the door, she returned to the living room to leave Max a note. 'Max, managed to get in touch with that bed and breakfast and booked for a few days.'

She was pleased that her writing was firm and clear. 'I'll call you when I can and text when I arrive.'

Am I shutting the door on my life with Max? Should I stay and listen to his explanation? Common sense was urging her to, but that was the adult Morgan. The child in her said run and get time to think.

She loved her car. The BMW three series estate felt like home when she settled into the bucket seats. It was a great driving car and despite being upset she looked forward to the drive on the coastal road as the car hugged the corners and the gear change felt right.

She felt strangely detached, driving the car, from what had just happened. It was almost as if by leaving the flat she'd gained more control.

The drive would take a few hours, but already she could feel her spirits lifting. She left Edinburgh under a dull and cloudy sky, but by the time she got to the Ayrshire coast the sea was shining blue and calm, the sun glinting on the waves that splashed on the rocky foreshore.

She stopped at a spot just past Turnberry to look at the grey seals sunning themselves on the rocks. She could see hundreds of birds feeding close to edge. In the distance the granite island of Ailsa Craig shimmered in the sun, looking like a giant Christmas pudding. She must have sat for about

20 minutes feeling the wintry sun on her face and decided she needed a coffee.

She reached Girvan quickly, it was only another hour till she reached Portpatrick but she needed a boost.

She found a car park on the shore and parked up.

There was a mobile coffee van and she bought a latte and sat in the car looking at the sea. Just as she was enjoying the view an old camper type van pulled in front of her blocking her view. *I should have parked there myself*, she thought.

The back of the van was covered in stickers and Morgan spent a few minutes looking at the badges for the Camper Van association, the National Trust, and many more. It looked about 30 years old and on its last legs.

A few minutes passed before she realised that she was almost in a trance watching the van. She couldn't snap out of it. Her coffee was growing cold in her lap, and although she could hear the voice in her head saying *Get back on the road!* loud and clear, she stayed where she was. She couldn't stop thinking about the text to Max with the breasts and she couldn't get the image out of her head. The image of a naked Max in bed with a young student kept playing, it wasn't useful thinking.

Watching the van kept her mind off everything else. She saw the back door of the camper open and a beautiful looking young girl with long brown hair, step out. She was wearing strangely old- fashioned clothes. Strange outfit for a young girl, Morgan thought. The girl stood for a few minutes watching the sea and then turned as an older man with long grey hair and a woman got out of the front seats of the camper van and joined her. They set off to walk along the coastal path.

Morgan watched them for a few minutes, taking her mind off Max and reminding her it was time to get on the road again.

It was after lunch when Morgan arrived in Portpatrick – too early to check in, she took the car down to the village, parked up and went for a walk.

The village looked a bit like Cornwall, she thought. A harbour with some small fishing boats tied up, a couple of smart looking yachts and a lifeboat. It was surrounded by hills. A large hotel stood on one cliff and big houses seemed to sit above the village. That will be where my bed and breakfast place is, she surmised.

Walking along the shorefront watching a fisherman bringing in his lobster catch, Morgan felt herself relax, almost forgetting why she was there alone, she was just a tourist, looking for a place to eat. The sun was shining and not a cloud in the sky.

She bought a newspaper and found a coffee shop. She'd switched her mobile off while she was driving and resisted the urge to switch it on. She didn't feel like talking to Max or anyone else.

The coffee shop was quiet. Just Morgan, a man on his own and a couple sitting in the corner huddled together.

She sat quietly, relishing the peace. But it wasn't long before a blonde thirty-something woman she took to be the owner brought her coffee and, despite Morgan pointedly giving her full attention to the paper, started talking to her.

'Are you down on holiday?' she asked. Morgan, looked up. 'Yes just a few days,' she smiled, hoping that was the end of it.

'Well,' said the woman, 'I hope the weather's ok. Snow's been forecast but the village usually misses it because of the gulf stream and in the ten years I've been here we've never had much. It was a bad summer last year for tourists and we need good weather for the season to get the most out of it.'

'I'm sure it's a struggle,' Morgan agreed, in as sympathetic a voice as she could find. The woman wasn't to know that Morgan just wanted to be left alone. She was tired, the drive and the drama had drained her.

She finished her coffee and glanced at her watch. She still couldn't check into the bed and breakfast for another hour and as she looked out of the window the sun was sparkling on the choppy sea. A walk around the harbour was just what she felt like doing. Wrapping her scarf around her face she stepped out and began walking briskly.

Just then a fishing boat started to come into the harbour and as Morgan stopped to watch she felt a presence beside her.

'Hello,' It was a deep, male voice. 'You here on business or holiday?'

Morgan turned her head to be met by what looked like a caricature of what she always thought a fisherman should look like. Big bushy beard, wild hair and a ruddy complexion, dressed in overalls and a hat that looked like it had been on his head for decades. She dreaded to think what was underneath it.

For the first time that day Morgan felt herself smile. 'Hi,' she replied. 'I'm just down for a few days' holiday.'

The man stuck out a big hand and introduced himself.

'Hi. I'm Tam Mitchell, harbour master and lifeboat captain.'

She shook his hand and almost winced. It was like being clasped by a giant. She saw him glance at her left hand. Checking for a wedding ring?

'Hello, I'm Morgan, pleased to meet you,' she grinned. He still had hold of what looked like her tiny hand in his big paw.

'Where are you staying?' Tam then asked. 'It's still early

in the season and people haven't really started arriving yet – if they ever do.'

Morgan told him about her booking at Seaview Bed and Breakfast.

Tam gave a knowing nod: 'That's a good place. Mike and Mary have been running it for several years. It's actually quite busy this week, I was told. There are a few couples and a family staying and a single man.' He paused, his eyes actually twinkling in the craggy face. 'And you'll be the single woman!'

Morgan felt it was time to move on, pulling her hand free. 'Lovely to meet you Tam but I need to go and check in and have a rest after the drive.'

'Aye lassie enjoy your stay and come and see me if you need anything. I have my "office" at the harbour most days or in the pub on the corner.' Tam sauntered off leaving Morgan to continue her walk.

Back in the car Morgan sat for a few minutes, soaking up the view and letting the sea air and the whole experience relax her and lift her spirits. Her thoughts turned to Max and what the future might be for them. That is, if they had one – worryingly, she wasn't sure if either of them wanted one. Perhaps I'm not meant to be with anyone, she thought.

She had been on her own for three years before she met Max. When she moved in with him, she'd kept her old flat and she had a tenant in and it would take time to sort out... *Stop it! It hasn't got to that stage yet. It might be a big misunderstanding and Max can explain it.* But she still didn't switch on her mobile.

She really did feel as if she'd left the city and her life there. She focused her attention on the wave-battered rocks and the little strip of beach which gleamed in the sunshine, watching seabirds scavenge on the sand.

Morgan could feel her shoulders drop and realised she'd been hunching them up to her ears with the stress and the driving. It wasn't just Max but her job as well, sitting at a desk all day.

She checked her watch. It was just after 3 pm and Morgan thought check in would be open and she could get to her room for a rest and a cup of tea. Then she remembered. What about dinner? She saw a seafood restaurant 100 yards away and got out of the car to see if anyone was in to book for 6.30p.m. That way she could eat and leave before the restaurant got busy and she had to talk to anyone.

The Lobster Pot had lights on, and when she rang the bell, a young man came to the door. She explained she was visiting. Could she have a table in a quiet area about 6.30pm?

'Yes, of course,' he said.

Feeling pretty organised and pleased with herself Morgan found the SeaView Bed and breakfast up on the hill above the village and parked in the adjacent car park. There was just one other car, a large black Jaguar.

Before she had a chance to ring the bell, the door was opened by another tall man. This village seemed full of them, Morgan thought.

'Hello!' he greeted her. 'I'm Mike, the owner. You must be Ms Cooper? Welcome to Seaview and the village.'

Morgan was glad to get into her room and away from the curiosity that was already beginning to grate on her nerves. *Where are you from? Are you on holiday? Are you seeing old friends?*

It seemed as if everyone wanted to know her business, and after living in the city for so long she'd become used to being anonymous. All these questions had begun to make her uncomfortable.

Now she wondered if she was just too touchy. Her life had been so busy, working long hours, rarely going out at night because she was so tired and spending the Saturdays recovering from the week and Sunday preparing for the next week.

Mike had told her that there was another single room occupied, as well as three couples staying at the moment. He'd told her that one couple had been coming for the last few years.

She made a cup of tea and lay on the bed. She must have been exhausted because when she woke up it felt like late afternoon and her tea was cold. She must have been asleep for an hour. *She decided to switch on her mobile before she took a shower. Then she would go down to the village to eat.*

The phone sprang into life- seven missed calls from Max and a message. She would call Max after a shower. As she passed the window she glanced down into the carpark. There was the large black Jag she'd seen earlier, and, sitting next to it, a camper van. It was too dark to see it properly but for a moment she thought it looked just like the one she'd seen on the journey down.

Once she had showered Morgan felt stronger, and calmer than she'd felt all day.

She switched on her phone again and listened to Max's message.

'Morgan I just need to know you're safe. Have you arrived at the village? Let me know you are all right. I love you.'

She sat on the bed to call him back. 'Hi Max. I got here safely and had a good drive down. Are you ok?'

There was a silence and then Max started to speak. 'I've been sent home this afternoon. I was at the University and summoned to a meeting with the human resources people. It seems that an image was also sent to the University.'

'Oh my God Max that sounds serious. What on earth has happened? I just saw that text and assumed the worst, I am afraid. I didn't even want to hear your excuses.'

'No excuses. I was stupid Morgan. I went to the pub with all my students and got a bit drunk and ended up back at the flat of one of them. I am not proud of myself but I was going to tell you all about it. Then this image was sent. I don't who sent it. I can't think it's this girl Suzy, she's gone home to her parents in Skye. Everyone seems to know what I did. The University are talking of calling in the police.'

'Max I'm not perfect but going to the home of a student, a very attractive student, after too much to drink and staying the night is just asking for trouble.

'It's not the time for recriminations, we need to get this sorted. You're still my best friend. But it doesn't mean I'm ok about it.'

'Morgan, this is nothing to do with you. Well not much. I just felt lonely. You're always working and then if not working too tired to talk or go out. Then, do you remember that meal we went out for a few weeks ago? I asked you what you thought of our future and if we would marry and have kids someday. You said you weren't planning on having children, you wanted a career. I was stunned and not sure we were on the same wavelength. We haven't really talked much since then. This girl just gave me lots of attention and I must say I liked it. She made me feel special and alive. Stupid I know, but it's done now.'

'I know you don't mean it Max but it sounds like you're blaming me for you spending the night with one of your students. When you asked about the future I was taken by surprise. I think it was instinctive reaction as just now I couldn't think of having children and balancing a job working long hours. It doesn't mean I don't love you and want a future together.

'Look, this isn't the sort of thing we should be talking about on a phone. I'm going to stay here for a few days and think things through. But keep in touch and let me know what is happening. You will get through this Max. Speak soon and take care.'

Morgan sat on the edge of the bed trying to work through in her mind what she had just heard. She must have sat staring into space for about 30 minutes when she heard a noise outside and got up to look. Another car had come into the car park. Then she felt her stomach rumbling. She needed food.

She looked in her case and found fresh jeans and a jumper. It felt cold.

The restaurant was right at the harbour. It was painted white with black windows. Inside was dominated by a giant fire with the surround covered with lots of brasses.

Morgan was given a small table at the window. She ordered and looked around. There was just one other table occupied. *It was a dark-haired man in his mid thirties, casual in jeans and a jumper. He was studying his Ipad.*

The food was delicious. She rounded the meal off by ordering a coffee and then planned to walk back to the bed and breakfast to read and get a good sleep.

Just then she noticed the man at the other table get up and come towards her.

'Hi,' he said. 'I recognised you from the bed and breakfast. You're staying there too, aren't you?'

Morgan was a bit taken aback. He looked very tall. It didn't help that as she stared at his big brown eyes and smile, she found herself struggling to say anything. It had been a long time since a man had smiled at her like that.

'Yes,' she mumbled.

'Can I join you?' He held out a hand. 'My name's Cameron Steel. I'm here for a few days.'

He just seemed to glide into the chair next to her and she could feel herself smile at him. Careful Morgan, she thought, he's just being friendly.

She said she was down for a few days rest and needed to escape from work.

Cameron nodded. 'I'm here for the funeral of my aunt in Stranraer and the village was a good place to stay.'

Morgan mumbled her condolences in a way that she hoped sounded sincere, but he was still confiding.

'I work in security consultancy, mostly in the London area, and before that worked at the Met. I drove up early today,' he smiled. Before she had a chance to respond, he had started to rise from the table. 'I thought we could walk back to the bed and breakfast together? I haven't seen anyone else although the owners said they were expecting more people to arrive.'

As they left the pub the cold air hit them. There was a bright moon shining on the sea. It looked very cold. The sound of the sea was almost hypnotic and neither of them said anything.

Morgan said: 'Do you mind if we walk up the main street and the big hill to the bed and breakfast? I don't fancy the cliff walk in near darkness.'

Cameron nodded: 'Yes good idea. The sea and the sky look a bit threatening. It's absolutely freezing. I thought it would be slightly warmer at the end of March.'

As they walked Cameron told her more about the village and its reliance on tourism and fishing. He told of growing up in Stranraer and leaving to join the police when he was 17.

It seemed to just take a few minutes to reach the bed and breakfast. Morgan wished him good night and went straight to her room.

She slept well and when she got down for breakfast and opened the dining room door the dining room was quite full. There were two other couples sitting at opposite ends of the small room and Morgan looked around to find her table at the window.

She didn't like to stare but stole a furtive look at the other two couples. One was a middle-aged couple with walking gear on and a map laid out on the table.

There was another couple. He looked much older and had a leg amputated above the knee with two crutches beside his table.

She saw Cameron at another table deep in thought and wearing a smart suit. She smiled at him and he raised a hand.

Mike came over to ask her if she wanted tea or coffee and anything cooked. She asked for porridge and tea, getting up to fetch some fruit and yoghurt. Just as she was returning to her seat the door opened and a couple with a young girl came in. They nodded at everyone and sat at a table for four. Morgan looked at the tall grey haired man, his wife with her mousey brown hair and the beautiful young girl with them, who Morgan assumed was their daughter, although she didn't look much like either of them. It looked like the family at the car park at Girvan, Morgan thought.

She was enjoying her porridge and watching the sea out of the window when she felt someone beside her table. She looked up, and Cameron was there.

'Hi I'm just off to Stranraer for the funeral. I'll be back this afternoon. Perhaps see you later? Have a good day.'

Back in her room she got her jacket and decided on a long walk across the cliffs. It seemed very cold outside but the sky was clear.

The owner seemed to sense when someone was going out. He asked her what her plans were for the day and if she needed any tourist advice. There are lovely gardens nearby, Mike suggested.

'I'm not feeling like driving today so think I'll just have a long walk and a coffee and then decide what to do in the afternoon. I might sit in your lounge and read a book.'

Mike nodded: 'Sounds good. The weather forecast is warning of snow but says it might come in later but the village is usually very lucky and in all the years I've been here we've never had much.'

'It feels cold enough,' said Morgan, 'but I'm not that worried. I have a few days here so it will pass by then and I have some good books to read. I was hoping for a quiet time anyway.'

She started along the road towards the cliffs but turned back. It was such a bitter wind she could feel the cold piercing her head and decided she needed her hat from the boot of the car.

The walk was just what she needed, a bracing wind and no one around. Her thoughts went to Max and for the first time she realised that perhaps all was not right in their relationship.

In the last few months, they had barely seen each other during the week.

Morgan walked for more than two hours across the cliffs to a lovely wood where the trees were bent away from the sea at right angles as if they wanted to escape the incessant wind. They were almost bent double, gnarled and their growth stunted, looking like old men struggling against life. The sea looked pretty rough and the sea birds were being carried on the wind screeching as they landed on the cliff face.

It was good to walk and have time to think, and she resolved to call Max later. She wandered down to the village and found a coffee shop to have a cappuccino and a sandwich.

When she got back to the bed and breakfast just after

3p.m. the car park was empty except for the camper van and her car.

As she went in the communal lounge door was open and she saw a group of people sitting having tea and shortbread. Morgan wasn't sure why she went in but before she could think, she was inside saying hello to everyone. 'Hi I'm Morgan, here for a few days from the Edinburgh.'

The tall grey haired man was the first to speak: 'I'm Reverend Artemis MacNeill and this is my wife Christine and our daughter, Rebecca.'

They all smiled at Morgan. She sat down and helped herself to some of the homemade shortbread.

Then the other woman, part of the couple, said: 'I'm Mary Benson and this is my husband, Charles. We're down to open up our caravan for the summer season and make sure it's survived the winter. We come most summers and spend several weeks in the village. We usually stay here for a few days each Spring to allow us to get the caravan aired and freshened up and put clean sheets on.'

Morgan said: 'Do people usually come here every year?'

The Rev looked up and seemed to hesitate. 'My wife and I come here every year. We come down from the north to see my family and usually stay here for a few days.'

Morgan looked directly at the young girl.

'Do you like it here Rebecca?'

Morgan noticed she looked at her mother before answering: 'It's lovely. I've been to the village before and usually stay on the family farm but this is the first time I've been allowed to stay here. It's great.'

'Are you at college?' Morgan asked

'Not yet, but that's what I want. I want to go to music school.'

Her mother looked up and said: 'Rebecca plays the violin and everyone who hears her says she has a real talent.'

Morgan said: 'Did Rebecca learn the violin at school?'

Christine shook her head. 'I home schooled Rebecca. She learnt the violin from my family in the Highlands.'

The conversation sort of dried up and Morgan made her excuses to escape to her room. When she got there a note had been slipped under the door. It was from Cameron and suggested they met in the pub around 7p.m.

'Why not?' thought Morgan. She dismissed the thought that she was getting back at Max.

Time for a shower and a rest before I call Max and get down to the pub to meet Cameron.

At about 6.15 she finally switched on her mobile and noticed no more missed calls from Max. She dialled his mobile and he seemed to take ages to answer.

'Hello Morgan,' he finally said. 'It's good to hear from you.

'I understand you are upset. You should never have seen that text. I've done something I'm ashamed of, but being apart has made me realise I would never have done anything if things had been all right between us.'

Morgan said: 'But you have never said anything about things not being right. What's going on?'

Max said: 'I'm not sure what's happening. I am just waiting to hear from the police and the university. It's all on social media and the students are having a ball making fun of me. It's awful.'

'Oh my God Max. What a mess. What are you going to do? Is there anywhere you can go for a few days? What about your brother?'

Max said: 'I'll let you know as soon as I know Morgan. I'm going to go now. Speak soon.' Morgan was amazed at this new cold, matter of fact Max.

Just before 7p.m she left her room and made her way downstairs. She was deep in thought, replaying the conversation with Max. She felt powerless to help and part of her didn't want to. This was his mess to clear up.

She noticed the walking couple still in the lounge. She waved at them and they both smiled back. The camper van family were nowhere to be seen but she noticed the van still in the car park. And there was no sign of the bed and breakfast host Mike.

It was starting to get dark and when she opened the door it was bitterly cold. She could see the stars and the cold seem to catch her throat as she walked down the hill to the harbour.

It took just five minutes to get to the pub and Cameron was already at a table near the wood burner.

'Hi,' he said. 'Let me take your coat. It's freezing. I hope it's not going to snow as I have to get back to London soon and work.'

Morgan felt she should ask about the funeral. 'How did the funeral go?'

'It was fine: another funeral of an aunt I hadn't really seen for about 10 years. It was good to catch up with all the family though. That seems to be the only time I see people these days with work and living in London.'

Morgan nodded in agreement. 'Work seems to take up all our time these days. It seems to have got busier over the last few years with fewer people doing more work.'

Cameron said: 'What do you do Morgan?'

'I work in communications for a power company. The business is doing well and I enjoy the work but I am starting to feel I have been there too long.'

Cameron asked her where she lived and she explained that she lived in a flat in the centre of Edinburgh with her partner Max. No point of telling him her relationship was shit.

Cameron said he was single after a relationship broke up when his girlfriend got fed up with his working hours and no indication from him when that would change.

'She just got bored and I can't blame her. My job was relentless and now I'm working on my own its still busy. I had to take a week's holiday to get up for the funeral. I am hoping to leave in the next couple of days and stop off on my way back to London at the Lake District.'

Morgan realised she could hardly hear what Cameron was saying. She looked around. In just ten minutes she had been in the pub it had become packed with people. She saw a large noisy crowd at the bar and noticed harbour master Tom holding court at the centre.

Just then Tam looked over, waved and then beckoned them to join them.

'That's Tam the harbour master,' said Morgan. 'I think he wants us to join the group at the bar. Are you ok with that?'

Cameron nodded: 'Don't think we have much choice. It might be fun.'

They got up to move across and Tam's loud booming voice said: 'What are you drinking Morgan and what about your boyfriend?'

'Ha, Ha Tam. This is Cameron, another guest at the bed and breakfast. I'll have a glass of white wine. Thanks'

Cameron said: 'A pint of the local beer would be great thanks.'

Tam then introduced them to all the people in the bar, all seemed to be locals and worked in Stranraer on the ferry or here in the village.

The wine was flowing and Morgan felt a bit lightheaded. She went to sit at a table and within a few minutes Tam joined her.

'These sessions in the pub can get a bit out of hand. But it's the only place people can come and relax with friends.'

Morgan said: 'It's great Tam. A good atmosphere and a lot of fun. Can I ask you a question?'

'Sure,' said Tam.

'Your accent seems slightly different from other people here. Is there a touch of Glaswegian?'

Tam said: 'Yea, spot on. I left Glasgow about 20 years ago to come here. I feel like a local now but I've never lost the Glasgow twang.'

Morgan said: 'Do you still have family there?'

Tam shook his head.

'No, just some distant cousins I never see. This is my home now. I belong here. I came here for the job but I also wanted a new start. I love it here. It's a great place to live. Quiet in the winter but the tourists come in the summer. When I first came here families used to come for a week or a fortnight. Now it's just weekends and the caravans.'

Just then Cameron came back to the table.

'I thought I could drink but they know how to enjoy themselves here. They're a great bunch.'

Tam said: 'I thought you would both be going back to the bed and breakfast and the concert?'

'Concert?' Morgan asked.

'Aye, that young girl Rebecca is apparently going to play her violin for a few people tonight. From what people are saying, she's worth hearing. I heard about it from a couple in a nearby hotel who were going along to hear her.'

Morgan said: 'Actually I feel like getting back. I might be struggling to walk soon if I stay here. We can check it out.'

Cameron said: 'That's fine by me. I might have to drive tomorrow morning and don't want to be over the limit. It's been great fun though Tam. Thanks.'

They waved goodbye to the growing crowd at the bar and walked out into the cold air.

It took just five minutes to get back to the bed and breakfast and even from a distance Morgan could see the lounge lit up and people standing around.

Mike the owner managed to find a space in the lounge for Morgan and Cameron to stand. At one corner Rebecca was sitting playing her violin and Morgan recognised the music as Tchaikovsky. Everyone seemed transfixed by the girl holding the violin. They couldn't take their eyes off her.

As she finished and the applause started Morgan glanced at her mother, sitting beside her and smiling proudly. The Rev was sitting apart watching the other people, it seemed.

Morgan looked around and saw most of the people staying in the bed and breakfast and a few other people who must have come from different hotels.

She glanced at Cameron who mouthed 'wow' and smiled.

It was then as the girl started to play again it came to Morgan where she had seen her before. She signalled to Cameron to come outside.

'I had a funny feeling I'd seen that girl before. I thought it was because I glimpsed her at Girvan when I stopped for coffee. But I've seen her before on Facebook and Tik Tok. The girls in my office are obsessed by her playing. Videos of her playing are posted on Facebook and they call her 'The Celtic Wonder.' I'm sure it's her.'

Cameron said: 'She's amazing. I find her music very moving but that could be the funeral and all the beer I've just had. She has that sort of something special about her.'

At that point they heard applause and then people started to come out of the lounge. It was just after 9p.m.

Morgan went back into the room and found Rebecca putting her violin away.

'Hi Rebecca. That was lovely. I wanted to ask you something. Ok?'

'Yes, of course,' said Rebecca.

'Are you same girl who posts on Facebook under the name 'The Celtic Wonder'?'

Rebecca looked amused and laughed. 'Yes. That's me but I didn't put it on Facebook. That was my cousins in Skye. They recorded me when I was playing and posted it. They record me every time I am with them in the Highlands. My Dad wasn't too pleased.'

Morgan said: 'It's wonderful. Everyone really enjoys hearing you. When did you start playing the violin?'

'About seven years ago. My uncles gave me this violin for a birthday present and I had a lesson every week. They all play musical instruments on Skye. I loved it the moment I touched it and I enjoyed learning to play it. Now I want to go to college to find out if I am good enough to make a career of it.'

'You seem to have a natural talent. Your parents must be so proud of you,' said Morgan. She smiled at the young girl and was struck by how happy she seemed sitting there in her own little world – just her and her violin.

Just then they were interrupted by a smartly dressed middle aged man who said: 'Excuse me interrupting, but my wife and I just wanted to say how special that was to hear you play. It was lovely. My name's Dave Campbell this is my wife Amanda and we're staying in a hotel along the road. I wonder if you can tell me where you learned to play. It was exceptional.'

Rebecca laughed and said: 'I just learned with family in the Highlands. I'm hoping to go to music school.'

Dave Campbell said: 'Is that where you live, in the north?'

Before Rebecca could answer her father suddenly appeared at her side.

'Rebecca – you need to get upstairs and get organised. I am sure these people will understand we have to be somewhere else.'

Rebecca quickly gathered up her violin and case and said quickly 'Sorry, I have to go' before leaving the room.

Everyone seemed deflated when she left and they watched as the Rev and his wife followed.

'Interesting,' said Cameron. 'It seems to me he didn't like Rebecca talking too much.'

'Perhaps they are meeting people. Or perhaps they just want to protect her. She has a prodigious talent and if the reaction in a small room like this is anything to go by, she will get attention. She seems very shy and perhaps they thought it was too much for her,' said Morgan. While Morgan was talking, she noticed Rebecca walking up the stairs. It was then she saw the man Dave Campbell and his wife watching her from the corner of the reception area. They seemed deep in conversation, well he was talking a lot, and just then Morgan heard him say: 'It must be her. It must be.'

His wife looked across at Morgan and then turned to her husband and whispered something to him. They both turned and walked out of the bed and breakfast.

Morgan said: 'They must have seen Rebecca on line as well. What do you think?'

Cameron said: 'Well he looked very excited. Who knows what's going on? I'm too tired to think and I'm off to bed. I'm thinking of seeing my sister in the morning and then getting back to London. I hope I'll see you at breakfast before I go. It's been good meeting you Morgan and spending time with you.'

Morgan: 'Yes, I need to get some rest. Too much wine for me. See you in the morning Cameron.'

CHAPTER TWO

Leaving she grabbed a newspaper to read. She glanced at the front page and in the top corner, not the main story, was a headline that said: 'Top University Professor in SEX Trap.'

By the time Morgan got to her room she felt dizzy. She sat on the bed staring at the newspaper. She wasn't sure she could face looking at it. She put the paper down and decided to make a cup of tea. As the kettle boiled, she sat on the floor practicing her yoga deep breathing, feeling her heart beating fast.

After about five minutes she felt strong enough to pick up the paper and open to the page. Apparently, someone had sent a picture of Max, in a strange bedroom, with a girl with blond hair, to the newspapers and posted it on Instagram. It was difficult to make out if was Max, but, she thought, it looked like his bottom, and the story was there.

It went on to say: 'The Professor and the University had no comment to make. The paper attempted to contact Professor Fraser at the home he shares with his long-term partner but no one was available. Professor Fraser was not at the University and his classes have been taken by a colleague. A neighbour at his flat said he had seen the Professor leave with a small suitcase the previous evening.'

She felt this was a story about someone else. Her mind was finding it difficult to connect it to Max, the man she loved and lived with.

Stop It, Morgan. This is his mess and whatever he has been doing he will have to deal with the consequences.

She was finding out a lot about Max these days. Not as quiet as she thought, obviously. But she knew he must be in a terrible state. She sat for a few minutes. Then her mind was made up. She would go back to Edinburgh and support him. She decided to call and let him know.

As she checked her phone, she noticed two missed calls and a couple of emails. Thinking it was Max she looked at the missed calls. Not him, but work looking for her. The chief executive's personal assistant.

It must be something serious, thought Morgan. I'd better call. Margaret, his personal assistant, answered immediately.

'Hi Morgan,' she said, how are you? Sorry it's so late but the senior team are here working. I know you are on a few days holiday but the boss wants a chat.'

Morgan waited till she was put through to John Stevens, the chief executive of the company.

'Hi Morgan, how are you? I heard you were down in Galloway having a break. Hope you're having a good time. I'm sorry to bother you while you're away, but I just wondered when you would be back? We have a big announcement coming next week and I could do with your advice on how to handle it. It's a tie up with an American company which will be good news for our shareholders and boost our core strengths. I could do with your input? Will you be back on Monday?'

'Yeah. I'll be back on Monday and keen to find out more. Perhaps you could email me some details and I can read it later today?' Obviously the first things that come to mind are – will it affect staff in our business; will there be any job losses; what are we telling people now?'

'As always Morgan you even work on your days off,' John laughed. 'Perhaps it's best if you are back. I need your advice and I like the way you think. You ask the questions that never come into my mind but can come back and bite me. I have another bit of news.

'Maybe I shouldn't tell you this but think you should know...' John's voice had dropped almost to a whisper. 'I had that deputy of yours in for something, nice lad, and he was very confident when I asked him how he was settling in. In fact, so confident he said he felt he could do your job.'

'Oh, did he? How interesting!' Morgan kept her voice calm even although she was shocked. 'It's good he's ambitious. He'll do his own job even better.'

'Glad you're seeing it that way,' John agreed. 'I was a bit surprised myself and nearly told him he was a cheeky and disloyal bugger but, in the end, I didn't say anything. I just thought you should know and keep an eye on him and handle it the best way you can. You know I will support you.

'How's the break in Galloway? I think you said you were going with your partner – Max isn't it?'

Morgan hesitated and then said: 'Actually I came on my own. Max was busy. I just needed a break and it's been good but very cold. I think I'm coming back to Edinburgh tomorrow so I will be able to look over the documents and work on them this weekend. I'll see you on Monday and will call you if there is anything I don't understand. But email me the background so I can go over it this weekend.'

He finished the call and Morgan just sat there with the phone in her hand. *What a bloody awful day and week*, she thought. *I need time to think but it looks I will be heading back to Edinburgh.*

Morgan sat looking at the newspaper report, her tea getting cold. She was just about to call Max when her phone rang again. It was Barry their upstairs neighbour in Edinburgh. What can he want? she wondered.

'Hi Barry. How are you?'

'Hi Morgan sorry to call you at this time of night but I couldn't get any answer at the flat and thought you should know about the journalists outside. I think Max has gone away. There are cameras as well.'

'I'm in Galloway for a few days. I don't know anything about it,' she lied.

Barry said: 'Have you not seen these stories about Max in the papers?'

Morgan decided she did not want to discuss this.

'No. I haven't Barry. Just ignore them and don't speak to them and they will likely get bored and go away if no-one tells them anything. Max might be away for work. I am planning to come back to Edinburgh tomorrow so I can sort it out. Thanks Barry.'

She ended the call and sat for a few minutes.

She tried Max's phone but it went straight to answer machine.

'Max. It's me. Its Wednesday night and I've seen the media. I'm coming back to Edinburgh tomorrow. Let me know where you are.'

Morgan couldn't sleep and decided to check her emails from work. The reports from work had arrived and she spent the next hour concentrating on them and trying not to think about Max and their lives together. Reading the reports must have made her sleepy because it seemed like the middle of the night when she woke up on top of the bed still in her day clothes.

She checked her watch – 3a.m There was a strange light in the bedroom and she felt disorientated. It was several minutes before she got up and opened the curtains.

It took her a few seconds to realise the strange light was snow. It was a white out.

The whole village was a blanket of snow and she could barely make out the cars. She could see the dark clouds coming up the Irish Sea. Blast, she thought. So much for the village never getting snow.

A feeling of helplessness in the hands of nature swept over Morgan. She quickly changed into her nightdress and took her make up off before getting back into bed. Face it in the morning, she thought.

She must have fallen back to sleep pretty quickly and it was nearly 7a.m when she woke up. She looked out and it was still snowing pretty hard.

She quickly showered and washed her hair. It was 8.30am when she went into the dining room, to find just Cameron sitting at a table.

'This looks bad Cameron. I don't see any of us getting anywhere.'

'I got up at 6a.m, intending to see my sister for breakfast and then start driving back to London and looked out of the window. I couldn't believe it,' he said. 'It surely can't keep snowing, and it's icily cold.'

Together they looked out of the window towards the sea. A big black heavy looking cloud seemed to get heading up the Irish Sea, straight towards them.

Morgan laughed. 'I think you might be wrong there. That is another big dump on the way.'

At that moment Mike came in.

'If you want warm food I would order now. We might not have power soon,' he said.

Porridge, they both said and laughed at the joint thinking of eating something warming.

As they waited the lights in the room started to flicker.

On no, she thought. She checked her phone. It was still working. She quickly texted a friend at work to say she might lose contact for a few days as stuck in snow in Galloway.

Mike came in with two steaming bowls of porridge and at that moment the lights went out. Two seconds later the mobile phones went dead.

Cameron and Morgan looked at each other, no-one saying anything. They just started eating as if they knew there might be no more hot food for a while.

It was then they released Mike was still in the room. He coughed in a rather embarrassed way and both Morgan and Cameron looked at him.

It was Morgan who spoke first: 'Are you all right Mike? I know we were both planning to leave today but obviously we can't but I'm sure we will be able to pay you for any extra days and work out how we all manage.'

'It's not that,' said Mike. 'I went up to let the other guests know that breakfast had started while we still had power. I knocked on the door of the Rev MacNeill and Christine, waited for a few minutes, but there was no answer. I don't normally do this but I unlocked the door. The room was empty and the beds had not been slept in. They told me last night they were taking Rebecca to the family farm for a few days but they would be coming back here. I knew her room would be empty but I thought they would be back. I checked and the camper van has gone.'

Cameron said: 'Perhaps there's a simple explanation. If they were going to see family, they may have decided to stay the night there, especially if the weather was bad. What time did the snow start?'

Morgan said: 'When I woke up about 3a.m there was already a lot of snow.'

Mike said: 'I think it started just after 1a.m. There's something else. The Benson couple are not in their room either. It's strange but I think I heard people going out this morning about 6a.m.'

'Bad decision,' said Cameron. 'If they have gone out in this, we'd better let someone know.'

They all looked out the window as the sky turned black and the big snowflakes just kept falling.

'It looks lovely but if they are out there then I would be worried. Is there anyone we can alert?' he said.

Mike said: 'A restaurant called to say they were taking hot food to older people stuck in their houses. They have a couple of quad bikes. I can ask them to keep a look out for the Bensons. They might be heading to their caravan to check it?

'There's no way of contacting the police and anyway they couldn't get here. The main road seems blocked about six miles towards Stranraer. They can't even get a helicopter in the air.'

Cameron interrupted: 'If they went out at 6 am that's three hours ago. Let's give it another hour before we think about a search party.'

Just then the man with walking sticks and his wife came in and sat down. They nodded and introduced themselves. I'm Richard Merry and this is my wife, Astrid. We live in Newcastle but come here every Spring for a few days.

Morgan thought if this was Mr Merry, he was anything but merry. He had the saddest face she'd ever seen.

Just then Mike's wife Mary came in. 'I usually stay in the kitchen but I thought I'd better come and tell you what I can do. I don't think anyone should go out in this weather and I hope the snow stops falling soon or we'll be in trouble.

'I am sure people are out trying to clear the road but they can't do much till the snow stops. The village seems cut off and the shops are talking of closing. They're working in darkness and the freezers are starting to melt.

'I've obviously no electric power in the kitchen but I have a portable gas cooker so I can heat soup and cook pasta so we should be all right for lunch and dinner tonight. It'll be pretty basic but I'll do what I can. It'll also be dinner by candlelight.' She smiled and said: 'I can make coffee and wonder if you would all like a cup just now.' They all nodded.

The house was starting to feel cold and they all stayed in the dining room and try and keep warm. Morgan went to her room and put on another jumper and grabbed a scarf.

The coffee was warming and the four of them sat at the table in the dining room looking out on the scene.

Cameron said: 'Did Mike tell you some of the guests are missing? He's hoping the Rev and his wife and daughter at their family farm. The other couple, the Bensons seem to have gone out this morning.'

Astrid said: 'Yeah, I saw them leave about 6a.m. They had walking boots and jackets on and were walking out of the village. I thought it was a bit strange as the snow was pretty deep.'

Cameron said: 'I don't fancy being out in this weather. You could get hypothermia very quickly.'

Morgan was sitting quietly watching everyone in the room when she felt tears spring to her eyes. She jumped up and said she was going outside to try and get into her car and retrieve a fleece and hat she kept for emergencies.

Cameron offered to come with her but Morgan said: 'No I'll be ok. Just need a couple of minutes to myself.'

She stood at the front door for a few minutes looking at the scene. It had an unearthly feeling about it, the silence washing over her like a blanket. It struck her there was no birdsong and this was Spring. Everything was in hiding.

Morgan knew why she was tearful. This was the first time she had been alone with nothing to do for more years than she could think of. This thing with Max had unnerved her.

It was seven years since she'd left Dorset and her family home to move to Edinburgh and a new job after working in London for ten years. It was eight years, she thought, since her mum died of motor neurone disease with Morgan nursing her for the last three months at the family farm. She'd felt really close to her father during those days but just six months later he sold the farm and moved into a luxury flat.

Dating websites were relatively new when he started but a succession of younger girlfriends followed. Morgan felt he was being disloyal but now, with the passage of time, she realises he was just lonely and grief stricken. He had loved Morgan's mother. She knew she'd been hard on him. Suddenly she had an overwhelming urge to call him and tell him she loved him.

She could feel herself almost crying again. She rushed to her car, the snow coming up to her knees, managing to get the boot open and grab the fleece and hat. As she made her way back to the house she looked out to the Irish Sea.

A massive black cloud seemed to fill the space. It looked as if the sea was coming to challenge the land. Morgan wondered how this lovely fresh white snow came from such a black cloud.

The snow started again and the snowflakes were coming sideways, swirling around, then straight down, bringing the biggest snowflakes she had ever seen.

She decided to take the fleece back to her room. She needed a few minutes by herself and bathe her swollen eyes.

She heard people talking in the lounge and slipped quietly up the stairs, locking the door of her bedroom.

It was cold but she huddled in the fleece and closed her eyes.

Her mind was racing. The silence was making her listen to her inner voice. She'd always kept herself so busy, busy.

'Perhaps I was just running away,' thought Morgan.

I ran away to Edinburgh and into the arms of Max.

She was just getting warm when she heard noises downstairs and the front door slam. She heard Cameron call her name. He was outside her bedroom door.

'What on earth,' she said to herself. She got up, checked her face and swollen eyes and opened the bedroom door.

'I'm here. What's the problem?'

'Morgan – the Benson's are back. They are both ok but very cold. I think the wife may have a touch of hypothermia. Have you got that fleece? Mary is getting them coffee.'

'I'll be right down,' said Morgan, grabbing the fleece and a thermal beanie hat.

When she saw the couple sitting on a couch, both of them looked exhausted and very pale. Mary was getting the woman's wet shoes off. Her trousers were soaked up to her thighs.

'What happened?' said Morgan.

Cameron said: 'It seems they went to check their caravan. Slightly mad decision, in my view. But they said they were worried about it when they saw the snow but didn't realise it was so deep and got a bit lost. Thankfully they met a villager who showed them how to get back. They didn't have the right clothes and their feet and legs are freezing. Mary's getting them coffee and some hot water. The woman looks worse. Really, she should be checked by a doctor but no chance at the moment.'

She saw him glance out of the window where the snow was coming down fast and furious.

She handed the fleece to Charles and he put it round his wife's shoulders and he mouthed 'thanks'.

Mike said: 'We can get a doctor here if needed. The lifeboat is going out soon to take a young boy with suspected appendicitis to the hospital in Stranraer. A helicopter can't come and the road won't be open for a few days, according to Tam. They can take the boat round to Loch Ryan and an ambulance can meet it. It won't be a pleasant ride for the wee boy, and they can bring a doctor here.'

Cameron said: 'So the lifeboat is an option if someone's ill?'

Mike said: 'It's the only way out of the village at the moment. Once back from Stranraer they will go down the other way to check on a couple of people who live down that way and a luxury hotel, they will have guests staying and he wants to check they are ok.'

Cameron nodded at Morgan to go outside.

'Are you all right Morgan? 'You looked a bit upset.' Cameron was looking at her intently, too intently.

'I'm fine, just not enjoying being stuck here.'

She tried to steer the conversation away from her saying: 'What do think of the missing couple and their daughter?'

'I think the Bensons were very lucky they got back here safely. The Rev and his wife? I suspect they're all warm and cosy in a farmhouse and staying till the roads get cleared. I checked the visitors' book when you were out as I remembered they took our registration. I checked the Rev's. Guess what it is, or looks like?'

'Go on,' said Morgan. 'I need a laugh.'

'It looks like REV 333 from what I can read of his handwriting. It seems apt for a preacher.'

Morgan said: 'That's handy to know if we need to get the police involved. I'm just hoping they turn up when the snow stops.'

They heard Mary come back into the dining room and went in to find coffee and sandwiches for lunch. The Benson couple looked human again and the woman was actually smiling.

They ate in silence watching the snow continue to fall, blanketing the village. As they watched they saw a quad bike in a street in the distance. It was the only thing that moved.

Morgan decided to go back to her room and made her excuses, saying she had some work to look at. It was also a good excuse to have a couple of hours to herself.

She sat in the chair and tried to read her work but her eyes kept going to the view from the window. The sea looked so grey and uninviting, she shivered, letting her mind wander. She remembered her mum and how much she missed her. She felt very peaceful and it was something to do with the fact she couldn't go or do anything at the moment. There was no Max and there were no meetings she had to be at, it was just her. She sat there for what seemed a few minutes but when she checked her watch it was actually nearly two hours. She was starting to feel cold, shivering and made up her mind to go back downstairs. It must be warmer with more people together.

When she got down just after 5p.m. Cameron, the Bensons and the Merrys were already there. The room felt warmer.

Mike and Mary came in and asked if they were all ready for "dinner." They all laughed and said anything warm would be good.

Mary said: 'I have pasta with tomato sauce and garlic and there's a bottle of red wine. I can make coffee on the hob as well. Is that ok?'

They all nodded, grateful for anything at this stage.

It was then Cameron said that he was going to walk to

the nearest hotel and find out if there was any food there.

Morgan looked out of the window. 'Is it safe to go out?'

Cameron laughed. 'I'll be fine and back in a few minutes.'

Within five minutes he was back. Pointless he said, the hotel said all the food they had was for their customers. 'It's very icy out there and not at all pleasant.'

He added: 'This snow must stop sometime and then we can find out the damage and what we need to do to dig ourselves out. Perhaps tomorrow, if it stops snowing, we can go down to the village and find out what's happening. I could talk to Tam to see if he has any news.'

Morgan heard herself say. 'Let's just eat and stay as warm as we can. It might be difficult sleeping but I'll just sleep in my clothes. It's too cold to get undressed.'

Mary had worked miracles. A glass of red wine warmed them up and Cameron had everyone laughing at some of the stories from his time as a policeman in London.

After about an hour it was just Morgan and Cameron left in the room. It was dark outside and as they watched they saw two young deer walk across the garden. She felt very safe sitting with Cameron and her mind was at ease for the first time in days.

She was tired but she didn't feel like going to her cold dark room just yet. She got a fresh coffee from the kitchen.

'Do you miss being a policeman Cameron?'

'Not really Morgan. I left Stranraer when I was 17. I needed to escape. When I was 16 and my sister 21 our parents were killed on the A75 coming back from a trip to Carlisle and their car hit a lorry heading for Europe. It's such a dangerous road. I went off the rails a bit and got expelled from school. It was my uncle who suggested the police and helped me apply to get into the Met in London. I was lucky and got accepted. He arranged for me to lodge with a friend of his for the first six months. The police gave me the stability to get my life back on track.'

'God that's awful Cameron. What a dreadful thing to happen to you and your sister. No wonder you wanted to get away.'

He nodded: 'But I left my sister to get on with things here, I always feel guilty about that. I didn't want to live here. I made a good life in London and it was a good career for me. I made Sergeant at 25 and spent the last few years in the firearms unit eventually being in charge as an Inspector. Then about a year ago I decided to do something different. I'd been with the Met for 14 years and I needed a change.'

'What do you do now then Cameron?'

'I am what people call a consultant. I got a job advising a major conference in London as security consultant. It paid quite well so I'm just trying to see what's available. I'm meant to be London this weekend to meet someone about other work. My sister thinks that now I have given up the police I might come back here. At the funeral I could sense people had been talking about it and hints were dropped.'

'You wouldn't consider that?' Morgan asked.

'I don't think so. My life is in London and I like it. I will look at coming back more often though.'

At that moment the candles in the room started to flicker. It was 9p.m, still snowing and the village was in darkness. Morgan used a torch Mary had found for her and went to her room to try and sleep, wrapped in three layers of clothes.

CHAPTER THREE

In Edinburgh Max was sitting in his flat wondering how his life had got to this stage.

It was funny, he thought, how one night, in a previously unblemished life could change everything. He had no idea what Morgan would do and he wouldn't blame her for just walking away. She must feel humiliated, he thought. She'd always said what a boring life he led, private school, no drugs and then Edinburgh University, now a professor at the same university.

It had started with drinks on a Friday night which had become normal for the last few months. It was a welcome relief at the end of a week and Max knew he was flattered to be asked by the students to join them.

The girl, Suz, was always the life and soul of the party, about 21, clever but also stunningly attractive with great legs.

Max had been aware of her in classes but never thought beyond that. He was happy with Morgan and they'd a good life together. But the students were fun to be with, and he found himself talking to Suzy most of the night.

Too much drink and too much attention and when they all left the pub at 10p.m it seemed natural to say 'yes' when she suggested coffee at her place.

It was a lovely flat and she said her father had bought it for her while she was at university. She lived alone and had recently split with a controlling boyfriend.

Max remembers feeling guilty as she opened the door. But that feeling soon disappeared as she pressed her body against his and he realised she had no underwear on. They never made coffee and all Max can remember is falling onto her bed, helping her out of her clothes and lying helpless with lust as she took his penis in her hand. He didn't remember much after that until he woke up at 6a.m, not having slept much. The other side of the bed was empty. Just a note saying, 'Gone to the gym, make yourself coffee and see you again, Love Suz.' He got dressed and left, scared someone would see him.

It was Saturday morning and Max made it back to the flat before Morgan woke up. He managed to shower and change and sit at the breakfast table before she got up.

She said: 'I didn't hear you come in last night. Was it a late night?'

Max felt himself blush but managed to answer in a normal voice: 'Yes someone's birthday and it got late so I slept on a colleague's couch. Hope you weren't worried.'

Morgan said: 'No, you deserve a night out. It's been pretty busy for the last few months and we all need a night out. Remember we are away to Galloway next weekend. Do you fancy going out tonight? I feel like we haven't seen much of each other?'

'Let's go for a walk and lunch and chat and just relax tonight. Feeling a bit washed out.'

Max managed to behave normally, he thought, all weekend. When he went back to the University on Monday everything seemed as normal.

He looked for Suz in class but she wasn't there. He thought she was away for a few days. Nobody said anything apart from one student who passed him and said: "Enjoy Friday night Prof?" and winked.

It was two days later when he left his phone at home, probably more stressed than he realised, and when he saw the text drop into his ipad at work, ran home, in a panic, his heart racing, in the vain hope Morgan hadn't seen his phone.

When he opened the door all he could see was Morgan holding his phone and looking confused and angry. Morgan left and told him to sort it out. She didn't even wait for much of an explanation, mind you what would he say except he had been a plonker.

The next night he was sitting at home alone when his mobile rang. He didn't recognise the number. But he answered.

'Hello is that Professor Fraser?' When he answered yes, he realised it was a mistake.

'Hello James Vincent from the Daily Post. We are working in a story about a young student who claims she was taken advantage of, by you, her Professor at the University. What do you have to say about that?'

Max could feel himself get angry and he never handled it well when he was like that.

'I have nothing to say,' he said.

James Vincent added: 'That's fine Professor, we have the story from a friend of Suz and the pictures. We just wanted to give you a chance to give your side of the story.'

At this point Max ended the call and sat on the couch stunned. The phone rang again and he could not bring himself to answer it. It was a nightmare. He knew he had to get away before the media came round to his house.

He called his brother Tom in Inverness and asked if he could come to stay for a few days. His brother said: 'Are you in trouble?'

Max answered: 'I think I might be. I have been very stupid and need to get away from Edinburgh and the University for a few days.'

'Of course,' said Tom. 'We can talk when you get here.'

Max emailed the University and said he was sick and needed a few days off. He would be in touch, he said.

The drive to Inverness was like escaping from a hell of his own making. No matter how far he got up the A9 he seemed to know it was going to get worse. He switched his mobile off and when he stopped for a coffee kept a baseball cap over his face. He felt like a criminal, not a respected member of the University Faculty. One night, he thought, and one night with the wrong person. One stupid mistake.

He knew he would have to explain to his brother but resisted the urge to call his mother in Perthshire and explain. She never took much interest in his life anyway and he wasn't even sure she liked Morgan. Perhaps she thought he could be better. She was in for a surprise now.

When he arrived in Inverness his brother was still at his job at the local enterprise company. Using his spare key, Max let himself into the city centre flat, lying low was what he thought was best.

He took his brother out for dinner that night to explain. It wasn't exactly a relaxed night out. His brother said little as he explained and at the end he just said: 'You stupid arse.'

Funny thing was Max totally agreed with him. Back at the flat he tried to ring Morgan again but her phone was switched off.

The next morning his phone rang and he recognised the number of his friend Pete. 'Hi Pete,' he said.

'Where are you mate?' said Pete.

'I'm in Inverness with my brother keeping my head down. I did something really stupid and got involved with one of my students. I've already had a journalist on the phone and I just don't know what is going to happen with work now.'

Pete said: 'I'm sorry to tell you this Max but pictures of you and this student in bed have been posted on social media and in a newspaper. I can't think who took the shots but someone has got hold of shots in her bedroom. It doesn't look good.'

Max was stunned but before he could say anything else another call was trying to get through. Thinking it might be Morgan he told Pete he would ring him back.

When he answered a strange voice said: 'Is that Professor Max Fraser?'

Max confirmed it was. The voice said: 'This is Inspector Robbie Brown from Police Scotland. We're investigating the distribution of pictures on social media and it's been established that you are one of the subjects in these pictures. This is not a criminal investigation yet but we will need to talk to you at some point. Where are you at the moment?'

Max said: 'I'm in Inverness just now but I've just found out about this. I need to find out more. I plan to come back to Edinburgh early next week. Is that ok?'

Inspector Brown added: 'Yes, just keep in touch with me at Police Scotland in Edinburgh and I can update you. These are pretty offensive pictures and our priority is to find out who distributed them and get them taken down as soon as possible.'

Max found himself asking: 'What are they and who have they gone to?'

Inspector Brown said: 'I'm sorry to inform you Professor but these are pictures of you and a young woman who I believe is a student of yours in her bed at her flat. We don't believe these pictures have been distributed by the girl but we need to find out how they were taken and why.'

With that he rang off leaving Max stunned on the couch. Then his phone rang again. Without thinking he answered it. It was Florence Jones, the head of human resources or people management at the University.

'Hello is that Professor Fraser?' she said. 'We've been contacted by Police Scotland about the distribution of some images which seem to involve yourself, Professor and a student.

'In these circumstances, while an official police investigation is ongoing, we feel it best if you do not come into work for the next week or so.'

Max heard himself ask: 'Am I suspended?'

'Let's just say it's best if you don't come into the university in the meantime. Of course, we will be carrying out our own internal investigation into the relationship between one of our senior Professors and a student. We'll be in touch.'

Max started to say: 'There is no relationship'.... But the phone went dead.

Oh my God, he thought. His next thought was to call Morgan.

Even that was not working out for him. Her phone was just going to message.

Just then his mobile rang again, it was his neighbour at the flat – boring Barry. He said: 'I don't know if you know but there have been journalists here all night asking for you. There is a van parked outside the flat. I told them I didn't know where you were.'

Max said thanks. 'Both Morgan and I are away for a few days,' he said. 'I can explain everything when I get back.'

Barry then said: 'Yeh I saw Morgan a couple of days ago and she seemed upset. Is she all right?'

'Yes thanks, she is. We'll see you soon.' He ended the call. He put his head in his hands and felt like a fugitive. It was all getting too much for him to handle and he realised he needed Morgan and missed her.

He was on the couch when his brother found him a few hours later with the curtains shut and the television off.

Tom shook him. 'Come on Max, it's not the end of the world. We can sort this out, but just lying on the couch isn't going to help. What about Morgan?'

Max said: 'I can't get through to her, it just keeps going to message. I think she is in Galloway in a bed and breakfast for a few days but when we last spoke, she was talking about coming back to Edinburgh and to the flat. I need to warn her there are journalists outside and I assume calling the flat phone. I just hope she doesn't go back to that.'

Tom said: 'Did you say she was in Galloway? If so, then she won't be getting back to Edinburgh very soon. If you'd watched the news a large part of Galloway is completely cut off by the heaviest snow for 40 years. Whole villages are without power, mobile phones dead. They are talking of using lifeboats to get supplies in and medical emergencies out as even helicopters can't get in. They are working hard to get the roads open but until the snow stops, they can't get an idea of what needs to be done. She might be stuck there for days.'

Max looked worried: 'I hope she's all right. So, that's why I can't get through on the mobile. It's probably a good place for her to be right now while this nightmare goes on. I just don't know what to do but could I stay here another couple of days to lie low before I have to go back to Edinburgh. The police and the university need to speak to me.'

Tom said: 'What do you think is happening? Did this girl send out these pictures?'

Max said: 'I don't know but the police seemed to suggest it was someone else. I've been so stupid and let my ego get out of control. How I thought a night with a student was going to work for me privately and professionally I just don't know. In one way I don't really care about the university but Morgan is a different story.'

Tom punched him on the arm. ‘Come on Max pull it together. Get smartened up, dark glasses on and we will go out for a long walk and lunch. It will do you good to get out and some exercise. No one will bother you.’

CHAPTER FOUR

Morgan woke up the next morning amazed that she'd managed to sleep in the cold.

She checked and it was just 6a.m. She looked out and though there was more snow it had stopped falling. She lay in the relative warmth of the bed realising it was the first time for many years she didn't have to get up to do something, go to the gym, a meeting or even seeing anyone. It was the strangest mindfulness break she had ever been on. At the moment she didn't mind it but knew she would be bored after just a couple of days.

It was about 8a.m when she made her way downstairs. The Bensons and Cameron were already in the dining room drinking coffee.

'Hi everyone. Did you get some sleep?'

Mary Benson said: 'Not much. Both of us kept waking up and worrying about the other couple. What if they are out there?'

Morgan nodded and said: 'I'm sure they're ok. We need to keep thinking that until we hear otherwise.'

Just then Mary and Mike came into the room. Morgan thought she had never been so grateful for instant coffee in her life as they came in with two trays, and – amazingly – croissants and jam.

Cameron said: 'I'm thinking of trying to walk down to

the village and see what is happening and if any of the shops are open. Does anyone want to come with me?'

Mike said: 'You might manage as the villagers have used the quad bikes to make a path down the hill to the village. You can walk without sinking into the snow. It's still about three feet and worse in places where it has drifted.'

Morgan found herself volunteering.

Just then they heard banging on the front door. Cameron looked out the window and said: 'It's the lifeboat guy Tam. Maybe he's got some news?'

Just then the dining room door opened and the Merry man and his wife Astrid came in.

Astrid said: 'We smelt coffee so we came down. Our room is really cold. There's something serious going on out there. Mike and that man are in deep conversation and they look very worried.'

Just then the living door opened and Mike asked Cameron to come outside.

He went out to find Tam and Mike at the front door.

Cameron said: 'What is it, Tam? You look very serious.'

Tam said: 'As you probably know we had to take a boy by lifeboat to the hospital yesterday. When we returned, we planned to take the lifeboat down the coast, the other way, to check on guests in a local hotel and a few people that live there. But the weather was so bad we had to abandon that trip. We got up early this morning and as the snow had stopped at 6a.m we took a run in the boat to the hotel. They're fine but it was when we were on the way back, I spotted something.'

Cameron said: 'What was it?'

Tam said: 'I noticed something red on the rocks that looked like a jacket. When I got my binoculars I saw, what I was certain, was a body. We couldn't get close to the shore as I didn't have the small inflatable with me but I am certain there is at least one body there.'

Cameron said: 'Could it be someone washed up in the storm from a boat?'

Tam said: 'Not sure. It seems pretty high up the water line to have come from the sea. I got back about an hour ago and used the radio at the lifeboat shed to call the police in Stranraer. That's really why I am here. Our Inspector is Tom Driver. I believe you know him, Cameron?'

'Tom Driver, I know him or rather did. We went to school together. When I went off to join The Met he joined Strathclyde. I didn't realise he was back here,' said Cameron.

Tam said: 'Yeah, he's been back a few years. When the Inspector heard you were back home for a funeral he asked if you could help.'

Cameron said: 'I'm no longer a serving officer. I left about a year ago.'

Tam said: 'He knows that. But he asked if you could come out with me in the boat to check what's lying there. He needs two people he can trust. I can take the lifeboat and a smaller boat to get in close. He's hoping we can see what is there and report back. Are you game for it?'

Cameron said: 'Of course I'll help all I can. I assume we aren't telling the other guests. They are already worried.'

Tam said: 'Entirely up to you. I just want to find out what it is.'

Cameron said: 'I might mention it to Morgan. She knows something's up.'

Tam said: 'I'm going now to get the boat ready and some gear for you. How about I see you at the harbour in 30 minutes?'

Cameron said: 'What should I wear?'

'Something warm and I can get you waterproofs, hat and boots. You look like a size nine,' said Tam. With that he left and set off down the hill to the village.

Cameron went back into the living room and nodded at Morgan and hoped she got the message to follow him. She was right behind him.

'What's going on? It looked serious.'

Cameron nodded: 'It might be. I'm not meant to say anything about it but I thought you would want to know. Tam says when they were out, they noticed something on the rocks on their way back to Portpatrick. Tam thought he could see a body on the rocks. He wants me to go back out with him to check. He says its ok with the police as the senior policeman knows me and wants me to be there.'

'Do you think they've been washed up off a boat or something?'

'Tam thinks it's too high up the waterline to be from a boat. He thinks it's more likely they came off the cliffs. I'm just leaving now and Tam is going to get me kitted out.'

Morgan said: 'Wait a minute till I get a coat and I'll walk down with you. I said to Mary I would try and get some cans of soup and check what's happening in the village. I really don't want to be left here with Mr Merry and co.'

Cameron said: 'No problem. The path down seems ok. When I get back, I'll start clearing the cars. They should get the road open soon.'

It was hard walking but they made it down to the harbour in about ten minutes. Cameron said he would see her soon and left to make his way to the lifeboat. Morgan could see Tam and another man on the boat and a smaller boat tied behind.

She walked round to the main part of the village and stood on the front shore watching as the lifeboat left the harbour and turned left out of the village. Cameron had said they might be a few hours.

It was then Morgan looked around the village. It seemed empty of people. There was no noise except the sound of the sea lapping on the beach. As she stood staring at the cold grey sea her mind wandered to her mother. The image of her was fading and she would have given anything just to be able to give her a call and tell her what was happening. She suddenly felt very alone. She knew she was missing Max, well the old Max who only cared for her.

She shook herself and started to walk up the main street.

It was only because she saw someone come out of a door that she released the little shop in the main street was open. It was in darkness and in a far end towels and sheets were mopping up the water from the deep freezes. The owner looked really pissed off and said Morgan could see what she could find. All she could see were tins of mushroom and tomato soup, some crackers and cheese that still looked all right. There was no bread or fresh milk but she found some longlife cartons at the back of the shop. A couple of bottles of red wine and they'd enough for a day or so.

She couldn't see anyone else apart from the shop owner and the woman who had come out of the shop. Morgan decided to retrace her steps and went back down the main street. It was as she was passing the pub, she saw people through the window and decided to have a look. As she opened the door the heat and smell of alcohol almost overwhelmed her. It took a moment for her eyes to take it in. Packed with villagers, many of them very happy looking and a massive coal fire at the back.

'Hi, how are you? I'm Robert and I'm bar staff here. Do you want a coffee, or something stronger? I assume you're a visitor?'

Morgan put down her shopping and smiled. 'Yes, I'm staying up the road in the Seaview bed and breakfast. I'm from Edinburgh but obviously stuck here just now. It's not all bad it seems.'

Robert said: 'Yes there are less than 1000 people living in the village and I think about a fifth of them are here today. It's everyone who could get out of the house coming in for some soup and chilli and a drink.'

'That's great and I saw people out on quad bikes delivering food,' said Morgan.

'Yeah. The village is pretty cut off in the winter and we look after each other. It's a small community and we're used to storms but this is pretty bad. Some people here remember the 1963 snow storm and this seems almost as bad. The good thing is we have the fire, we have food we can heat up and we have wine.'

Morgan smiled and said: 'I would love a glass of red wine and some chilli? Is that ok.'

'Sit right down and it'll be with you in a few minutes.'

Morgan sat on a spare seat sharing with some of the locals, man and three women. She gave them a warm smile and said: 'Ok if I join you? I am just having a drink and something to eat.'

The man at the table was the first to speak.

'Of course, lass. Are you visiting?'

Morgan said: 'Yes, down from Edinburgh for a few days and possible a few days longer than I meant to.'

'Aye it's a bad storm. But they'll get the road open soon and we'll get back to normal.'

Morgan introduced herself to her table companions. There was Jimmy, his wife Jane and neighbour Nancy. The other lady was Maureen who lived next door to the pub.

Jimmy said: 'Did you see the lifeboat going out again. Wonder what's up this time?'

Morgan decided to keep quiet and thankfully just at that moment her glass of red wine arrived.

'Cheers,' she said to her table. She realised she needed a drink and the warmth of the fire was making her sleepy.

Funny, she thought. It's the sort of place you could stay all the afternoon just chatting and drinking. Just then the bowl of chilli arrived and Morgan realised she was hungry.

'Tuck in, you look like you need it,' commented Nancy.

Between mouthfuls Morgan decided to find out a bit more about the village.

'What's Portpatrick's history,' she asked.

Nancy said: 'Well the village was named after St Patrick, his footstep is meant to be on the wee island you see in the harbour there. It was called something before but it used to be important as the port for the mail deliveries across the sea to Northern Ireland. Then Stranraer became the main link with Larne and Belfast and for the last few decades tourism has been the mainstay of the village. We are so close to Ireland many people go shopping in Belfast rather than Glasgow or Dumfries. We're pretty isolated here.'

Jimmy said: 'Nancy's right. Not many jobs around here and a lot of young people leave to find work. Some come back, others never.'

Morgan realised she had been sitting in the pub for over an hour.

She said: 'Thanks for your company but I'd better get back to the bed and breakfast with the wine and soup for everyone else. They'll be wondering where I am. We already had two guests missing in the snow but they got back all right.' She didn't mention the MacNeill family issue.

Jimmy nodded and asked: 'Will you be ok getting back yersel?'She nodded she was fine.

It was tougher walking up the hill and by the time Morgan made it to the bed and breakfast she was exhausted.

She found Mike shovelling snow from the car park and trying to create a path.

‘I’ll just drop this stuff in the kitchen and come out and help you, if you’ve a spare shovel,’ said Morgan.

It took a good two hours of shovelling to get the cars cleared and their wheels exposed, then another two hours to start clearing the path to the exit gate of the bed and breakfast. But there was no sign of anyone clearing the main road or even the little hill down from the golf club.

Morgan wondered what her work colleagues would think of her now. Hair unwashed, same clothes as yesterday and no makeup, she realised she didn’t care. It was just good to get something done outside. She would have gone mad stuck inside twiddling her thumbs, she thought.

At sea, Cameron was concentrating on staying upright on the lifeboat as they made their way along the coast. He was full of admiration for Tam and his colleague as they manoeuvred through the waves. The sea seemed much rougher after they left the safety of the harbour. Thankfully it took less than 30 minutes to reach the bay where they were going to anchor. It was surrounded by massive cliffs though Cameron could see a small cottage sitting on the foreshore so there must be road. But there was no time to talk and ask questions. He could see Tam giving instruction to his crewmate as he started to untie the small boat behind them.

‘Can you get yourself in that Mr Steel?’ shouted Tam.

Tam manoeuvred the small boat as close to the shore as he could and they both scrambled onto the rocks.

Cameron shouted: ‘Which way Tam?’

Tam pointed to the left and they started to make their way over the rocks.

After what seemed like an hour they turned the corner of the cliff. They could see something up near the cliff base. It looked like clothes.

As they got closer the full horror of what lay mangled

on the rocks at the bottom of the cliffs became clearer. There were two bodies lying close together, their heads at a strange angle. At first Cameron thought they looked like mannequins.

Their limbs seemed all broken and their bodies lay only feet apart among plastic and rubbish thrown up by the high tide in the stormy conditions.

'I think that's the Rev who has the family farm not a million miles from here,' said Tam, and that looks like his wife.

'I think they must have been here for a while.'

Cameron thought there was something strange about the way the bodies were lying.

'Tam I'm not sure they've fallen. That's a fall of over 100 feet and they don't have those injuries consistent with a fall. I could be wrong but I think they've been placed here.

'I think we need the police team here as soon as possible.'

Cameron took his eyes away from the bodies and looked around. He saw the cottage sitting in the bay about 100 yards away as he turned to look along the coastline, he spotted something lying among the rocks about 50 yards away.

'What's that over there, Tam? I see a piece of clothing. Let's take a look.'

They scrambled over the rocks and seaweed covered stones and found another body.

'My God. What the hell's going on here?'

He looked at the body of a man in his 40s wearing a strange looking coat. He was lying on his back but Cameron could see dried blood on the stones below him.

'Tam, I think this guy might have been shot. The other two don't look like they've been shot but he has. It's very mysterious. We can't touch him or move them but I saw you had some tarpaulin on the boat. Can you get it to cover the bodies till we can get police forensic team here?'

'Tam nodded: 'Of course. I'll get it and radio the police when I'm on the boat.

'I can drop you in Portpatrick and then go straight to Stranraer to pick them up.'

As they walked back towards the boat he said:

'We should check that holiday cottage. It should be locked up safe. People aren't due till Easter. A guy in the village keeps an eye on it.'

Cameron said: 'Yeah. Let's check once we get these bodies covered and as safe as we can.'

It took them an hour to arrange the tarpaulin and weigh it down with big boulders. They took one last look before heading back to the beach.

Cameron was first at the cottage and out of habit turned the handle on the back door. It opened immediately. He turned to Tam and said: 'Interesting. It's open.'

They both went in. On the kitchen table was a packet of opened biscuits and when Cameron looked in the fridge there was fresh milk.

Tam said: 'I've checked the bedroom and I would say someone has been staying here. The bed has been slept in.'

Cameron said: 'Let's go. The police can check it out.'

As they left Cameron stopped.

'Look fresh tyre tracks. These look as if they come from a big vehicle. Could it have been the MacNeill's camper van was down here?'

It seemed a shorter journey for Cameron as they made their way back to the village. It was early afternoon when they got back to the harbour. Tam had already alerted the police. He set off for Stranraer, the sea its usual choppy self.

Morgan was busy shovelling snow from around the cars when she saw Cameron coming up the hill.

She stood watching him, and then out of the corner of her eye she saw someone else walking towards them. It was Dave Campbell who was staying in the nearby hotel. He walked towards Cameron and shouted. Cameron didn't seem to hear him and Morgan realised he had ear phones in, probably listening to music. She moved towards him and indicated he looked behind him.

Cameron turned and saw Dave Campbell. He took his earphones out and said: 'Hi.'

Dave Campbell said: 'Sorry to trouble you but I just wanted to check how things are with you all? I saw you went out on the lifeboat. What was that about?'

Morgan could see Cameron looking uncomfortable.

She said: 'Wasn't it to help the lifeboat deliver food?'

'Yeah. We took stuff down to the hotel on the coast,' said Cameron.

But Dave Campbell wasn't giving up. 'Is the Rev and his wife still missing? What about the girl?'

Cameron said: 'I'm not sure. People seem to think they are at the family farm and hopefully they're all safe. I'm just worried about more snow and not getting out of here.'

Dave Campbell turned and walked away and Cameron waited till he was out of earshot before he said: 'Thanks Morgan. You obviously saw that I didn't want to say too much at this stage to a stranger. Mind you, if we're stuck, everyone will know soon.'

Morgan said: 'You look upset Cameron. Can you say what you found?'

'It was the bodies of the Rev and his wife and a third body lying at the bottom of the cliff. Tam is away on the lifeboat to bring the police here. It's police business now so best we don't say anything at the bed and breakfast.'

'My god that's awful. It obviously wasn't an accident,' said Morgan.

'It doesn't look like an accident but they'll need to get the bodies out of there. Listen, I think we'd better get inside. It looks suspicious us talking out here and I think there's more snow coming.'

He turned and pointed to the sky south.

'Oh, shit,' said Morgan. 'The shovelling and clearing we did today was a waste of time.'

Cameron nodded: 'I know. I wondered if the police would bring a helicopter here, but the weather's too bad. They will have to do it the old way. I assume Tam is going to take them down to the site on the lifeboat and then work out what to do.'

CHAPTER FIVE

It took Tam Mitchell and his crewman less than an hour to make their way round Corsewall point and into Loch Ryan before bringing the lifeboat to a halt at the harbour, making sure he kept away from the big ferries leaving Loch Ryan for Larne and Belfast. There was no snow at all in Stranraer and waiting for him at the harbour was Inspector Driver and two plain clothes officers.

'Welcome Tam,' said the Inspector. 'Let's go to the office and get you a cup of coffee to warm you up.'

Once seated Tam explained: 'You know I spotted something in the rocks down near the hotel yesterday. Well, I went back this morning with Cameron and we managed to get onto the beach. We think we found the Rev and his wife who have been missing from the bed and breakfast since the night of the first snow. We also found a third body and he may have been shot in the back. I am not sure who he is but I suspect he's the brother of the Reverend who lives at the family farm with his two sisters. I've seen him around the area.'

Inspector Driver said: 'Do you have an idea how they got there?'

Tam said: 'I don't think they fell and neither does Cameron. There's a small road that comes down to the bay for the holiday cottage. They could have been brought there but there was no vehicle left there. Someone must have driven it away, and it wasn't the Rev.'

Inspector Driver said: 'I think we need to go see this now. Can you take us? I'll come with a couple of my team and we're arranging a boat to bring a forensic team and get the bodies out of there. I thought about getting a helicopter to land on the cliff but the forecast is more snow so that's not feasible.'

Tam said: 'Anytime you're ready. It'll take just over an hour and we brought a small dinghy to get into the bay. Make sure you all have good footwear. It's pretty treacherous out there.'

Inspector Driver replied: 'I will get an update from the emergency team who are trying to get the main roads open again. We know there's more snow forecast but we're hoping it won't be too much at this stage. The snow seems to be coming up the Irish Sea and then continuing up towards Glasgow. I don't like the sound of what is happening in the village but I am reassured that Cameron is there. He was a good police officer and he'll know what to do.'

As Morgan and Cameron made their way back to the bed and breakfast Morgan suddenly remembered. 'What about the girl, Rebecca? Was there any sign of her?'

Cameron said: 'No. Let's hope she's safe at the farm. We can tell the police when they get here.'

Morgan said: 'What the hell is going on here Cameron? I'm glad you're here because I am finding all this more than a bit strange. People disappearing and found dead at the bottom of a cliff. And all this snow. This was meant to be refreshing and restful break away from the city and work. Instead, we are stuck here and awful things are happening.' Morgan felt her eyes well up.

Cameron said: 'I agree. There's a really funny atmosphere.

Let's get into the semi warmth of the house and wait for the police.'

They found Richard Merry and his wife Astrid sitting in the lounge with the Bensons and a plate of sandwiches and coffee. Morgan and Cameron were just about to help themselves when the Merry wife suddenly sprang to her feet and started shouting: 'You bring us bad news. I can sense it, death and pain,' she announced. Then she rushed out of the room, looking very distressed.

The husband Richard apologised: 'Sorry, my wife's a bit of a prophet of doom. She thinks she has a special relationship with the spirits. I assume nothing has happened?'

Cameron said: 'I think the police are here now looking into things. We will know more soon.'

Just then they heard the doorbell.

It was Mike again. He said: 'I have a local farmer here, Roger Farrell, and he needs to speak to the police. He has a farm outside the village. He says he's found something.' Both Cameron and Morgan left the dining room.

At the bottom of the stairs stood a very unhappy looking man in what looked like three overcoats and big wellies. Outside Morgan could see a tractor with a sort of snow plough on the front standing in the driveway.

'I'm Roger and I live on a farm up the lane over there.' He pointed south. 'The snow hit my sheep stock hard. It came so quickly we could not get about 200 ewes and some of their lambs into shelter quickly enough. I have been out for the last 24 hours digging out their bodies and it's made me feel sick to the stomach. That's the problem for a lot of farmers around here.

'But that's not why I am here. As we made a path on the single track road, we found a camper van abandoned in the snow and lying off the road in a field. We managed to clear some of it and opened the door and thankfully there was no one inside. There was a handbag on the floor and it looked like they'd left in a hurry. I'm just worried they left the van in the snow to seek help and are lost. I couldn't call the police and I heard in the village that a policeman was staying here so I thought I would try here.'

Cameron said: 'I'm not a policeman now. The police are actually on their way to the village now in a boat but they have to call somewhere first so I'm not sure when they will arrive. But that might be the camper van of the couple who were staying here with their daughter and went missing on the first night of the snow.'

Roger Farrell said: 'I could take you both up there now in my tractor to have a look. I will be out on the farm for the rest of the day and try and get part of the road into the village cleared.'

Cameron and Morgan looked at each other. 'I think I should at least go and check this out for the police. They will not even be in the village yet,' said Cameron.

'If you're going then I'm coming too,' said Morgan. 'I can't stay here any more doing nothing.'

The farmer nodded: 'Get some warm boots on and a jacket. You can sit in the cabin with me. It'll be fine. I can get you back here later or if the weather turns bad you can stay the night at the farm.'

It was just after 1p.m. when they left. As Morgan climbed into the cabin of the tractor she thought back to her life in Edinburgh. Thankfully all that hill walking and gym work had kept her fit. This was a bit out of her normal day.

Roger's tractor was moving pretty fast on a track he had made in the road on top of what looked several feet of snow. Within minutes they were out of the village and travelling up a hill past some caravan sites. They passed an old castle and several farms before Roger pointed out a farm building on the left. 'That's my place. My wife will be wondering where I am but it's better we look at this vehicle before any more snow comes,' he shouted above the engine. Cameron nodded.

It took about another ten minutes before they saw the camper van sitting in a field just off the road. On the right were snow covered fields, rough stones from the walls peeking out, then the cliffs and the cold looking sea.

Roger stopped the tractor on the road and they got out. The snow was pretty deep and they struggled to get close to the camper van.

'I cleared the snow from the van really to make sure no one was inside. It's a mystery,' said Roger.

Cameron managed to open the passenger door. He saw a battered old leather handbag on the floor at the front. He climbed in and looked in the back of the camper van. There was clothing and a suitcase lying, and sort of bedding at the back of the van and in an alcove above.

'I can't see anything. How long do you think it's been here?'

Roger said: 'It must have been here before the snow. There are no track marks into the field. It's looks like it was parked up but there is nowhere close for people to go. No-one came to the farm if the van broke down.'

Cameron said: 'The police will have to see this but we think this is the camper van of the Rev MacNeill and his wife who were staying in our bed and breakfast and went out the night before the snow arrived.'

Roger said: 'If it's his camper van then his family farm is not that far from here. About a couple of miles further along the road and into the left it lies in a dip in the hills. They might have gone there.' Cameron put his head down and just nodded, not saying anything about the bodies. There would be time for that conversation, thought Morgan.

As they stood talking it started snowing again.

Morgan said: 'While we've been talking have you seen that black cloud coming up the sea and taking up most of the sky?'

They all looked south and Roger said: 'More snow. I think we'd better get back to the farm and get some shelter till we see how much snow comes.'

Cameron nodded and turned to Morgan. 'Before we go Morgan could you do something? I am too big to climb over the front seats and check the back of the camper van and the doors are all frozen solid apart from this passenger door. It must have been sheltered by the stone wall. I think just in case there is something there.' Cameron looked at Morgan.

She laughed: 'I'll try if you think it's important.'

She climbed in the passenger seat onto her knees. Then she started to manoeuvre her body between the seats and managed to squeeze through.

She shouted back: 'There just seems bedding of some sort pushed against the walls and some sort of kitchen at the back end. Hang on. There's something on the floor. It looks like smudged blood to me. I'm not going any further.'

She managed to back out of the camper van and turned to look at the two men.

'That definitely looked like blood or something very dark smudged. It looks like something was pulled along the floor.'

Cameron said: 'Let's secure it as best we can and leave it for the police and forensics. Someone parked it here and left it. We just don't know who.'

Morgan said: 'I'm freezing and not just by the cold. The snow is really getting to me. Could we just go? I could do with some warmth.'

'Don't worry lass. The wife will have the fire on and some tea and scones,' said Roger. 'We can see what the weather is like after some food and rest and decide if we can get you back to the village this afternoon.'

As Roger went to get the tractor started and make sure it was headed in the right direction, Morgan grabbed Cameron's arm and said: 'There was something else there but I didn't want to say anything in front of Roger. There was some writing on the back window. It was done on the inside and said something like 'they stole her.' It looked like it was written with a black marker pen. You can't really see it outside on the window with the snow.'

'That could be nothing,' said Cameron 'or it could be something. Let's hope the police get here soon. Do you think they'll be in the village yet? I think we'll have something to eat and warm up and then get back to the bed and breakfast as fast as we can. Let's hope the police are there and can take over.'

Roger was waving at them to climb into the cabin of the tractor and the noise made it impossible to say anything. Within minutes they were back at the farm gate. As they came into the farmyard Morgan saw the pile of dead lambs and sheep in the corner of farmyard.

'That's horrendous,' she said pointing to the mound.

'Aye lass, it's awful. But that's what farming's about. We are used to it but this is a bad blow at the start of the season. Let's get in and warm up. We're hoping we'll get some help or compensation but that's a conversation for another day.'

As they walked into a wall of warmth and a cheery looking woman smiling at them.

'Hi I'm Maggie. Come away in and get warm. I have some soup and bran scones that'll heat you up.'

'Hi. I'm Morgan and this is Cameron. We're both staying in the village and somehow got caught up in this. I must say your soup's very welcome.'

'Nae bother. We're glad to see people especially such a bright young couple. We haven't seen anybody for days. Thankfully we have the fire and can cook and a lamp for light.'

Morgan let the couple comment pass and tucked into the warm soup. She was starting to feel normal again.

Cameron said: 'Thanks for all this. I wonder once we have eaten and warmed up you could take us back to the bed and breakfast Roger?'

Maggie interrupted: 'I was hoping you were going to stay?'

'No Maggie. These young people know what they are doing. If they need to get back, they need to get back,' explained Roger.

CHAPTER SIX

On the lifeboat Inspector Driver was doing his best to keep his eyes on the land, while his stomach was telling him to jump off. He looked behind to see the Coastguard boat, requisitioned to bring a forensic team to this storm battered coastline. Even the rocks on the shore looked cold. He could see snow clouds forming in the distance and knew they had only a small window of time to examine the scene and get the bodies out of there. Within minutes they'd put down anchor and Tam was getting the small boat ready. The other boat had also stopped and within a few minutes the Inspector, his sergeant and the forensic team were on the beach.

Tam pointed to the left and they started walking. Tom Driver saw a small cottage on the right and a road leading up the side of the cliffs back to the B road that ran all the way along the coast.

They found the bodies easily as the bright yellow tarpaulins had done their job pretty well and protected them from the worst of the snow storm.

The forensic team got to work fast. They unfolded their black bags and started to lift the tarpaulin. Inspector Driver got his first sight of the two bodies together, a man and woman in what looked like their 60s.

He turned to Tam. 'You think this is the Rev MacNeill and his wife?'

Tam nodded: 'Yeah, I've seen them before and Cameron thought it was the Rev and his wife who disappeared from the bed and breakfast the night before the snow. They were all worried about them.'

Inspector Driver said: 'Right then, who's that guy over there?'

They scrambled over the rocks to the body of a middle aged man lying about 200 yards from the first two bodies.

'I can't be sure but I think that might be a relative of the Rev there, he lives at the farm nearby with two sisters, twins I think, and a bit strange looking.'

As the forensic team started to lift the body into the bag Inspector Driver stopped them.

'That looks like a gun wound in his back. Cameron was right when said he might have been shot. I couldn't see any obvious injuries on the other two but they're lying strangely. Do you think their necks are broken?'

Tam said: 'I'm no expert but they do look strange the way they are lying.'

'We'll know more once they've examined them. Let's get them back to Stranraer as quickly as possible. Much of the forensic material will have been lost with them lying here for a few days in the open but our pathologist needs to see what's going on. They might have to go to Dumfries or Glasgow.'

Tam said: 'It doesn't look like an accident.'

'No,' said Inspector Driver 'It looks suspicious. Do this MacNeill family come from here Tam?'

Tam said: 'I think they all come from a farm about two miles further up the road there. But I don't think the Rev and his wife live there. They seem to be visiting. I know locals said the farm was owned by old MacNeill and his wife, Betty. They had four children, the Rev, two sisters and another son and people think they still live there. It's a pretty old-fashioned place and nothing has improved since the parents died about 20 years ago.'

The bodies were loaded onto the second boat and instructions given to get them to Stranraer to be picked up by transport to take them to the pathologist in Dumfries.

Inspector Driver and his sergeant Peter Ford and his PC Ed Jones went back on to the lifeboat with Tam to head to Portpatrick.

'Tam, we're going to need to find Cameron at his bed and breakfast.'

Tam said: 'Aye it's the Seaview up on the hill near the golf course. You know the one. They should be there. The snow is starting again and it will be getting dark by the time you get there. Are you going to stay the night?'

Inspector Driver said: 'If its ok with you Tam I'd like to get back to Stranraer tonight. I might leave the Sergeant here if that's ok with him. I'm going to ask Cameron if he can get to the farm and see if the girl Rebecca is there.'

They all lapsed into silence as the lifeboat made its way through the waves and the snow.

CHAPTER SEVEN

Max returned to his flat in Edinburgh after three days with his brother, who told him to get back and face whatever was happening. Max thought it was just because he was so angry at him that he wanted him out of his house.

He'd checked with Barry his neighbour to see if the media was still hanging around but he said they'd gone after two days, he was yesterday's story and the news had moved on. The local evening paper had reported a man, a former boyfriend of the student for distributing pictures taken on a hidden camera in her bedroom to the procurator fiscal. He seemed to be another student. Great, thought Max, how am I ever going to face them again? He found himself feeling guilty about the damage to that young girl's reputation, but reminded himself it was her old boyfriend who had caused most of the problem.

He realised his night of madness, fun madness, he admitted to himself, may be with him for ever. His relationship under threat and on top of that he had been suspended by the University.

Everyone at work seemed to know what happened.

He had had some supportive messages but one saying what a tube he was, and some threats the university was looking into.

More worryingly, he'd heard nothing from Morgan and

sitting in the kitchen of their flat he realised he was missing her.

Checking the large pile of mail, he passed the mirror in the hallway. *God, I look haggard*, he thought.

He picked up his phone. He'd been keeping it switched off. There was a message. Hoping it was Morgan he decided to listen. No – it was actually two messages, and neither of them raised his spirits. One was the police and the second, the University.

He took the decision to do nothing about them today. His only activity, he decided, was to open a bottle of red wine and binge on box sets. Time enough tomorrow to face the world.

The wine and the loneliness of being in the flat without Morgan meant that he slept only fitfully that night, waking up the next morning tired and lethargic. Checking the BBC online it said the road to Portpatrick was still closed but hoped to be open in a day or so. He found himself hoping that Morgan would be back in Edinburgh soon as he needed to talk to her.

When he listened to the messages it didn't improve his mood. One was from the police saying they would be in touch to organise a meeting. The other one was from the university basically saying he shouldn't come back. They fell short of saying for ever and he wondered if he would ever get back. He had no idea what he would do but he was starting to feel that his life was not in Edinburgh.

CHAPTER EIGHT

Rebecca was starting to find the light from the ancient oil lamp very creepy, casting strange shadows, in the old fashioned living room of the farm.

She glanced across to her aunts, sometimes it was hard to tell them apart. They were twins and always dressed the same and always had the same hairstyles. Normally she could tell them apart as Effy, or her Sunday name Euphemia, had a large mole on her upper lip. Her sister was Agnes but always known as Aggie.

They'd been getting increasingly tearful in the last day, huddled in front of the lounge coal fire and spending every hour worrying about their brother who lived with them and looked after them doing all the jobs, leaving the sisters to drink tea and watch television. They barely mentioned their older brother or sister in law, her parents. It was the night the storm came in when they left the farm in the camper van and they'd heard nothing from them since. They'd brought Rebecca to the farm to stay and said they were going back to the bed and breakfast.

Rebecca knew her dad was angry at her. He had shouted at her about playing her violin in the bed and breakfast. But the arguments had been going on for weeks and Rebecca knew it was because he didn't want her to go away to study.

This wasn't the usual trip for Rebecca. They usually brought her here every May for three months to help with the harvest and the hay on the farm, but they'd never come here in March before.

Once they got to the farm her father disappeared to Uncle Quintas' bedroom. Rebecca has never been in his bedroom as he always locked his door and spent hours up there on his computer.

Rebecca was downstairs with the aunts that first night and they could hear her father shouting at his brother, her mother was with them.

Rebecca couldn't hear much but knew the arguments were about money. She had worked out that the farm was losing money and her father was blaming Quintas.

The row went on for about an hour with Quintas saying nothing, with her aunts sitting close to the fire, not saying anything. Then they heard something smash upstairs and Quintas shouting: 'What are you doing? That's mine. Stop touching it.' Rebecca could hear her mother trying to calm them both down.

Just to do something Rebecca said: 'Should we feed the animals? Isn't it time for the pigs and the sheep in the shed?'

Aggie looked up: 'I don't like what's happening. Artemis shouldn't have come back here and caused all this trouble. I don't like it. We were happy till he came back and started shouting.'

'Neither do I,' said Effy. 'You go and feed the animals Rebecca. I want to make sure Quintas is ok.'

Rebecca put on an old coat and went out to find hay and straw, leaving her aunts sitting by the fire.

Rebecca was standing in the farmyard, delaying going back into the farmhouse, when she saw her father, mother and Quintas come out of the back door.

Her father nodded at her and said: 'We're going to the village to have coffee and a chat with Quintas. We should be back in a couple of hours. Look after your aunts Rebecca.'

Rebecca wasn't worried. Her mother had told her that her father did not like upsetting his sisters. He would be going somewhere quiet to continue the chat with his younger brother.

She finished her work and went back into the farmhouse to find Aggie and Effie pacing around the room looking agitated.

Aggie stuttered: 'Artemis is really angry at Quintas, saying he's been spending all the family money on gambling and videos. Artemis says the farm is in trouble and it's all Quintas' fault. This is our home. This was our parents' home and we can't, we won't, leave it.' Both sisters were crying, their heads sunk into their chests and a look of misery on their faces.

Rebecca felt she had to say something. 'Look, Dad will sort it out. You won't have to leave here I'm sure of it. I'll make some tea and we can have dinner. It'll be all right. They'll be back soon.'

Effie said: 'Play us some music Rebecca. It will help us relax. I don't even want to go up and see what they did upstairs. I'm too scared.'

Rebecca got her violin and settled down in the almost dark lounge to play a tune from memory. She couldn't read music in this light.

As she started to play her violin, she felt almost sorry for her uncle. She knew how strict her father was and careful with money. Gambling would be the devil's work to him.

She thought back to when she was younger. Every morning her father spent an hour reading from the scriptures, teaching her about right and wrong. That was before she started her home schooling with her mum. One day she told him she just wanted to play outside. He was so furious he didn't speak to her for a week.

She had missed having friends but she found some with her mum's family. She'd cousins who played with her. Now she was 17 she didn't really enjoy coming here to Galloway and the farm.

They sat in front of the fire and ate some food waiting for the family to return. It got to 10p.m. and when they had still not come back the sisters became even more agitated. They refused to go to bed and Rebecca felt she couldn't just leave them.

It was about midnight when it started snowing and the sisters sat on the couch rocking back and forth in unison crying and repeatedly saying 'where are they?' Rebecca was in an old armchair, dozing, when she was woken by the sisters telling her to get down below. This was to a room below the lounge floor which had been fitted out with a toilet and bed where Rebecca had been sent to stay when they had visitors. She told them she wasn't going anywhere.

'I'm not going down there again. I hate it.'

It was then as Rebecca looked out of the kitchen window and saw, in the light of the moon, the shadow of a man going into one of the outhouses. She resisted saying anything to her aunts but instinctively went to lock the back door. She could see the light of a torch moving around outside.

She put out the lights in the kitchen and in the sitting room. When no one came to the door she decided it must have been a tramp.

When the snow became heavy Rebecca convinced her aunts that her mum and dad would not want to travel back in the heavy snow and were probably staying in the bed and breakfast with Quintas. That seemed to calm them and eventually they fell asleep on the couch.

The next morning the power went out but it didn't seem to faze the aunts. They were used to power cuts and immediately brought out the same oil lamps their parents had used more than 50 years ago. The smell was awful and Rebecca could feel her lungs filling up with the fumes. She was glad to get out of the house and take food to the animals. She saw footprints in the shed but couldn't see anyone. It was a bit scary, though.

The aunts were become increasingly depressed, sitting for hours on the couch and not eating much. Rebecca realised how much they relied on Quintas. Even playing her violin didn't seem to raise their spirits. They had no mobiles and the main telephone line had been broken for months.

They just sat on the couch rocking back and forth, back and forth.

The next two days seemed the strangest Rebecca had ever spent. All the times she had been before, Quintas had been there and, although his sisters were busy, he was in charge and they looked to him for guidance. They did what he told them. Now he wasn't there they seemed to have lost all their confidence. They wouldn't go to bed and slept on the couch facing the front door. They wouldn't help feeding the animals and Rebecca had to make them eat, often just bread and tea, water heated on the open fire. They drank the tea and ate the food but they were talking about the past mostly.

Rebecca just let them talk. It was interesting. They normally never talked about the family but started saying she was an angel every time she brought them something.

They told her Artemis had met his wife at a church in Edinburgh. They tried for several years to have a child and had given up.

Effy said when they brought baby Rebecca home, they'd never seen Artemis so happy. He told them Rebecca was a blessing. God's gift, he said.

By the third morning Rebecca was getting worried. The sisters hadn't slept much and kept repeating things. She decided to get help. She felt something was wrong, her parents would have got a message to her if everything was all right.

She said: 'Effy, Aggie can you hear me? I'm going to try and walk to the nearest farm and get help. I have stoked up the fire and left some food but we need bread and milk. I'll not be long.'

Effie said: 'Don't you go as well Rebecca. You can't leave us here.'

Rebecca went over and gave her a hug. 'I'll be back soon and I'll bring help. I'll going to try and find where mum and dad and Quintas are.'

Rebecca put on her best boots and only coat she had and set out. Shit, she thought, this snow is pretty deep and it's freezing. She would never swear out loud if her dad was around. It made her feel guilty but her cousins in Skye had taught her a lot of swear words. It was good to swear when she couldn't master difficult pieces on her violin and this trip was the right time to swear. Miles from anywhere and snow still falling and up to the tops of her boots.

CHAPTER NINE

Morgan woke early, she checked her watch and it was 5a.m. Dressing quickly she realised she was nervous but glad to have Cameron and a policeman with her, worried about the girl Rebecca and if she was safe. Cameron had made the decision to get to the farm and see if the girl was safe there and who else was there. He hoped they would be in time.

As she started down stairs, she saw the giant tractor of farmer Roger idling at the bottom of the steps and both Cameron and the Sergeant dressed in warm jackets and boots waiting to go.

'Roger says his wife has coffee and porridge ready for us at the farm. They're going to show us where to walk,' said the Sergeant. Morgan wondered how they would all fit in the cabin of the tractor.

It took the tractor only about half an hour to make its way over the tracks in the snow and up the hill to Roger's farm. It was not as comfortable with four people in the cabin and Morgan found herself virtually sitting on Cameron's lap.

'This is the highlight of my day,' said Cameron bringing a touch of humour to the chill of the morning.

Morgan was shivering by the time they got there. It wasn't really the cold but anxiety over what they would find.

She glanced at Cameron and said in a quiet voice: 'You don't think we're going to find more bodies at this farm, do you?'

'We'll just have to see. We have no idea what's going on or why these people were killed and their bodies dumped on the beach. We need to check the farm to try and understand what's happening.'

Cameron put his arm around her and gave her a squeeze. 'It'll be fine. You'll be back in Edinburgh before you know it and this will just be a bad dream.'

Roger turned to them and shouted above the engine: 'We can stop here at my farm for a while and Maggie has the porridge ready or I can just continue and take you back to the camper van.'

Morgan immediately said: 'Porridge and a warm up first please.'

Cameron nodded and they all scrambled to get down from the cabin. Even Sergeant Ford seemed glad to get down from his position in the small cabin.

The warmth hit them when they opened the door and Roger's wife Maggie was spooning out steaming porridge into bowls. She'd made coffee and there was local honey sitting on the table.

She hesitated and then said: 'I don't know much about what goes on at the MacNeill farm. I think there are two sisters, twins, and a younger brother. They might be triplets but he is the boss, and an odd one. Never speaks and hardly ever comes into the village. The sisters are seen in Stranraer sometimes, dressed identically in some strange clothes. They all lived there with their mother and father until they died. I don't think the farm has changed much since then. The sisters and the brother run it like a small holding. Every summer they seem to get some help from a young girl. I've seen her getting the cows in and feeding the sheep.'

Cameron said: 'That could be the girl Rebecca who went missing with her parents from the bed and breakfast. We're hoping she's safe at the farm.'

Sergeant Ford said: 'If you can drop us back at the site of the abandoned van, how long will it take us to walk to the MacNeill farm?'

Roger said: 'The snow is pretty deep up there and it could take you an hour or so. Once you get to the farm road there should be a sign saying 'MacNeill farm'. It's about another mile inland from there. It's pretty isolated and off the beaten track.'

Maggie said: 'It's going to be difficult walking in that deep snow. It's compacted so you might be able to walk on the top. We can give you a small shovel if you need it.'

'Thanks. We'll take that offer up.' As he spoke Sergeant Ford got up and started putting on his jacket.

'Think we should set off. If we find anyone, are you ok if we need to bring them to the farm?'

Maggie nodded and said: 'Yes, anything you need.'

Cameron said: 'Are you confident the phones will come back on?'

Sergeant Ford said: 'I'm hoping. When I left Stranraer, they were talking of getting the main road between Portpatrick and the town open today. There also reports they're close to getting power back on. The electricity people have been working 24 hours a day to get reconnected. My thinking is if there are people up there, they must be pretty cold and miserable. I hope they have a coal fire to keep them warm.'

Roger said: 'I've made a decision. I'm going to take you up to the road that leads to the farm on the tractor. It's going to be difficult to walk it for a long distance. It means you just have about a mile to the farm which will be bad enough.'

It took Roger just a few minutes to get them back to the camper van. He continued past it with the snowplough on the front of the giant vehicle making a sort of path through the deep snow. Then it seemed to get deeper and he stopped.

'I don't think I should go any further in his beast. I can't afford to get bogged down. I need the tractor to find any sheep. Can you manage from here, do you think?'

'I'm sure we can,' said Sergeant Ford climbing down and reaching to help Morgan out of the cabin.

The three of them stood watching as farmer Roger turned his giant tractor very carefully and moved back down the road, leaving them alone in the bleak landscape. Morgan saw what looked like a large grey castle in the distance.

'What's that castle?'

'That's Dunskey Castle, abandoned long ago and in need of some repair,' said Sergeant Ford.

'It's right on the cliffs and pretty dangerous, it's not that far from where we found the bodies, the bay where we found them is just a bit further on,' said Cameron.

'Let's get going,' said the Sergeant.

Morgan checked her watch – 9 a.m. They started walking or sort of walking, falling into deep snow and having to be pulled out time and again by each other. Morgan's thigh muscles were burning and it took them well over an hour to make it to the entrance of the MacNeill farm.

They stood exhausted, sweat pouring down their faces. Just as they were getting their breath, their chests heaving with the exertion and not speaking they heard a ping, then another ping and then another.

'Think that's the phones back on. Hallelujah,' said the Sergeant.

Morgan pulled out her phone to find a load of missed calls, a text from a friend and about 20 Whats app messages.

Cameron said: 'That's good because we can find what's happening from the Inspector and get help if we need it.'

Sergeant Ford nodded. 'Yes, big help. Let's get on and find out what's going on at the farm.'

They set off feeling happier and only had about a mile to go. They were half way there when they saw a figure coming towards them on the farm road, long dark hair blowing in the wind.

Morgan said: 'I think that's Rebecca.'

She waved and the girl waved back. It took them about ten minutes to reach her and Morgan said: 'Rebecca, it's Morgan from the bed and breakfast and Cameron. Do you remember us? This is Sergeant Ford. We were just coming to check you're all right. Is it just you there?'

Rebecca smiled. 'Hi, of course I remember. It's good to see you. We haven't seen anyone for days and my parents and uncle have been missing since before the snow came. My aunts are there but they're not well. I was coming to get help.'

Morgan said: 'Let's take one step at a time. What's wrong with them?'

'They're getting very upset. They miss their brother Quintas and want to know where he is all the time. I can't tell them anything. He left with my parents, I think three days ago at night and they haven't come back. I told them they couldn't because of the snow. Now we're running out of food and I set out to find the nearest farm to get help. I've been managing to feed the animals but it's a lot and I need help,' she said, sounding stressed and very tired.

Sergeant Ford said: 'Let's get back to the farm and check on your aunts first. We've phones working now so we can get help. You don't need to do this on your own. We'll help.'

Rebecca said: 'Thanks but I'd better go into the farmhouse first. They don't like strangers.'

As they walked towards the farmhouse Morgan was beside Rebecca and felt her arm link through hers, as they stumbled and fell into deeper snow.

Morgan could feel the girl's exhaustion and suspected she hadn't slept much since her parents left. She also felt that she wanted to tell her something.

'Is there something you want to tell us Rebecca?'

'I just wondered if the people who've been coming to the farm have anything to do with mum and dad being missing.'

'What sort of people do you mean Rebecca?' said Morgan.

'I'm not sure but my aunts mentioned a man who comes every year to see Quintas. They don't know his name but he stays in a caravan near the village and they just go up to Quintas' bedroom to talk. They don't like him, smarmy, they said.

'There seem to be other visitors but the one they were frightened of was a guy who came last week to the farm. They saw him arguing with Quintas in the farm yard. He seemed to be looking for me or that's what the sisters thought. I also saw someone in the farmyard the night my father went missing, wandering around with a flash light.'

Morgan put her arm round her and said: 'You need to tell the police about this Rebecca. It might be important.'

She tried to keep her talking with one ear listening to the Sergeant on the phone to the Inspector. She couldn't hear much but he was asking something about a helicopter and help.

When they reached the farm Rebecca signalled that she was going into the house first. The three of them stood waiting, watched by a wary collie dog sitting in a corner. Morgan could hear animals in the shed, thinking it all looked pretty old fashioned, old sacks and containers randomly scattered in dilapidated sheds.

Just then Rebecca came out and beckoned for them to come in.

'They are ok but not speaking much. I told them you'd come to help. They're ok about you coming in. Come inside and get warm at the fire.'

They walked through a dark kitchen dominated by an old black range. Then into a large lounge with a large fire throwing shadows on the dark old Victorian furniture. It was gloomy and it took Morgan a few seconds to see two women huddled together on the old settee.

'Hello I'm Morgan Cooper and I'm here with Sergeant Ford and Cameron. We're here to help you.'

One of the women looked up and said: 'Where's Quintas? Artemis and Christine took him away. It's not fair.'

Sergeant Ford said 'I'm a policeman. We're here to help you. We need to get you all to hospital to get checked out and then we can explain everything.'

He turned to Rebecca and said: 'We must get them away from here as soon as possible. I'm just going to phone and arrange it.'

He left the room and Cameron followed leaving Morgan with Rebecca and the two sisters.

'Rebecca is there any way to make a cup of tea for everyone?'

'Oh sorry,' she said 'I should have asked. I can boil water on the fire but there's no milk.'

Morgan said: 'Just hot tea will help everyone while we work out how to get you all away from here.'

Rebecca said: 'If we go to hospital how will my parents know where we are?'

'Let's get tea organised and then we can find out what the police have arranged,' said Morgan. This seemed to calm Rebecca. They were just handing out mugs of tea to the sisters when Cameron came into the lounge and signalled Morgan to come outside.

She only realised Rebecca was behind her when she walked out the back door.

'I want to hear what's happening,' said Rebecca. 'I think something has happened to my parents and you don't want to tell me.'

Sergeant Ford said: 'You're right Rebecca. I'm sorry to tell you that your parents and uncle have died. It seems they died the night they left here. We are just starting to investigate what happened but I need you to stay strong and not tell your aunts until we get them to hospital and assessed. They don't look very well to me.'

Morgan looked at Rebecca and thought she seemed in shock.

'Did you suspect something had happened to them, Rebecca?'

'I didn't at first but the more time went on I knew my mum would have been back even if she had to walk through the deep snow. When I didn't hear I knew something was wrong. Did Uncle Quintas harm them?'

'No. We don't think so,' said Sergeant Ford 'But we don't know what happened yet. What makes you think your uncle might have harmed them?'

'My father was so angry with him. I heard them arguing in his bedroom and things being thrown around. It wasn't just the missing money and the farm not being looked after. There was something else and I heard my father say he was taking Uncle Quintas to the police station in Stranraer. I don't know what was going on but I had never seen my father so angry. My mother was trying to keep the peace and calm things down but my father was determined.'

She started crying and Morgan went to put an arm around her.

'The police will be able to explain things to you when we get to Stranraer.'

Sergeant Ford said: 'Rebecca we need to get your aunts out of this house and to safety. The main road has been opened to Stranraer but getting them to that road is an issue. Your aunts are not in any fit state to walk in this snow.'

Cameron said: 'Could the helicopter come with medics and airlift them? I can't see any other way as no vehicle can get down here yet. I think we can walk with Rebecca back to the farm and Roger will give us a lift back to the bed and breakfast.'

Sergeant Ford nodded: 'I agree. The inspector is planning to come to the village. He can meet us there. He wants to speak to Rebecca and he can get us up to date with what's happening.

'Rebecca, a helicopter is on its way with medics. Can you get them ready? Pack them a nightdress and anything else they might need. Will they understand that they'll be winched up to the safety of the helicopter and taken to hospital? It can't land.'

'I can explain but they'll want me with them, they're feeling very vulnerable and scared. We all are,' said Rebecca.

Sergeant Ford shook his head. 'I'm sorry but there's not enough room in the helicopter. You'll need to come back with us to the bed and breakfast. We'll get you to the hospital to be reunited with them as soon as possible. Ok?'

Rebecca nodded: 'Ok. I'll try and explain to them.'

As they heard the helicopter approach Rebecca appeared in the kitchen ahead of the two aunts dressed in identical pink outer coats and matching hats, looking scared and helpless.

The medics and one of the helicopter team came into the kitchen. They spoke to the Sergeant and then led one aunt outside and strapped her in and winched her into the helicopter. They were fast and within five minutes both women were in the helicopter and it was gone.

The mood in the farmhouse changed.

Cameron said: 'I think we should get back to Roger's farm as soon as we can. Rebecca, do you want to make the fire safe? Can you get what you need and switch everything off?'

Sergeant Ford looked towards her. 'We'll need to make the house as secure as we can.'

As Rebecca left to go to her bedroom Sergeant Ford said: 'This is now a crime scene. We need to get into that guy Quintas,' what a strange bloody name for a farmer, bedroom and a forensic team here as soon as. I've already briefed the inspector and I'll come back with them. The inspector says he knows more about what happened to the Rev and his wife and the uncle. He'll brief us all when we get back. I want to get Rebecca away to hospital as soon as we can to get checked out.'

Cameron said: 'I went upstairs and had a look. That guy's room has about four locks on it, it's been locked. The other rooms are just open. The sisters have a twin room, there is a bedroom for Rebecca and a spare, I assume for the Rev brother.

'It's very dark up there and old fashioned, the wallpaper looks about 50 years old.'

Rebecca appeared in the kitchen with her winter coat on and a small suitcase with her. She also carried her violin case.

'Is it ok if I take this? I can't leave it here.' she said.

'No problem. Let's go,' said the Sergeant. 'Cameron and I can help you carry anything. Don't worry.'

'What about the animals? Rebecca started to look distressed. 'I fed them this morning but they will need feeding tonight. Who will look after them?'

Sergeant Ford said: 'We're going ask the farmer Roger to come up later and look after them. Then tomorrow we'll make arrangements. Don't worry. We'll take care of everything.'

As they started walking away from the farm Morgan saw Rebecca turn and stand looking at the farm, tears running down her face. Morgan couldn't think of anything to say but just put her arm around her and said: 'Let's go. It's too cold to stand around.'

It took them over an hour to walk back to Roger's farm. He'd arranged a bigger tractor to take them all back to the village. As the bed and breakfast came into view, they saw the lounge of the bed and breakfast lit up and the Inspector sitting at a desk.

CHAPTER TEN

Inspector Driver was busy getting his temporary office set up in the living room of the bed and breakfast. Thankfully, with the phones back on he knew his Sergeant, Cameron and Morgan plus the missing girl were on their way back to the village.

He had news for them but wanted to see what state the girl was in. The post mortems on the three bodies had been carried out and the report had come through and didn't make pleasant reading. Inspector Driver now had a triple murder investigation to lead. The father and mother had had their necks broken, a professional job the pathologist said, and the brother was shot. It looks like he was trying to get away when he fell. They found some blood under the snow about 100 yards from the camper van.

The village was so quiet he heard the tractor before he saw it pull up outside the bed and breakfast, watching as his Sergeant jumped down first, then Cameron helping Morgan and the girl.

He saw his Sergeant stay to speak to the farmer as the other three made their way up the steps. Mike opened the door to greet them.

Cameron said: 'Hi Mike. I'm just going to see the Inspector in here. Could you make sure Rebecca and Morgan get something to drink and eat? It's been pretty cold and miserable out there. I'll be through in a minute.'

Morgan said: 'Yeah, we need to get freshened up. You ok Rebecca?' The girl nodded, keeping her eyes lowered.

By this time the Inspector had opened the door. 'Glad to see you all back safely. Come inside Cameron and we can have a chat.'

Rebecca looked like she wanted to say something but shrugged and went into the kitchen.

Inspector Driver closed the door.

'I hear the sisters are in a bit of a state Cameron. What's the girl like?'

'She seems very sensible and practical. But that could be shock. She knows about her parents and the uncle. She kind of forced the question and I think the Sergeant felt he had to be honest. She took it ok.'

'Good,' said the Inspector. 'We need her to be strong. She's going to have identify the parents and uncle and we'll take her to Dumfries for that.'

At that moment the door opened and Sergeant Ford stepped in.

'I've asked the farmer to stay around. I suspect you might want me to go back to the farm?'

Inspector Driver smiled: 'You know me too well. I think it might be an idea. A forensic team is being dropped by helicopter in about an hour and I need you to make sure everything in that guy Quintas' bedroom is bagged. I know he had some secrets and I want to know what they are in case they're the reason they've been targeted.'

'Ok no problem. I might see if they have spare bedroom here for later. Any news before I go?'

'Yeah, sit down both of you,' said the Inspector. 'The post mortem results came in last night. The Rev and his wife died of broken necks. They don't think that happened in any fall. They think they were killed in their camper van and then the bodies taken down to the bottom of the cliff. Perhaps the killer hoped they would be washed away or people would think it was an accident. The brother was a different matter. He was shot in the back, perhaps as he was trying to run away. Finding any blood is a matter for the forensic teams going there today. So, it looks like we have a killer on the loose. The big question is why these people? It also looked a pretty professional job. Why were they targeted, why kill a Minister and his wife and a farmer, in Portpatrick of all places? Nothing like this happens here.'

Cameron said: 'So you think they were driven down to the bay by the killer?'

Inspector Driver nodded: 'Think so, as no other explanation. We'll check for fingerprints in the camper van and tyre tracks on the beach. It's going to be difficult moving around with all this snow but at least the main road is open and the power back on. Once that girl Rebecca gets some food and a rest, we'll get her to Stranraer. Her aunts are in hospital and asking for her. They're in pretty bad way and seem to have regressed back to another time, blocking out what happened at the farm and the disappearance of their brother. We're looking at where we can take them for safety. Then we need Rebecca to go to Dumfries to identify her parents and uncle. I'm hoping Morgan can go with her, not a policewoman or social worker.'

Cameron said: 'Rebecca told Morgan that some people had been coming to the farm. One guy arguing with Quintas in the yard and another who comes regularly and goes to the brother's bedroom. It seems there was someone looking around the sheds the night the Rev and his family left.'

Inspector Driver turned to his Sergeant: 'Something strange seems to have going on there. Make sure any computers or phones in Quintas' bedroom are taken as soon as possible to the digital team. We need to see what he has been doing up there. The team have already established that he had an iPhone and they are tracing the calls on that. I am looking at all the financials as money seem to have been an issue in the family. We need to see if this guy Quintas was the target and the Rev and his wife collateral damage. They seem to have met their killer on the road the night before snow started.

'I'm looking at what resources we have and Glasgow say they can help if needed. If you can be in charge of the search of the farm Sergeant that will be one aspect covered. Can you ask the farmer if he can feed the animals tonight and tomorrow and I'll get animal welfare to take over?'

Sergeant Ford made to leave and Cameron said: 'It'll be good to get your thoughts on how they lived in this farm. There seems to be a basement fitted under the lounge where they used to ask Rebecca to go if there were visitors. She seems to have been stuck at that farm for months and no one ever saw her in the village. That's not normal for a young teenager. It would be good to find out about the dynamics of life there. I think the sisters and brother were left to run the farm, not very well from what I can see.'

Inspector Driver said: 'You haven't lost it Cameron. I'm hoping you can stick around. I've cleared it with the bosses and they are glad of your help. We might need Morgan as well as Rebecca seems happier with her around and trusts her and we can't seem to get social work at the moment.'

In the kitchen Rebecca was still not speaking but eating toast and sipping her tea, which Morgan had put two spoons of sugar into. She didn't look quite as pale.

Inspector Driver came into the kitchen and said: 'Rebecca we have a car to take you to Stranraer to see your aunts and get checked out at the hospital. I've arranged a hotel for you to stay if you don't need to be in hospital. Then, tomorrow I'll see you at the police station. A car will come and get you.'

For the first time Rebecca looked up and said: 'Can Morgan come with me? I don't want to be alone.'

Inspector Driver looked at Morgan and she nodded.

'I'm sure that will be fine Rebecca. Morgan will stay with you. Once you've been checked out, we'll make sure you see your aunts. They've been told that their brothers and sister -in -law are dead but I'm not sure it's sunk in. We'll have support with you when you see them.'

Once Morgan and Rebecca left in a police car the room fell quiet.

Inspector Driver started packing up his documents.

'Do you fancy a coffee and chat before I get back to the office in Stranraer? I need to see how the girl is then arrange for her to get to Dumfries to identify the family. I can't ask the sisters. There're not well enough. What plans do you have Cameron?'

'I'm going into Stranraer to see my family and then I need to get back to London soon but I'll play it by ear. I keep thinking there's a killer living in this village. Do you think whoever did this is still around?'

'Yes, I do strangely. I think there's a lot we still don't know. It's why I like having you here, another experienced hand. Once this snow melts, we can get back to some sort of normal life. The village is almost back to normal, whatever normal is. The main road is open but many of the side roads are still blocked so that's making our job difficult. I'm going to have a look at all the characters living around here. As you know people often come to rural areas to escape something or find a quiet life and a lot of Irish people have moved her and bought land and homes. Tam Mitchell came to live in the village after some family tragedy. Everyone has a story. Whether there's a killer here I don't know. It could be someone from outside with a grudge or just a random killing.'

Cameron added: 'There was that strange message on the back window of the camper van. What was all about? Who stole her and who is she?'

'Yeah,' said the Inspector. 'I've asked the team to get a picture of that. We can't get the van out of there yet which is a problem.'

They were finishing the coffee Mike had brought them and were getting ready to leave when they heard a knock at the front door.

They heard Mike answer and a voice saying: 'I'm Dave Campbell. I must see the inspector now. I have information.'

Inspector Driver looked at Cameron. They heard Mike saying the Inspector was in a meeting.

Cameron said: 'I've met that guy. He's staying in another hotel but was here listening to Rebecca playing and asking questions.'

Inspector Driver said: 'Let's hear what he wants.'

He opened the door and told Mike to let him in.

The three of them sat round the table.

'Hi Mr Campbell. I've asked Cameron to sit in on the chat. You wanted to speak to me. Fire away as I need to get to Stranraer as soon as possible.' said the Inspector, sitting back and folding his arms.

Dave Campbell took a file from the briefcase he was carrying, putting it on the table and looked like he was composing himself.

'I believe I have some information that might be pertinent to your investigation. I am a lawyer in Glasgow but this is not about work. I have come to see you as I believe the girl called Rebecca is my missing niece.'

He stopped speaking, waiting for his statement to sink in.

Cameron let the Inspector take the lead.

'What do you mean your niece? She's the daughter of the deceased Rev and his wife surely. We are talking about the same person, aren't we? Have you confused her with someone else?'

Dave Campbell nodded. 'I'm convinced she is my niece who has been missing for 17 years and taken, we believe, from a crashed car by the Rev and his wife. A crashed car which killed my sister, the mother of this girl.'

'That's a very serious allegation Mr Campbell. What proof do you have?' Cameron thought even the inspector's voice sounded full of doubt and amazement.

Dave Campbell cleared his throat and said: 'Let me explain. I need to go back 17 years. My sister, Lizzie Campbell, was one of Scotland's rising stars in the musical world. She was a world class violinist and the week before she died was giving a concert in the Royal Concert Hall in Glasgow.

'It was the last time I saw her alive and the last time my parents saw her. We thought it was the start of a great career and she was hoping to get a job offer from an orchestra. She was happy and she had her little girl. Her daughter was just three months old.'

Inspector Driver: 'Who's the child's father?'

Dave said: 'We think it was her boyfriend at the time, an Indian student at Edinburgh University who returned home at short notice.

'Lizzie had been a quietish girl growing up near Glasgow. She started playing the violin when she was about six. She'd already been playing the piano, and was naturally gifted. When she went to Edinburgh to study music, she met a new crowd and never talked about her life apart from the music. I was in Glasgow training as a lawyer and I didn't see much of her in that period. We each had our own friends and social life. When she was in her fourth year, she came home one Sunday and told my parents she was pregnant by her boyfriend.

'They'd been in a relationship for more than a year but he seems to have left Edinburgh and his course very suddenly. She said she had told him of the pregnancy and he was delighted and they talked of a future together.'

Inspector Driver: 'Did the boyfriend ever turn up again?'

Dave shook his head: 'No. She went through the pregnancy herself and then when the baby was born my mother went through for a couple of weeks to her flat in Edinburgh to help her. She very much wanted that baby, and played it music every day while she was pregnant. She named the baby Sophie. I don't think she put the father's name on the birth certificate but I could be wrong. It was tough for her at first but once Sophie got to three months things got a lot easier. We all loved that baby. Lizzie didn't seem to get any money from the father but managed with her savings. She didn't seem bitter and loved being a mum.'

'What happened then?' said Cameron.

'When the baby was four months, she called my parents to say she was going to take Sophie and have a few days driving around the Highlands and visiting a friend in Inverness, spending a couple of nights in Wick with an old school friend. Her plan was then to head back to Inverness, cross to the west coast, visit a friend in Oban and then stop at my parents in Ayrshire. But she never made it.

'That was the last we heard from her. On the fifth day she seems to have left Wick and was driving back down the road quite early when she crashed. Her car seems to have left the road and smashed into a tree.

'When they found her, she was dead, and Sophie gone. No baby seat, nothing. It was as if she didn't exist. I went up there and found the bed and breakfast she stayed in and they said she had breakfast with Sophie in the dining room early and left with her. There didn't seem to be any problem.'

Inspector Drover said: 'What do you think happened?'

Dave said: 'I don't know but it wasn't right. One thing the media were not told by the police, was that although Lizzie had been injured in the car accident, what they did not disclose is that she would have survived if medical help had been found quickly. It was about half an hour before they got to her and she died in the ambulance. They found out later that her car had been tampered with. I think someone wanted her dead. I think Sophie was taken by the person who killed my sister. On top of that they left my sister dying in that car, something I will never forgive.'

Inspector Drover looked shocked and said: 'Are you seriously telling me you believe your sister was murdered and her baby stolen? I assume this will be in the police report?'

Dave voice sounded bitter: 'They thought it had been a professional job. As it was the media interest died down pretty fast. No one seemed to care what happened way up there out of the central belt. My parents were heartbroken, as all the family was, but they never believed that they would not find their granddaughter. The death of their daughter, Lizzie, was too much to bear but the loss of Sophie was the final straw, it took the life out of them, they were never the same and it was as if a light had gone out their lives.'

Cameron indicated to the inspector that he wanted a word and they left the room, making an excuse to Mr Campbell.

Cameron said: 'Strange it's the same message about someone being stolen that was on the camper van. Do you think there's a connection?'

Inspector Driver said: 'I've no idea but this certainly puts the cat among the pigeons. That poor girl Rebecca seems at the centre of all this. Is there is a link between what happened 17 years ago and what's happening now? Let's get back in.'

They couldn't stop Dave Campbell talking. It was almost as if he was giving out 17 years of frustration.

He said: 'The whole thing devastated my parents. As well as losing their only daughter in awful circumstances the granddaughter they had come to love, and their link to Lizzie, had disappeared.

'Over the next five years they did everything they could, spent thousands of pounds on private detectives and still found nothing. It was almost as if Sophie had disappeared off the face of the earth. At one point, police thought she might have taken abroad and all horrible thoughts went through our heads.

'In the end not knowing and the constant worry killed them both. We all put our lives on hold. My father died five years after Lizzie and my mum a year or so later. They said it was cancer killed my mum but I always felt it was a broken heart. To lose your daughter and granddaughter in one day was too much for them. Perhaps if they'd known what had happened to Sophie they could've coped. But not knowing was like having your heart ripped out. My mother described it as living with a heavy heart every minute of every day.'

Inspector Driver said: 'What makes you certain this girl Rebecca is your lost niece?'

Dave Campbell starting pulling more stuff out of his briefcase.

'I have been searching social media for as long as I can remember, looking for someone that I thought was Sophie. Then I saw this girl playing on YouTube and I did some research and decided to come down here and see if it was her.

'I have a video of my sister playing the violin and one of Rebecca. They've different colour hair- Lizzie was blonde and this girl has darker hair. But I know it's Sophie. When you watch those videos you'll be convinced too. I need the police to take this seriously and do a DNA test,' his voice rising with stress.

Inspector Driver put up his hand. 'I don't need to see them now Mr Campbell. We are in the middle of a murder investigation. I want you come to the police station in Stranraer tomorrow at 11a.m. and we can go through everything. I need you to go back to your hotel and not mention this to anyone. Can you do that?'

Dave Campbell nodded: 'Yes, I'm content you're listening to me and taking this seriously. I'll be glad to come and show you what I have tomorrow.' The inspector nodded and Dave Campbell got up and left, obviously satisfied that what he wanted to say had been taken on board.

Cameron and the Inspector watched him walk down the pathway before they sat down.

Tom said: 'Cameron can you get us both a coffee and then we can have a chat. I need to make a couple of calls.'

Cameron nodded: 'What on earth do you make of that?'

Tom said: 'I'm not sure and I need some time to think things through. We will know more tomorrow. But I assume you think like me and this makes Mr Campbell a suspect? 'He's very smooth, isn't he?'

Cameron said: 'I'll get two strong coffees, ok?'

When he got back to the room the Inspector was just finishing a call.

'I just called Morgan and asked her if she could stay in Stranraer with Rebecca tonight. They are keeping Rebecca in hospital and she wanted Morgan with her. There is a police guard outside her room. I also asked Morgan if she would go with Rebecca tomorrow in the police car to Dumfries to get these three victims formally identified. She agreed that she will stay with her in a hotel and they will come back to Stranraer the next morning. It's good of Morgan and she says she's been able to speak to her work and arrange time off.'

Cameron said: 'I think I'll stay another couple of days and see what happens. Is that ok with you?'

Tom said: 'I'm glad you are both staying around. I'm going back to Stranraer now to do my research on this accident 17 years ago. I've already called the office and asked them to look out the police reports from that time. If you are bored you could try the library in Stranraer and see if you can find the media reports.'

Cameron said: 'Good idea. I'm going to Stranraer anyway to have a coffee with my sister so I'll call into the library. I'll stay here tonight and come to the station tomorrow.'

Inspector nodded: 'Good, we have Mr Campbell tomorrow morning and I would like you there. It's also good Rebecca is away when we see him. I hope we can get a DNA sample from him tomorrow morning.'

CHAPTER ELEVEN

Rebecca felt better after a night in the hospital. She'd slept and felt safer knowing Morgan was in a room next door and a policeman outside the door. She knew she had a tough day ahead, perhaps seeing her dead mum and dad would make this whole nightmare real.

She thought she was dreaming and couldn't get her head around it. Even music didn't make sense or make her feel any better, strange as it had always been such a comfort and somewhere she could escape to when she felt down or her parents were angry with her, which they always seemed to be, now she was 17 and with a mind of her own.

She found the journey to Dumfries in the back of the police car pass in a flash. She was holding Morgan's hand and could feel the warmth from another human being seep into her body, neither of them speaking. She felt almost detached from her own body and her brain was struggling to cope with all that had happened.

She couldn't believe she would never see her mother and father again.

Her aunts had looked so strange in the hospital. They seemed to have shrunk and weren't that bothered to see her. They were lying in twin beds in a room to themselves and just holding hands and staring into space. The nurses were kind to them but when Rebecca tried to tell them that their brothers were dead it didn't seem to make any impression. They just kept asking for juice.

Rebecca knew she was going to have to leave the hospital and the aunts and go to the mortuary.

Morgan didn't say anything in the car going to the hospital mortuary. She knew Rebecca was going over everything in her head and preparing herself for the next challenge. The hospital visit to the aunts had been stressful enough but to have to identify her parent was going to be difficult. As the car stopped at the mortuary, she felt her hand being gripped more tightly.

She turned to Rebecca and said: 'I can stay with you if you want and come in with you. You don't have to do this alone.'

'Thanks,' said Rebecca. 'That would be good.'

They were escorted to the entrance and met with a friendly woman who took them into a room.

She told Rebecca that a curtain would be pulled open and she just needed to nod if she could identify her parents and uncle.

Rebecca watched as she stared at the three tables in room. On one was her mother, the second her father and her uncle was last. After looking at each table Rebecca turned and said: 'Yes, it's them. They look like they're sleeping.'

She started crying softly and Morgan put her arm around her.

'That's it over with. They won't feel any pain again. Let's go and get a coffee.'

The policeman told them he was to take them to their hotel. The plan was for them to stay the night in Dumfries and be taken back to Stranraer tomorrow morning. He said he would be on duty at the hotel all night to make sure they were ok.

Morgan made sure Rebecca was comfortable in her room and suggested they went down and had a coffee or something. 'How are you doing, Rebecca? This has been an awful time for you. Do you want to stay and have some food or eat in your room and rest?'

Rebecca said: 'I'd like to be where there are people. I would feel too lonely in the room by myself. I don't even feel like playing my violin. I feel so alone and everyone who cared about me is gone. My father always told me to be brave in everything I did, and to pray, but it's hard.'

Morgan said: 'I lost my own mother Rebecca not that long ago. They are always in your heart but you need to give yourself time. You must have some family up north who can support you?'

Rebecca nodded and Morgan felt it best to leave the conversation and organise food.

They ate downstairs and by 9p.m. Morgan could see Rebecca's eyes closing with tiredness.

'Let's get an early night. We'll see what tomorrow brings and what the police can tell us.'

Morgan left Rebecca in her room and made her way to her adjacent bedroom. She was exhausted and realised she hadn't thought about Max for the last few days. It was over, she thought. She didn't really understand why he would want to cheat, when she thought the relationship she had with him was enough, but she didn't feel anger towards him. Perhaps it was time for them to end before they did something stupid like marry. She resolved to call Max in the morning and check how he was. She hoped she could get back to Edinburgh in the next few days but had promised the Inspector she wouldn't leave Rebecca until she was safe with relatives.

The visit with Rebecca to the mortuary brought back memories, memories she had buried, seeing her own mother lying in a hospital bed, slipping away from her for ever.

She could feel the tears starting and curled up in bed, crying herself to sleep.

She woke an hour later. The crying had been good for her and she resolved to sort her life out, and time to live on her own for a while. She also realised her work was boring her and she was not bothered about her deputy taking her place. In fact, it would be good to find something new. Once she had made the decision, she felt happier and drifted back to sleep.

The next morning their plans to go back to Stranraer were interrupted by the duty police officer. He said Inspector Driver wondered if they could stay in Dumfries another night and not come back to Stranraer till the following day.

When she met Rebecca for breakfast Morgan decided to make it sound like fun.

'It looks like we are here for another day Rebecca. How do you fancy doing some shopping and getting you some new clothes and some lunch? The police officer can come with us to keep us safe,' said Morgan.

'You mean shop and choose my own clothes? I've never done that before. Mum always bought all my clothes. I didn't like them sometimes. I saw clothes online I liked but I never had any money.'

They had a good look around the area and Rebecca chose some jeans, tee shirts and track shoes. When they got back, they were laden with shopping bags.

'I think we'd better just eat at the hotel. I'm exhausted,' said Morgan.

'I want to go and try on my clothes,' exclaimed Rebecca. It was the first time Morgan had seen the girl happy.

'Let's meet in the dining room in an hour. Ok?' suggested Morgan.

They had spent a pleasant day managing to talk without mentioning what was happening in Stranraer.

But at dinner that night Rebecca wanted to talk.

She said: 'I used to wonder why I looked so different from the rest of the family. I asked once if I was adopted but my dad said what he always said when there a difficult question "it was God's wish or God's gift." My mum never said anything and I stopped wondering and asking. They looked after me and loved me. I didn't want to upset them.'

The next day they were ready to leave at 10a.m. visiting the aunts who were now in hospital in Dumfries and then going to Stranraer.

Morgan felt better this morning. The previous night she'd managed to speak to her boss John Stevens. She had sent the document he needed the night before and told him she would not be back for a couple of weeks.

He said he understood her need for time off and agreed with her that her depute could manage the announcement.

'I've trained and prepared the team for this. They can manage without me. In fact, when I return, I want to talk to you about my future. I'm no longer sure it's with the company.'

John Stevens said: 'Morgan, I still think this company needs you. Look, take the time off, as much as you need and come back and we'll talk.'

The journey back to Stranraer took less than two hours and Morgan was deep in thought when she was jolted out of her dreaming by her mobile ringing. It was the Inspector.

'Hi, Morgan here.'

Inspector Driver said: 'Hi. How are things? A text said you're close to Stranraer. I've booked two rooms at the big hotel on the seafront for you both. I think you should get settled in there. I took the liberty of getting your stuff packed up from the bed and breakfast and your car into the town so they're all waiting for you at the hotel. If you can get Rebecca a coffee or something I can contact you at lunchtime and arrange to meet both of you. I assume Rebecca's ok? Thanks for all you're doing.'

Morgan said: 'Really, it's ok. I feel happy to help out and be here for Rebecca. She's doing really well.'

As she spoke, she looked across at Rebecca and was pleased to see her smile back.

In Stranraer Inspector Driver was sitting at his desk behind piles of documents with his head in his hands, exhausted after working through the night, and had just finished a meeting with his forensics team and it was still just 8a.m. He saw Cameron outside his office and beckoned him in.

'Hi Cam. I'm glad you're here. I want to tell you as much as I can before Rebecca and Morgan get back at lunchtime. Dave Campbell is coming in at 10a.m. so we have a couple of hours. I've ordered coffee for us. The team are still at the farm but what they're finding is very disconcerting. I'm not sure if it's connected to the murders but we cannot rule it out.'

'Sounds interesting. Can you tell me much about it?'

The inspector sighed: 'Where do I start? I'll start with this odd fellow, Quintas. He was a nasty piece of work, it seems. Apart from his gambling, and that might be where all the family money has gone, he had letters from the National Lottery and emails telling him to take a break and correspondence from a lot of online gambling companies showing he was spending about £1,000 a week online. If Rebecca's right then the Rev was spot on that the farm was in financial trouble. There were bills for animal feed and final demands piled up in his bedroom.'

Cameron nodded: 'The farm looked abandoned, like no one lived there.'

'It's worse. It seems the Rev threw his brother's iMac, brand new, onto the floor in anger. Now our teams have managed to have a look at it and no wonder the Rev was angry. It seems our little farmer was heavily into child pornography. He was exchanging videos and had the technical skills to make new ones. In fact, he had a list of his clients and our obscene publications team are on their way to Portpatrick to a caravan owned by a couple from Glasgow, who have a caravan, whose identity was found in his house.

'He's a client and visited the farm in the last few days to see Quintas. He needs to be interviewed.

'More worrying was that there was a camera set up in the basement and very carefully hidden, obviously to film Rebecca. We found some videos going back a few years. I don't think he did anything except look, a bit of a voyeur.'

'Oh My God that's creepy. I suspect the sisters had no idea what he was up to. I don't think they ever went into his bedroom.' Cameron stood up.

'Don't go, Cameron, there's more.'

'What on earth now?' Cameron said as he sat back down at the table.

'When Rebecca was in the hospital getting checked they took her DNA. We have the DNA of the Rev and his wife. Guess what, they are not related. The Rev and his wife are not her parents.'

'Bloody hell,' said Cameron. 'Does that mean there might be something in this story by Dave Campbell. Is this the missing baby?'

Inspector Driver nodded: 'I've had a quick look at the police file for that accident and the timing is about right. It was 17 years ago. I am going to ask Mr Campbell to agree to a DNA test. We can then see if he is any relation to this girl. It could be just his imagination but I'm interested in what happened all those years ago. I don't mind you sitting in on the interview this morning, you might get a different perspective on this whole mystery. Sergeant Ford is still at the farm and won't be finished there till later. Then we can let the girl go back for a look if she wants.'

'Until we start to understand why these people died, I suspect we'll never find our killer. I am becoming more and more certain that what happened almost two decades ago is behind this.'

Cameron said: 'I keep thinking of this poor girl Rebecca or whatever she is called. She's lost people who loved her, even if they were guilty of taking her, they've looked after and loved her for a long time. She will need help understanding all this.'

The Inspector nodded: 'I've never dealt with this sort of thing before. It's usually pretty clear cut in my job as I expect you know. Dealing with a triple killer is difficult enough with our resources but a missing baby is another thing. Anyway, Mr Campbell is due in any time now. Let's not mention anything about the DNA of Rebecca and the Rev. I just want to see what he says. I'm sure he'll be happy to give a DNA test.'

Just then there was a knock on the door. One of his team said a Mr Campbell was downstairs.

Dave Campbell came in carrying a laptop and a pile of documents under this arm.

He said: 'Let me show you both this now.' He opened the laptop and on one side of the screen he had a grainy video of a young woman with long blond, wavy hair playing the violin on a stage. On the other side was Rebecca playing a violin in the lounge at the bed and breakfast.

'I know they have different colour of hair. That's my sister playing at Glasgow Concert Hall just weeks before she died. This is Rebecca. When I watch them side by side, I know they are mother and daughter. They have the same mannerisms, the play the violin like twins. Look, can you see?' he implored the inspector.

'Yes, I can see some similarities but we need to study them more. Can you send these videos to me? Also, Mr Campbell can you provide us with a DNA sample today? That would help establish the full facts.'

Dave Campbell nodded: 'Happy to do anything you think might get to the truth. I feel, for the first time, that my niece is here. I'll do anything you say.'

The Inspector nodded: 'Can you tell us more about your family, your parents and Lizzie?'

Dave Campbell seemed all too willing to talk.

'We grew up in a house in the Newton Mearns area. Dad had his own engineering plant at Kilmarnock. We were never short of anything but not extravagant. No foreign holidays, just down south to see family. Lizzie was six when she started on the violin, she'd been playing the piano for about a year before switching to the violin, and within months the music teacher at the school recognised her talent. My parents were delighted and did everything they could to help her, driving her to lessons, buying the best of equipment. When she was 12, she started getting lessons with one of the top teachers at the music school in Edinburgh. At the time I never paid much attention. I was four years older and only interested in football.'

Inspector Driver said: 'Did you and your sister get on well?'

'When we were children, we played together. When Lizzie got into her music, we took different paths. I was studying to be a lawyer in Glasgow and I hardly saw her. She never seemed to bring a friend home. It was all music and my parents encouraged it.'

'What happened when she went to music school?' Cameron intervened.

'My parents bought Lizzie a flat in the city in the west end of Edinburgh. They also got me one in Hyndland in Glasgow when I went to university. Dad's business was doing well and around that time he sold it to a big Glasgow engineering company.'

'What happened to that flat when Lizzie was killed?'

At this question Dave Campbell started to look uncomfortable.

He said: 'The flat is still in the family. You will need to speak my parents' lawyers in Ayr as they handle all Lizzie's money. My understanding is that my parents changed their will after Lizzie died and left money in trust for Sophie, always believing she would be found. She will be a very wealthy young woman.'

'Was that a problem for you Mr Campbell? Inspector Driver was looking at him intently.

'No that was their decision. I had my flat and was left equal share with my sister. I understood that my parents couldn't accept that Sophie wasn't coming back. I feel now they've been proved right. Really, if you want to know the details I would speak to Robertson and Son in Ayr. The old man Robertson who dealt with it is retired I think but his son, James, is in charge and still looks after my sister's assets. I still have a key for Sophie's flat in Edinburgh and just check it's all right now and again.'

Inspector Driver said: 'Thanks for your honesty, Mr Campbell and filling in a few of the pieces of the missing jigsaw. Getting your DNA will help explain it more. We should get the results tomorrow. I'll be in touch.'

The Inspector buzzed his PA and asked for an officer to come and escort Mr Campbell to get his DNA taken.

Inspector Driver said: 'Where are you staying Mr Campbell? I plan to look at these videos today and all the documents you have brought. How about we come and see you tomorrow morning in Portpatrick?

'Yes, I'm just at the same hotel. Just ask for me. I'm happy to go back there now and go for lunch with my wife.'

Cameron and the Inspector watched as Dave Campbell left in his car about 20 minutes later.

'Very interesting isn't it. The question is how does this tie in with the murder? We'll know more tomorrow morning when his DNA comes back. What's he going to do if isn't his niece?' Cameron looked at the Inspector who seemed lost in thought.

Inspector Driver said: 'Couple of thoughts. The hospital in Dumfries have been on to say the old sisters are a bit disturbed. The other thing is I'm arranging for us to go to Ayr this afternoon and meet the lawyer, James Robertson. I just got one of my team to call him and he said he'll bring his father in. He's retired but will have vital information about the Campbell family. He seems to have been their lawyer for 40 years.'

Cameron said: 'I'm up for that. But we need to find out about this father of the missing girl. Who was he and was he aware she was missing all those years ago?'

Inspector Driver said: 'We're getting Sergeant Ford back this afternoon. He's finished at the farmhouse and it's been made secure. The animals are all away and it's up to the lawyers to find out who owns it and what they do with it.

'I suggested they let Rebecca back into the farm to pick up anything she needs. You can meet Morgan tomorrow morning and update her about the DNA results and what it might mean for this girl we call Rebecca. You can check what state this young girl is in. Morgan obviously won't say anything to her until we know for sure.'

The Inspector drove Cameron the 60 odd miles to Ayr arriving at the firm's office just after lunch. James Robertson was waiting for them.

'My Dad's upstairs and very interested in what you have to say.'

They entered an old-fashioned wood lined office where a distinguished looking man was already seated at the round table. Cameron was struck by the timeless look of an old solicitors' office and the smart appearance of the lawyers, and struck by how wary both men looked.

Charles Robertson introduced himself and said: 'This has been a bit of shock. It's a long time since anyone asked about the Campbell family.'

Inspector Driver introduced himself and announced Cameron as a consultant on the case.

He's already planned in his head what he would say.

'We're here gentlemen because there is a suggestion that the missing girl Sophie Campbell has been located.' He waited to see the reaction and watched a look pass between father and son.

'Excuse me,' said the older Mr Robertson. 'Perhaps you will understand our lack of excitement when you know we have seen several claims of the child being found in the past few years. There is quite a large estate at stake.'

Inspector Driver said: 'What I can tell you is that we have found a girl, of about the right age for your missing Sophie, living with a family who have died in the last few days. DNA results show that she is not their daughter. We have Lizzie Campbell' s brother claiming that he knows this girl to be his niece. We have the girl's DNA and we will soon have the Dave Campbell's DNA. But more importantly, we have her mother's DNA sample which we are using to check if this is her daughter. Her DNA was kept by the police after the road accident in case her daughter was found. We should know if it is the missing Sophie tomorrow.'

Charles Robertson nodded. 'If this is true and she turns

out to be Sophie then I can only say I wish Lizzie and her parents were here. It was a tragedy. When Lizzie died her parents were devastated but the baby missing as well was a cruel blow. They had so many hopes for Lizzie in her career. I assume you know she was a very talented musician and on the verge of great stardom when she died.'

Cameron asked: 'What is your role with the family?'

James Robertson said: 'We've provided legal advice for more than 40 years for her father in his business and private life, they were our biggest clients. When Lizzie went to music school in Edinburgh her parents bought her a flat to live in. They did the same for their son David.

'When Lizzie died the parents came to me. They really believed they would find Sophie and spent more than a £100,000 on private investigators, to no avail. She'd just disappeared. They made sure her DNA was kept so that if a child was found they could check against her mother's. Do you know what happened to her?'

Inspector Driver said: 'If it's the missing Sophie then we think she was taken by a childless couple from the crashed car – they brought her up off grid really. She didn't attend school and has never registered with a doctor. They seemed to travel around Scotland a lot in a camper van, the father was a sort of preacher from Galloway and the mother from Highlands, her family there seemed to have just accepted the baby as hers. They stayed in Galloway some of the summer and both families never asked questions.'

Charles Robertson said: 'What's she like this girl?'

The Inspector brought out his iPad and showed the video of Rebecca playing the violin.

'Gosh,' said Mr Robertson. 'It's different colour of hair but she looks like Lizzie. So, she's about 17, is she?'

Inspector Driver said: 'If this is the right girl what sort of money would she have?'

'Quite substantial Inspector,' said James Robertson.

'Do you represent Lizzie's brother as well?'

Charles Robertson said: 'No, there was sort of falling out before the parents died. If I remember David tried to get the parents to give him Lizzie's flat in Edinburgh. They refused and he didn't speak to them for about a year.

'Mr and Mrs Campbell died within a year of each other. Broken hearts I think and despair. They left a sizable estate and David Campbell received around two million. A similar sum was left to Sophie. They were so convinced she would be found they left that money in trust for her. The flat of her mother's has lain empty in Edinburgh since she went missing. That belongs to Sophie as well. We keep it clean and modernised it but it has been cleared of most of Lizzie's belongings. It's a lovely two bedroomed Victorian flat in the west end of the city. Lizzie's brother has a key to check up on it but we manage it and pay the council tax. It was in the parents' will not to sell it.

'Strangely Lizzie Campbell took out life insurance when she had Sophie. Unusual for a young girl but I understood she was concerned for her safety. Something about nasty letters.

'Obviously over the years this estate has grown considerably. We invest for her through our investment arm. The estate is probably worth of excess of £10 million in today's money. She will be a very wealthy young lady.'

Charles Robertson added: 'I'm not sure if this is relevant to the investigation but the family went to pieces after Lizzie died and the baby went missing. The heart went out of it. The parents were never the same. The relationship between Lizzie and her brother had never been close. In retrospect the parents spent too much attention on Lizzie and her music. The brother felt left out. When Lizzie died the parents hardly saw David. It was so sad.'

Inspector Driver said: 'Thank you for all your candour

and help. I will contact you tomorrow when I know for sure who this girl is. She may not be the daughter of the people who raised her but she may not be Sophie either. I don't want to get ahead of myself until we know the science. Tell me what you know about Lizzie's boyfriend and the father of the baby?'

Charles Robertson said: 'We don't know much. He seemed to just disappear one day and we never heard anything. Lizzie told her parents he had to go back to India as his mother was very unwell. Lizzie seemed to be pretty sure he was coming back to Scotland and told her parents they planned to marry. But when Lizzie died, we never heard from him. We tried to track him down but no luck. His name was not on the birth certificate so that was strange. Lizzie called him Malik. That's all we know?

Inspector Driver said: 'Thanks, very helpful. If you can keep these inquiries under your hat, I will let you know once we get the results of the DNA.'

Absolutely,' said James Robertson. 'We won't mention this at all until we hear from you.'

Inspector Driver added: 'Just one more thing. You don't happen to have any of those letters?'

'Sorry, no,' said Mr Robertson.

CHAPTER TWELVE

Morgan was in her room at the hotel with an hour to spare, before going back to Dumfries to see the aunts moved from Stranraer to a hospital, sitting on the bed preparing to call Max and have the first real conversation with him. She felt calm and ready to talk.

Just then her phone rang. It was Max.

'Hi Max,' she said. 'That's strange as I was just about to call you.'

'Great minds think alike, or something like that. How are you, Morgan? How's life in the snow in Galloway?'

Morgan laughed: 'I'm ok Max. The snow is disappearing fast and I'm still here committed to helping the police with this young girl who has lost her family. I wanted to call you to say I hope to be back in Edinburgh in the next couple of days. I thought we could talk.'

Max said: 'That's why I wanted to call you. Listen I'm sorry for what's happened and for hurting you. I never meant to.'

Morgan said: 'It's ok Max. This time away has given me a chance to think. I don't feel angry with you, just a bit sad we've grown apart. What's happening with the University?'

'The University have still suspended me. The police are investigating some ex-boyfriend of the student for distributing the video. I'm still a laughing stock, but otherwise ok. The thing is I have some news.'

Morgan said: 'What is it?'

'I got a call a couple of days ago out of the blue. It was a big museum in New York sounding me out about a job. I took about 20 minutes to realise I wanted away from academia and into the real world. I did two interviews on Zoom and got offered the job. The upshot is I'm away tomorrow to New York. The museum has got me a flat for six months and a good package to allow me to live. Once there, I'll email you contact details. I wanted to tell you but also to say you must stay in the flat. I don't plan to sell it any day soon and it's your home.'

'That's fantastic news Max. I'm so pleased for you. I think we were both in a bit of a rut. Funny I'm thinking of changing jobs as well.'

'I'm glad you're taking it so well. I really want to get away from Edinburgh and the University and this mess. I'll have to come back if there's a trial, but there's nothing to keep me in Edinburgh now, apart from you that is.'

Morgan said: 'We'll always be friends Max. Let me know when you arrive in New York and that you are safe. I'd better go now as I need to be somewhere. Again, I'm really pleased for you.'

Morgan rang off and sat for a few minutes on the bed. Well good for Max, she thought. She realised she felt pleased for him. She just needed to get her own life sorted. Contacting her dad was a priority.

On the short journey to see the sisters, Morgan said little, her mind going over and over the call with Max, Rebecca just watching the scenery. The time passed in a blur when the police car drew up at an imposing Victorian building on the outskirts of Dumfries.

They were met at the door by a nurse who said: 'Come

this way Ms MacNeill. Your aunts are just in here. I told them you were coming. You must be Ms Cooper?'

Morgan and Rebecca entered what looked like a hospital ward. At the far end were two rooms. In one, they could see the sisters in twin beds sitting up, alert and awake.

As they entered the room they looked up. Their eyes passed over Morgan and when they settled on Rebecca it seemed there was some recognition.

'Hi, Aggie and Effy. It's me Rebecca. How are you both?'

Morgan watched as the two women, dressed in fresh night clothes and bed jackets, sitting on the twin beds holding hands, smiled at Rebecca.

One of them, Morgan couldn't say which one, said: 'Hello, we're waiting for Quintas to come and have tea with us and look after us.'

Rebecca sounded distressed as she said: 'Do you not know who I am? I'm your niece Rebecca.'

Just then the door opened and a tea lady came in with two steaming cups of tea and a biscuit for each of them. The sisters' whole attention was on the tea.

The nurse spoke quietly to Morgan: 'Perhaps leave Rebecca with the aunts to have a cup of tea. I can chat to you in my office.'

Morgan left Rebecca sitting at the aunt's bedside and left with the nurse.

'Hi I'm senior nurse Jane Smith. 'I was told by Inspector Driver to let you know about the sisters. They seem to have regressed back to being young girls, constantly asking for their brother Quintas. We're still assessing them but they seem quite happy and certainly don't want to go back to the farm. I get the impression it was pretty miserable for them there. They like their room and regular meals cooked for them. They have company and enjoy some of the activities.'

Morgan said: 'That's good. Are they talking about what happened at the farm or have they blocked out the bad bits?'

'The latter I think,' said Senior Nurse Smith. 'They've never said anything and seem to be sleeping ok. They don't seem to be having nightmares. We're just going to keep them here till we see how they are and what we do with them.'

Morgan waited outside the room and watched as Rebecca sat with the two sisters gently smoothing their hair and touching their faces.

An hour later they were back in the police car and Rebecca said little on the journey back.

Morgan asked: 'Do you feel they are ok Rebecca?'

She replied: 'They seem fine, a bit distant. But that's nothing new. They always lived in their own sort of world, just the two of them, so I think they'll be ok. They weren't really interested in me, in the past or now. They asked about Quintas, but I never said anything.'

It was lunchtime when they got back to Stranraer and the arrangement was for them to go straight to the farm. It looked neglected and all in darkness. No animals could be heard. Morgan realised you could almost by pass this farm on the road, it was so well hidden. The snow had almost gone, just some left lying in the field. The policeman had brought a torch.

Morgan warned: 'This could feel very strange Rebecca. The house has been empty for a few days and police forensics will have been in. It probably won't look like it did before.'

Rebecca said: 'It's ok. I just want to pick up a few things like pictures and some clothes. Can you come in with me?'

The policeman indicated he would remain in the car as they got out to look around the farm yard.

'Where are the animals?' asked Rebecca.

'I think they've been moved and given new homes. They will be well looked after, I'm sure. You don't have to worry about them,' said Morgan.

Rebecca had a key for the back door of the farm and as they entered the small kitchen Morgan remembered the scene when they first came. She shivered, and had a strange feeling someone else was in the house. She was about to go back outside to get the policeman when Rebecca suddenly moved into the lounge, Morgan following. It looked forlorn and shabby. Just as they moved towards the fire Morgan became aware of a man coming down the stairs.

Before she could say anything, he spoke. He was dressed like he had been living rough, a sort Rambo style guy, unshaven and dirty looking. He was quite stocky in build but fit. He looked intense and scary, thought Morgan.

He didn't move, just stared at Rebecca and said: 'Its ok, I'm not going to hurt you. I just want to make sure you are ok, Sophie.'

'My name's Rebecca and what are you doing in our house?' She sounded indignant.

He didn't say anything but turned and went back up the stairs. He turned round and just said: 'You're safe now Sophie.' Then he disappeared up the stairs.

'Let's get the policeman Rebecca. Come back outside quickly.'

Morgan ushered her out and closed the back door behind them. She ran to the police car and told him a man was inside the house.

He told them to stay in the car while he checked.

He was gone just a few minutes. 'He's gone and seems to have used the bedroom window at the back. There seems to have been a rope left out of the window. I've looked to see where he went but I can't see anything, there's too many footprints in the snow to make out. It looks like a few people have been around. It's safe to go back in but I'll come with you while you get what you need. I think we need to get back to Stranraer. I'll call the station from the car and report to the inspector. They need to get forensics back out here.'

Morgan stood with the policeman in the lounge as Rebecca gathered a few photographs from the lounge area. He then went upstairs with her to gather some clothes. They were gone for just ten minutes and Morgan looked around the lounge. To her untrained eye it looked as if it had been searched, probably by the forensic team looking for something.

Within 15 minutes they were back in the police car.

Rebecca said: 'I never want to see that house again. It gives me the creeps now. It doesn't feel like a home any longer.'

Morgan said: 'I wouldn't worry about that just now Rebecca. You don't have to live here any more.'

Rebecca said: 'I wonder where I will live now? I have no one left.'

Morgan didn't reply and just held her hand as they were driven back to their hotel in Stranraer.

At the hotel she saw Cameron waiting for them in the reception.

'Hi, how did you get on?' He was looking at Rebecca.

'It was ok,' she said, 'but there was a strange man in the house and he kept calling me Sophie. I don't want to go back there. I never really liked it before but when my mum and dad were there it wasn't too bad. It's a bit creepy now.'

Cameron nodded: 'You don't need to go back Rebecca. The inspector wants you to go to the police station tomorrow morning about 10a.m. I suggest we three grab something to eat here and then get an early night.'

Rebecca said: 'I want to go and get a shower to freshen up. Can I meet you here in an hour?'

Cameron nodded and Morgan said: 'Good idea Rebecca. I'm going to get a cup of tea and catch up with Cameron. We'll just be down here.'

Minutes later they were in a quiet corner of the hotel coffee shop and Morgan could see Cameron had some news.

She said: 'That was a bit strange that guy in the house calling Rebecca by another name. Do you think it's connected to the deaths?'

Cameron said: 'I've just been with the Inspector for a couple of hours. He said to keep you up to date so tomorrow he will let Rebecca know that she really is Sophie Campbell. The family, working with the police, kept the DNA of Lizzie Campbell just in case they found her daughter. This confirms that she is Lizzie's child. They took the DNA of the uncle but it turns out he was adopted, so his DNA wouldn't have matched. It's lucky they still had Lizzie's. They haven't told the uncle yet. That will be tomorrow afternoon. The Inspector wants to make sure the young girl is all right first.'

'My God,' said Morgan 'What a turn up for the books. You don't seem surprised Cameron.'

'I'm not really. I could never put that lovely young girl with that family at the farm.

'There's more. The Inspector and his team have been doing a lot of digging into this accident that killed Lizzie Campbell more than 17 years ago. Tom got hold of the original file. What he found was another file of a complaint Lizzie Campbell made to Strathclyde Police about six months before she died, so likely about three months before she gave birth to Sophie. It seems she thought she was being stalked and followed. In those days they didn't take it too seriously. In the file is a card she gave them from a florist with a message, not signed by anyone, saying "Red roses are for the beloved, and yellow roses are for the forsaken." It seems to have been yellow roses sent to her when her boyfriend was back in India. There were also letters expressing admiration for her music and her kindness.'

Morgan shuddered: 'That's really creepy. Poor girl.'

Cameron nodded: 'There's something else. There was also a letter in the file from someone different. This was a really nasty letter saying she was useless, talentless and a disappointment and worse. The file says they were going to ask Lizzie for more of these letters but there are none there. When she died the investigation would go cold.'

'Where would these "other letters" be then?' said Morgan.

'Probably lost. But what is clear is that this young girl, Lizzie, was under a lot of pressure. No wonder she wanted away from Edinburgh.'

Just then Rebecca came down the stairs, the conversation stopped, and they tucked into fish and chips in the bar.

The next morning Cameron was waiting to take Morgan and Rebecca to the police station. The inspector was waiting for them and asked if they could stay with Rebecca during the meeting, making sure a social worker was present.

He spoke in a gentle voice as he said: 'Rebecca I know this has been a difficult time for you. I want you to know that we are making progress in finding out who killed your mother and father and uncle. But during our investigations we discovered a link between their deaths and the death of a young musician in the north of Scotland more than 17 years ago. In that accident a baby girl was taken from the crashed car and disappeared.'

Morgan was watching Rebecca's face as she started intently at the Inspector.

'What exactly are you trying to tell me?' asked Rebecca. Morgan thought her voice sounded a bit stressed.

Inspector Driver said: 'We know you are not the child of the Rev and his wife. DNA confirms what we suspected. We've now confirmed that you are that missing child from 17 years ago, Sophie Campbell, and your mother was Lizzie Campbell.'

Rebecca said nothing then she attempted a sort of rueful smile.

'I used to ask my parents if I was adopted. When I was ten, I realised I was different from them and when I questioned them, they never really answered. Did they take me from the car?'

Inspector Driver nodded: 'We think so. I know they probably did wrong but they did care for you for 17 years. We don't know all the circumstances yet and I can't give you all the answers. We've found an uncle, the brother of your mother, who's been searching for you. You will be able to meet him tomorrow. Ok? Actually, he found us as it seems he has been looking for you for many years.'

Rebecca looked shocked and Morgan could see her trying to understand all that was happening to her.

Morgan said: 'Do you fancy coming for a walk on a beach with me, give you time to think. It's a lovely day and we could find one locally away from any snow.'

Inspector Driver said: 'I think Sandhead beach would be good. Stay away from Portpatrick and the farm just now. I'm going to get a police car to take you and keep an eye out. Do you want to talk to a social worker just now?'

Rebecca said: 'No thanks. I would prefer going for a walk to think and try to understand all this.'

Cameron watched Morgan walk out with her arm around the young girl. They'd been gone for just a few minutes when the car driven by Dave Campbell arrived. He was checked in and was soon sitting in the Inspector's officer. He looked strangely energised and excited.

The Inspector had arranged coffee and after a few minutes he said: 'Welcome Mr Campbell, it seems your gut instinct was spot on. We can confirm that this girl Rebecca is your missing niece. She's Sophie Campbell and we have double checked the DNA, against your sister's, which was kept by the police after she died. We have told the girl and she is trying to understand this drama in her young life.'

'Can I see her?' Mr Campbell interrupted.

'I think tomorrow best, give her time to get used to the idea. We can arrange for you to meet each other, perhaps in a hotel. But while you are here, I need you to tell me more about Sophie's dad.'

Dave Campbell said: 'I only met him a few times. He was Indian and a fellow student in Edinburgh. She never talked about him much so when she said she was pregnant and they planned to marry I was shocked. Then he seemed to disappear. I seem to remember he had to go back to India for a family issue.

'One thing Lizzie did say was that he had a sort of bodyguard with him. His parents had bought him a flat in a new luxury complex and the father bought two so that he had a flat for his son and one for the bodyguard. She said it made meeting up difficult and they usually met at her flat. He apparently told her his father was worried about his safety. As far as we know he left the university and flat about three months before Sophie was born. When I checked after she died both flats had been sold.'

Inspector Driver said: 'What was his name? Also, if you have the address we can look back at records for owners or occupiers which might lead us to find out who this boyfriend was.'

Mr Campbell looked embarrassed: 'I only remember his first name, Malik. The flats were in the West End. I can't remember the address but I probably have it somewhere.'

Inspector Drover said: 'I understand Mr Campbell and thank you for your help. I'll let you go now and take all this information in. I'll arrange where and when you can meet.'

'Thanks Inspector. I just feel relief. My parents never accepted Sophie was dead and now they have been proved right. I hope they're watching. You know I was adopted but I always considered Lizzie my little sister.'

On the beach Morgan and Rebecca walked in silence for about half an hour. They were paddling in the strangely warm waters. Rebecca explained it was the Gulf Stream, and was watching the blue sea lap gently on the shore when Rebecca broke the silence and said: 'Morgan thanks for being here for me and supporting me. It's been such a strange time. Now I find out that I am not who I thought I was all my life. I'm someone else. I feel like my feet have been taken from me. It's all so strange.'

Morgan put an arm around her shoulders. 'You could look at it another way. You now know who you are. You have a lot to take in, and it will take time, but you've your whole life ahead of you.'

Rebecca said: 'I'm meeting this new uncle tomorrow. I need to tell him and the Inspector that I have the funerals for my "old" parents. My aunt, my mother's sister, in the Highlands contacted me and said the funerals will be in Skye this week. I need to be there as the aunts are not fit to go. It's really my mother's family and they were very good to me. I know the Rev and his wife are not my birth parents but they cared for me and loved me for all my life. I know they are suspected of taking me from the car my birth mother died in but I can't think of that at the moment.'

'I fully understand,' said Morgan. 'I have to go back to Edinburgh soon but you have my mobile and I will always be there to help you. I think we've become friends so don't ever feel you can't call.'

'Thanks, Morgan I appreciate that. I really need to think about the future and I want to come to Edinburgh to study music. That's my dream.'

They got back to the hotel just after lunchtime to find Cameron waiting for them.

'Hi, the Inspector says he is coming over this afternoon to meet you for coffee Rebecca. Do you want a sandwich and a rest first?'

Rebecca said: 'Yes and I need to ask him if I can get to the Highlands in two days for the funerals of my parents. My uncle has apparently been buried at Portpatrick, but my relatives in the Highlands want the Rev and their sister buried in the family graveyard.'

They were all gathered in the lounge of the hotel waiting for the Inspector to arrive. Rebecca looked a bit spaced out, Morgan thought.

'Are you ok?' she asked.

'Just a bit confused and unsure who to trust. I know my parents, or rather the Rev and his wife, lied to me but they looked after me. I don't know anything about my real mother and I want to find out about her. But I'm nervous about meeting this new uncle. Now I don't know whether to call myself Rebecca or Sophie? It's all so confusing.' She looked around and then said to no-one in particular.

'Oh. But I trust you and Cameron,' she added.

Cameron said: 'Thanks Rebecca. Things will get much clearer, I'm sure. We'll always be your friends and you can rely on us.'

Just then the Inspector arrived.

He spoke directly to Rebecca: 'The meeting with your uncle Dave is scheduled for tomorrow morning at 10a.m. in a private room here in the hotel. I have invited your mother's lawyer, a Mr Robertson, to attend as well as he wants to talk to you about your mother and grandparents. They will want to call you by your birth name of Sophie, try not to worry about that. Your lawyer is determined to support you.

'He has arranged a driver to take you to Skye for the funerals, leaving tomorrow lunchtime. Is that ok with you?'

Rebecca said: 'Thanks for everything. I think I'll go upstairs to think about everything. I'll just order food in my room tonight and watch television. It's a lot to take in and try and understand. I've so many questions.'

When Rebecca left the Inspector looked around at Morgan and Cameron.

'What are your plans?' he said.

Morgan and Cameron both started speaking at once, Cameron nodded for Morgan to go ahead.

'I'm planning to go back to Edinburgh tomorrow afternoon. I'll check how Rebecca, or Sophie is, and she knows to contact me if she needs anything.'

Cameron added: 'I'm going to Edinburgh too as the Inspector wants me to check on something. We could meet up.'

Inspector Driver nodded and said: 'Is it ok if I have a chat with you both tonight? Perhaps we could go for a curry together?'

They all agreed to meet at 7p.m. Morgan decided to go to her room and have a shower and change clothes.

As she made to leave Cameron suddenly got up and wrapped her in a big bear hug. He was all warm and smelt good. She felt good in his arms and for a moment thought he was going to kiss her but he pulled away and said: 'Thanks for everything you're doing for that girl. I know it's making life easier for the Inspector.'

Inspector Driver laughed: 'It certainly is. I can concentrate on finding our killer.'

Morgan checked on Rebecca and she was already in pyjamas ordering a pizza to stay in. Morgan told her she was going out and not to answer the door to anyone. The policeman was still sitting on a seat along the corridor to check who came and went. The Inspector was obviously taking no chances.

Morgan felt better once had a shower and changed into fresh jeans and a shirt. She was getting sick of the clothes she'd brought and felt a yearning for her own bed and wardrobe.

The Inspector obviously wasn't just out for the night. When he said the meal was on him Morgan knew he was going to ask a favour. It was more than that.

Inspector Driver said: 'Morgan I've been lucky enough to have the help of both you and Cameron during these difficult days. The identification issue with this young girl has been troublesome and taken me away from the murder investigation. I'm more than certain they're connected, the death of that young woman in the North all those years ago has come to the surface again. Now we have established who she is really is, Sophie Campbell, it will be up to her lawyers and uncle to see to her future. It seems her lawyers have hired a security team to drive her up to Skye for the funerals tomorrow. She will be able to meet her relatives up there and have some company.

'I've asked Cameron if he'll continue to work for me for the next two months and he's agreed. He has been hired as a consultant on the case. I want him to go to Edinburgh to find out what he can about this girl's father and what actually happened 17 years ago.

'I'm hoping you'll still be able to help when you go back to Edinburgh, Morgan.'

She nodded: 'Yes, I'm going back to work but will always have my phone and can do whatever is needed. I also told Rebecca or Sophie that I will be always available for her.'

The next morning Rebecca didn't say much at breakfast and Morgan didn't push her.

Rebecca suddenly looked up and said: 'Who's coming this morning? Is it just my uncle?'

Morgan nodded: 'Cameron and I will be in the hotel if you need us. But I think you are meeting this guy Dave Campbell who seems to be your uncle, your mum's lawyer and the Inspector.'

CHAPTER THIRTEEN

Rebecca's brain was finding it difficult to take all the developments in. Sometimes she remembered her life at the farm and in the camper van, but that seemed like another world. She still missed her mum, but it was all so confusing. They had taken her from her other mum. But this was a mum she didn't know, she'd never even seen a picture of her. Last night she thought of searching online but couldn't face it. It felt like one of those soap operas she had watched with her cousins in secret when she went north. But this was real life, her life.

Thankfully Morgan went with me for a walk around the block and when we got back to the hotel, we went into a room that had been fitted with comfortable chairs and flowers, fresh water on the table.

The Inspector was waiting and introduced everyone to the lawyer, Mr Robertson from Ayr. Then he turned and introduced her to a man in his forties with blondish swept back hair and a tanned lined face. He was smiling and staring at her intently. She thought she had met him before.

'Hi, I'm your Uncle David. And you are Sophie Campbell. I have been looking for you for a very long time. I am so glad to have found you.'

'Thanks,' said Rebecca. 'This is a lot to take in. Can you tell me what happened to my mother? Do you have a picture?'

The Inspector left the room, hearing Dave Campbell start to explain the accident and the search for the missing baby.

He had an urgent text from his Sergeant and knew it was something about the murder. Sergeant Ford was waiting for him outside the door.

'Inspector we might have had a break. You know the character Morgan and the girl met at the farm. Well, we've been doing all the forensics on the rope we found. It was pretty clean but we did find something on the window sill. It's a fingerprint and we have a match. We think he was wearing gloves, in fact Morgan said he was, but probably took a glove off to swing himself out of the window. It was the window of the brother Quintas' room and we know he had a few people in that bedroom doing his business.'

Inspector Driver said: 'Let's go to my office. This is the first piece of luck we have had.'

Two minutes later they were in his office and the door shut.

'Right tell me all,' said the Inspector.

'He's in the system for a crime in Glasgow about 17 years ago. A former soldier, he left the army about 20 years ago, I'm not sure what he was doing after that. He came to the attention of police when he attacked his mother at her tenement flat in Partick in Glasgow and broke her neck. He then called the police to say he'd killed her. He said she'd been nagging him, calling him a failure.

'He appeared at the High Court but seems to have had some sort of breakdown, diagnosed with schizophrenia, and sent to Carstairs, the psychiatric hospital. He was released about a year ago. We don't where he's been living and we're looking for relatives. He's in the system as Charlie Trimble.'

Inspector Driver said: 'What the hell was he doing at a remote farm house in Galloway asking about Sophie? We need to find out all we can about him and if is still here bring him in for questioning.'

CHAPTER FOURTEEN

Sophie sank into the leather seats in the Mercedes as it left Stranraer and thought she should find this funny after spending most of her life in the back of a rickety and uncomfortable old van. But her brain was just starting to process all the information she'd just heard.

The most stunning thing was a growing understanding of how much the family she'd never known cared about her, and searched for her, and how much they'd loved her mother.

It was her mother, this beautiful slim blonde woman in a faded photograph, holding what Sophie now knows, is her as a new baby, with a shock of brown hair, that had left her speechless and breathless. The instant she saw the picture she felt a connection. Crazy, she knew, but it almost caused her to faint.

This new uncle seemed like a nice guy and he promised to speak more when she got back from the funerals. Funny she didn't feel anything when she met him. Her heart left like a heavy lump in her chest. All she could think was how her grandparents, her birth mother's parents, must have felt losing their daughter and their granddaughter in one day. It made her feel angry that her parents for the last 17 years had been happy to, at last, have a child while others were robbed. It was so, so sad.

Now she was sitting in the luxurious car with a driver and a security guard in the front. Her lawyer, or really her mother's lawyer, had arranged it to take her to Skye and the funeral.

She knew that after the funeral she would not want to be called Rebecca, but Sophie. Sophie Campbell, daughter of Lizzie Campbell. She repeated this several times to herself.

She sat back and looked out of the window at the Ayrshire coast, bathed in Spring sunshine and Ailsa Craig looking majestic.

The lawyer was a nice old man, a Mr Robertson, and she realises he'd known her mother and grandparents.

He got her a cup of coffee, asking her new Uncle Dave to leave the room, and calmly told her she was a very rich young lady.

She still couldn't take it in. It seems her grandparents left her a lot of money and it's been invested. Then her mother had insurance on her flat so Sophie now owns that. That was the most significant thing. She'd never had a home, never one of her own and now she had a flat in Edinburgh. The lawyer said they had maintained it and updated it and paid the bills and it was ready to live in.

Then he also told her that Lizzie had life insurance, taken out when Sophie was born. All in all, he said, I was worth in excess of £10 million. She looked after me, thought Sophie.

He told me not to worry about anything and was just glad to know that I had been found. He said my grandparents never doubted I was out there somewhere.

That's why he was making sure I was safe. He told me not to tell my relatives in the Highlands about the money, or anybody else. The way he said it sounded so serious.

Sophie's brain was full of so many thoughts and emotions, she was glad the two men in front never disturbed her. They only time they spoke was to ask if she wanted something to eat or a toilet break, stopping at a farm shop near Turnberry and picking up sandwiches.

She slept as the car sped up the west coast and woke up to see the bleak but stunning moorlands of Glencoe. It was a road she usually travelled in the back of the camper van, sometimes feeling sick and rarely seeing the countryside.

She must have fallen asleep again as she woke up to feel the car stop. It was outside her aunt's house and Rebecca saw her aunt and uncle waiting at the door. She checked her watch and it was 3p.m.

They came forward to hug her and Rebecca said: 'Hello Aunt Jean. It's good to see you.'

Jean said: 'It's all right Rebecca. The police have been to visit us and explain everything. You don't need to say anything but come in and have some sandwiches and tea. We're just glad to see you are ok. I'll take some tea and cake out for your driver, and his friend. He says they are staying to drive you to a hotel.'

Rebecca laughed: 'I think they've been told not to let me out of their sight.'

'You're safe here my love. Everyone is just so shocked and glad that you are all right. I can hardly believe what the police told me. We haven't said anything to anyone else as we want to get the funeral over with. I know they did wrong but your mum and dad loved you so much and they have been punished in the most brutal way. I want to bury them before the gossip starts.'

Rebecca said: 'They won't hear anything from me, Auntie. I'm like you and I want them to have a good funeral and be finally at peace. I can't be angry, it's in the past. No-one knows what really happened. Did you never suspect I wasn't their child?' asked Rebecca.

'We never gave it any thought. We knew they wanted children but it hadn't happened and we all thought they couldn't have any. Then we hadn't seen them for about a year and they turned up with you. We just thought it was a miracle and accepted it. We never imagined they would be so cruel as to take you from a crashed car and your mother. It has broken our hearts and, in a way, I'm glad they're dead as they would probably go to prison. How do you feel about them?'

Rebecca found tears springing to her eyes: 'I don't really know. I know I should feel angry or something but I don't, I just feel really sad. I never got to know my real mother. I think we should get the funerals over tomorrow and talk more.'

Jean nodded: 'Yes do you know your real name yet? Have you found relatives? The police wouldn't tell us anything about your new family. They just asked about Artemis and Christine. I made sure to tell them that Artemis was the boss and Christine did what she was told. Christine was my sister and I find hard to believe she carried out this deceit and that the idea was hers.'

Rebecca put her arm around her and said: 'Aunt Jean, there's no point blaming them now. They're gone. We have to look ahead. Whatever happens I will never forget my family here. You have been so good to me, teaching me violin and all the other things.'

Her uncle said little, just sat looking at her with sad eyes. She stayed for more than hour in a house she knew well, sitting by the coal fire and chatting about the last few days. The driver took her to a nearby hotel for the night.

The morning of the funeral was bright and sunny. Rebecca put on the black dress Morgan had found and a jacket to keep warm.

The driver and his silent security man, who had barely said a word since they left Stranraer, were parked outside the church.

Rebecca found her Aunt Jean and Uncle Neil and stood with them as they greeted other family members.

As they went into the church to take their seats Rebecca could feel her eyes transfixed by the sight of the two coffins, sitting side by side in the corner of the church.

She could feel her aunt take her hand in hers and squeeze it as the Minister took his place in the pulpit, which was placed so high Rebecca had to stretch her neck to see him. For an hour Rebecca listened to the voice of the Minister as he talked about sin and redemption. So apt, she thought.

Then it was over and they were standing in a line-up shaking hands, as one after another expressed their condolences, 'a shock for you, young lady, they loved you so much, to lose your parents.' To which Rebecca just said 'thanks.'

Then they were in the car, driving to the graveside on the slope of a hill. She saw the two graves dug, waiting for their occupants.

At least I can bury these parents, I never got the chance to bury my real mother, Rebecca thought.

She stood at the side of each grave, holding a cord, and saying a silent prayer for them both.

After they went back to a nearby hotel for sandwiches and coffee and Rebecca was not sure how she got through the next two hours chatting to people, some whom she barely knew but others she had spent her childhood with.

Eventually her aunt said: 'You look exhausted Rebecca. Shall we go back to our house for a cup of tea?'

'Yes. That would be great. I need to get away in about an hour and back to Galloway. The police need to see me and I have a lot to find out and sort out. I still haven't got my birth certificate. I promise I will come back up and see you all once I get things straight and find out where I am going to live and study.'

Rebecca was exhausted and slept almost all the way back on the drive to Stranraer. When she woke up, they were driving past Cairnryan and she knew they would be back at the hotel in a few minutes.

She went straight to her room, showered and got into bed. She didn't even feel hungry. The emotions of the last few days had exhausted her and all she wanted to do was sink into the bed and sleep.

Just then her phone pinged. She read the message. It was Morgan, 'Hi Sophie hope funeral went all to plan and everything ok? I'm back in Edinburgh so let me know when you are coming.'

Rebecca thought: 'That's the first time anyone called me Sophie.'

She sat for minute thinking and decided to reply to Morgan after meetings and knowing what her life was for the next few days.

Sophie, as she now called herself, spent the next day meeting with lawyers and getting to know her new uncle. She felt like a sponge and had to stop herself asking him question after question about her mother and her grandparents. The lawyer had organised her birth certificate, for the first time Sophie knew when and where she was born. At 1.45 am in a hospital in Edinburgh on December 1, 17 years ago. It said her mother was Lizzie Campbell but the space for her father was missing. Interesting, she thought.

Her uncle suggested taking her to Edinburgh to see her flat as he had a key, but the lawyer thought they should stay in a hotel in Edinburgh.

Dave Campbell insisted: 'I have my flat in Glasgow and we could stay there and just go through to Edinburgh to see the flat and have lunch. What do you think?'

'I'd like to have Morgan and Cameron with us when I go to the flat. I wonder if I could stay with Morgan in Edinburgh and we could all meet up. I can text her.'

Before Uncle Dave answered the lawyer said: 'I think that's a very good idea. It will give you space to get used to things. Can you call her?'

Sophie glanced at her uncle and saw a look of annoyance on his face. But he soon smiled and said: 'Good idea. I can drive Sophie up to Edinburgh tomorrow.'

Sophie went back to her room and called Morgan. She answered immediately.

'Hi Morgan, its Sophie.'

'How are you? I'm back in Edinburgh but strangely missing the lovely village of Portpatrick.'

Sophie seemed to hesitate and then said: 'I'm fine and planning to come to Edinburgh to see my flat. I wonder if I could stay with you for a few days. I feel I don't know my uncle well enough to stay with him at his flat in Glasgow and I don't want to stay in a hotel by myself.'

'Of course, you can stay. Just check with the Inspector that he's ok with that. I have a spare room with its own bathroom and I'll be glad of the company. The flat feels pretty empty.'

She could hear Sophie talking to another person but she said: 'I'll check with the Inspector now. We plan to leave tomorrow morning and be with you early afternoon. I have another favour. Would you and, if he can, Cameron come with me and my uncle to see the flat I now own. I'll call you when we are nearly at your flat tomorrow. I have the address.'

Morgan was amazed at the confidence this young girl

was showing and agreed that she would accompany her to the flat if that was what she wanted.

Morgan had just returned to her flat in Edinburgh, finding it strangely empty, with none of the usual mess that Max left in his wake, papers all over the flat, empty coffee cups and dirty towels on the floor.

When she had finally pulled into a parking space outside the flat, she'd hesitated in the car before getting out. So much had happened, it felt like weeks ago she left stunned by Max's betrayal and foolishness. Now she was back, a different person. When she had called work, they said they were looking forward to seeing her the next morning. The chief executive had a half hour slot to see her.

Sophie was due to arrive tomorrow afternoon and Morgan planned to see her boss first, then come home.

She was just looking around the flat when her mobile rang. It was a Whats App call from Max.

'Hi Max. I hope you're safely in New York and settled in?'

'Yes, where are you? Yes, I'm settled in. I've been in a hotel for the first week and now an apartment on the upper east side for three months, all paid by the museum, while I look for somewhere to rent. How are you anyway? I assume you're back in Edinburgh.'

'Yeah, just back. The flat seems really strange. I'm going into work for a chat tomorrow and then this girl we found in Galloway is coming to stay for a few days. I'll be glad of the company, to be honest.'

Max gave a big sigh: 'I know, I'm sorry about it all. It's been such a mess.'

Morgan laughed: 'It's certainly been a strange time. What's happened with the university and the investigation?'

'Well, the university have still got me on suspension. They don't seem to know what to do about me. I wanted to go back to the university but when I got this call from the Museum in New York I suddenly realised this was the right opportunity at the right time, a change will be good for me. It's more money and more responsibility. I told them what happened here and they weren't bothered. Different approach than the university.

'The police investigation is just carrying on. They seem to have charged a former boyfriend of the student so I assume I'll have to come back for a trial.

'I like New York simply because I can forget all about that business and get back to work. I've met some good people at work and I think I can be happy here for a while.

'I miss the flat, I miss you and Edinburgh and I haven't given up hope that we can both live there together again in the future if you can ever forgive me.'

Morgan said: 'It's nothing to do with forgiveness but we've both been through a lot and I think we need time to think. You've moved to a new city and an exciting job. I'm thinking about what I do with my career. At the moment I've got involved with something in Galloway so I want to see that through. I miss you but I'll enjoy the summer in the city as a single woman again.'

Max said: 'I was hoping you might come out and see me and have a holiday in New York. We could do some travelling.'

Morgan said: 'Let's just see. Ok?'

Max said: 'Listen, I'm going to go, but before I do, I left you a small gift under the pillow on my side of the bed. I hope you agree with what I am suggesting. I'll leave it at that and call next week.'

With that he ended the call. Fascinated, Morgan went into the bedroom and found the white envelope under the pillow. It was simply addressed to M.

In it were two letters, one from Max and one from his lawyer. She opened the one from the lawyer first and it seemed to be a legal agreement that said the flat was now owned by Max Fraser and Morgan Cooper.

She immediately opened Max's letter. It said: 'This has been your home for a while now and I want you to always feel it will be your home. I know you have your flat which you rent out but I want you to have a half share of this flat with me. I know I can't make up for the hurt I've caused you but this is my way of saying sorry.'

Morgan said 'Wow.' She then put them in a drawer and thought – deal with that later.

She checked her watch, it was after 9a.m. and she was due at work in an hour. She quickly went online and ordered a home delivery from the nearby supermarket. It was to be delivered at 3p.m.

She put on a smart trouser suit and left the flat. It felt strange putting on work clothes after living in jeans for two weeks.

She walked into the office to be met by the personal assistant to the boss. The chief was waiting at his door.

'Good to see you back Morgan. We've missed you.'

She felt a small rise in her confidence level and said: 'It's good to be back and I'm sorry about the snow and the problems. I only got back last night. I took holiday to cover.'

He said: 'Yes holiday. That was one of the things I wanted to talk to you about. Apparently, you have four weeks holiday due before the end of the year and that's this month. Human Resources are a bit worried about all the hours you've been working.'

Morgan said: 'I know that's just my temperament. I try to do everything and at a fast pace. I have been forced to take time off and it's made me realise some things. I have built a good team here and I can leave them to run things if I cannot always be there. I can't keep working at this pace.'

Her boss said: 'The team are fine Morgan but they lack your contacts and experience. We had a bit of a hairy issue last week and I could see they were looking for guidance from you. I don't think we have anything coming up so I am going to suggest you take at least a couple of weeks holiday and when you come back, I want to talk to you about a new role, with more money and responsibility.'

Morgan said: 'That sounds great. Thank you. Time off might be just what I need. While I was down in Galloway in the snow I got involved in an old mystery. What the police call a cold case but with a modern slant to it. It's been interesting but I'm actually still helping the police.'

She got up to leave and said: 'I'm glad we had this chat. I will be happy to meet when I get back but you need to understand I'm still thinking of moving on. Nothing is decided yet.'

She spent the rest of the morning meeting her team and catching up.

She told them she would be away for the next two weeks taking overdue holidays but would have her phone on all the time if they needed her.

She got back to the flat just after 1p.m and as she closed the door her mobile rang. It was Cameron.

'Hi Cameron. Where are you?'

'I'm just getting ready to leave Stranraer and arrive in Edinburgh this afternoon. Is everything ok with you? I've a hotel booked at the West End so pretty close to you. Do you fancy meeting tonight?'

'You know Morgan's arriving this afternoon,' said Morgan. 'She's staying here, her uncle's dropping her off, I think.'

'Yeah, I heard. I think that's a great idea. She needs a safe place and quiet haven.'

Morgan could feel her head nodding in agreement.

'I've got two weeks off work so I can be here for her. Why don't you come round about 7p.m. and I'll order a take away?'

'Brilliant,' said Cameron. 'See you later.'

Morgan made herself a coffee and sat down to think about what she needed to do in the flat before Sophie arrived. But as she sat there her mind was going over the events of the last few days and a thought popped into her head. The mother Lizzie had been a student at the music school. She decided to call the school and see if anyone remembered her or could look out her file. She could explain to Cameron tonight.

She dialled the number for St Mary's Music School.

A woman answered the call.

'Hello, St Mary's. Can I help you?'

Morgan said: 'Hello, I'm very sorry to disturb you. My name is Morgan Cooper. You're probably not able to help me but I'm trying to find out something about a former student at the school?'

The voice identified itself. 'I'm Margaret Young, I work in administration and I may be able to find something. We keep good records. What do you want to know?'

Morgan said: 'It's a bit difficult but I'm working with the police on a sort of cold case that involves a former student of the school. Her name was Lizzie Campbell and she was a student at the school almost 20 years ago.'

Margaret Young said immediately: 'Oh we all remember Lizzie, a very talented young woman. She was a sad loss to music and she had a great career ahead of her. It was tragic. Why are you trying to find out about her after all these years?'

Morgan said: 'The police will be able to explain the situation to you but I just wanted to find out if anyone remembered her?'

Margaret Young said: 'Actually, there is someone here who knew Lizzie very well. Her best friend was Rosie Murray who was a student with her and is now a teacher here at the school. I'm sure she would be more than happy to meet you.'

Morgan said: 'That would be brilliant. If I give you my number, could you see if she could meet myself and my colleague, a policeman called Cameron Steel, tomorrow afternoon about 4p.m. Can you let me know?'

Margaret Young promised to text and Morgan cut the call.

She spent the next hour tidying up the room for Sophie, waiting for the supermarket delivery.

The doorbell rang about 3p.m. and Morgan thought it was the delivery but when she opened the door, she found Sophie on the doorstep with a small suitcase.

'On your own Sophie? Welcome anyway. Come away in and we'll get you settled.'

Sophie smiled: 'Uncle Dave didn't want to intrude. We had a good journey and a good chat on the way up the road. He's gone back to his home in Glasgow. He seems very nice and has been talking about my mum. It's been lovely. He suggested we meet at my mum's flat tomorrow morning about 11am. Is that all right?'

Morgan said: 'That's perfect timing. Cameron will be here tonight and we can eat together. He can be around tomorrow. Why don't you get a shower and settle in? I'll make a snack.'

Sophie looked around and said: 'This is a great flat. There's so much space and such high ceilings. I'm used to a caravan and low ceilings.'

Morgan said: 'I suspect your flat will be just the same. They're all alike in this area. Victorian splendour.'

They spent the next two hours chatting over tea and

deciding what to eat when Cameron arrived. Sophie decided she would like a Chinese meal and Morgan looked out the menu in the kitchen. At 7p.m the doorbell rang and Morgan felt happy to see Cameron again. He was just good company, she thought.

The three of them spent a relaxed evening, trying not to talk about the murders and the new Sophie.

It was only as it got late and they talked of turning in Sophie said: 'I'm glad to be here with you both. It's so strange and confusing. The lawyers have been really good and suggested a counsellor and I've agreed. It's in Edinburgh so I'm hoping I can stay with you for a few weeks.'

'Absolutely Sophie. I'll help you in any way I can. Cameron is here working for the Inspector and we will both support you.'

Cameron nodded: 'I'll be here for a few days and then who knows where. The Inspector is talking of coming to Edinburgh so he can brief us on what is happening with regard to the deaths of the Rev and his family.'

Sophie said: 'I've been reading a lot about my mum Lizzie. Uncle Dave has been good at explaining everything. He showed me loads of newspaper cuttings and photographs. She seems to have been a wonderful person, and so talented. Sometimes I feel really close to her and other times she is so far away. I wish I'd known her.'

Morgan said: 'That's understandable. You're just getting to know about her.'

Cameron looked at his watch and broke the tense conversation when he said: 'Time for me to go. Thanks for a lovely night and I'll meet you both at Sophie's flat just before 11a.m. I have the address.'

It was bright and early when Morgan and Sophie arrived at the flat in Drumsheugh Gardens. Dave Campbell was already there. He hadn't gone in and Morgan thought he sounded a bit bitter as he said: 'Ah, Sophie has the keys. The lawyers didn't trust me.'

'Uncle Dave. It's not that at all. They just felt it was my first step to being Sophie, unlocking the door to the flat my mother left me.'

As Morgan and Cameron stayed at the back Morgan said quietly: 'I've found a friend of Lizzie's at the music school. She can meet us both at 4p.m. this afternoon. Is that ok with you? I haven't said anything to Sophie.'

Cameron said: 'No, that's absolutely brilliant. We need to build up a picture of this young woman and find out why she was killed. I am hoping there will be some clues in the flat she lived in.'

Morgan said: 'Don't get your hopes up. It is 17 years ago.'

They walked up the carpet covered stairs to a lovely old wooden front door. As they entered the flat the lounge door was open and Sophie's eyes grew bigger as she saw inside. The room was furnished with settees and a table but there were no personal items around, only a framed picture on the mantlepiece of the ornate fireplace. It was this Sophie was staring at. Morgan looked closely. It was the first picture she had seen of Lizzie Campbell standing on a stage smiling. Morgan saw a stunning young woman, with honey coloured long hair looking radiant, holding a violin. Sophie couldn't take her eyes from it.

It was then Morgan noticed the other item left, almost strategically placed, beside the fire place. It was a beautiful violin sitting in its open case on a chair.

She said: 'Was that Lizzie's violin?'

Sophie immediately moved towards the violin and before anyone could say anything she had picked it up and cradled it in her shoulder. Tears streamed down her face.

'When I am alone, I will play this violin. It's the most beautiful one I have ever seen.'

Dave Campbell said: 'When my parents were alive, they kept the flat just as it was. They were in shock at the loss of Lizzie and the loss of their granddaughter. But after they passed, I took the decision to clear out a lot of stuff like clothes and anything that Lizzie owned. I put some of it in boxes and it's in storage as we always hoped we would find Sophie. The flat was redecorated and upgraded about two years ago. The violin has been in the bank, along with the photograph. The lawyers had them delivered here yesterday. The violin is almost 400 years old and Lizzie's pride and joy. But it belongs to Sophie now, as does this flat.'

Sophie hadn't spoken a word and Morgan went over to check she was all right.

Sophie said: 'I just feel a bit overwhelmed. This is the closest I have ever felt to my mother. She lived here. I can almost feel her here. I can't explain it but I feel her in this room.'

They wandered round the flat, beautifully renovated. The flat had two bedrooms and what looked like a study but Dave said it had been Lizzie's music room and where she used to practise. Sophie lingered in the small room.

After about 40 minutes it was Dave who suggested they all went to a cafe to talk about what they were doing now.

Dave ordered tea for all of them and they sat around the table. Sophie seemed very subdued.

Dave said: 'Sophie wants some time to herself so I'll go back to Glasgow. The inspector called to say the social worker is going to contact Sophie at your home Morgan. Is that all right?'

After they dropped Sophie back at the flat, checked she was ok, it took just ten minutes for Morgan and Cameron to reach the music school and they found a smartly dressed woman in her late 30s waiting for them at reception.

'Hi I'm Rosie Murray. I believe you're Morgan Cooper who was asking about Lizzie Campbell.'

Morgan introduced Cameron, careful to mention he was a policeman with the Met, working for the police in Scotland.

Cameron took over and said: 'Perhaps I can explain what we are looking for. I work in London but I was recently in Galloway. Several things happened that encouraged the police in the area to re-open the case of the death of Lizzie Campbell 17 years ago. My job is to try and build up a picture of the girl and her talent with the violin.'

Rosie Murray led them through the music school to a cafe where she ordered coffee for the three of them.

She said: 'I am actually really glad you're here asking me about Lizzie. Her death hit the school hard and although the police came immediately after the accident and interviewed us, we heard nothing after that. It all seemed to die down.'

Rosie said: 'Now I'm interested why, something that happened 17 years ago, has brought you here. I spent three years with her at the school and I spent those three years in awe of her talent. She was destined for a glittering career with her natural talent and work ethic. She loved music and her life at the school, everything was just working out for her when she died. It was all too sad and it took me a long time to get over it. I still think about her almost every day when I work with students.'

Cameron said: 'What can you tell us about her private life?'

Rosie seemed to hesitate.

Then she said: 'I assume you know about Malik?'

Morgan said: 'Was that her boyfriend?'

Rosie said: 'He was a student from India studying law

at the university. She met him at a social evening at the music school and they hit it off immediately.'

She added: 'It's a long time ago and stop me if you know this already. They met when he was in his third year of law. She was in her final year at the music school. I know from what she said it was difficult to see him sometimes so they usually met at her flat. He seemed to have a flat but his father had hired a security person and put him in a flat next to Malik's to keep an eye on him and ensure he did his studies.

'They were pretty serious about a future together. His mother and father came over and the father took to Lizzie. In fact, have you ever seen her violin?'

Morgan said: 'If it's the same one, it's been in a bank vault for all these years but it was at the flat today. It looked old and very expensive to a lay person like me.'

Rosie said: 'Malik's father bought her it. It will be worth a lot of money. It seems the parents accepted her.

'When she found out she was pregnant she was so happy. She told me Malik was happy too and they planned to make a life together. I assume you know about the notes?'

Morgan said: 'What notes?'

Rosie said: 'I thought the police would find them in her flat. I only saw a couple but they were pretty nasty telling her to have an abortion and that the child was not pure. It was toxic and it really upset them both, Malik promised her it did not come from his family. She went to the police about a couple of things. She had an admirer who saw her play and started sending her flowers and love notes. It was a bit creepy. But the nasty letters really scared her.

'Then when she was about seven months pregnant Malik had to leave the University as his mother was dying of cancer in India. The parents sacked his security man, sold the two flats and he just left, it was very strange. Lizzie told me he had family issues and had to go back to help the father and the family business but he promised her he would come back.'

Rosie said: 'She had total faith in Malik and was sure he would get in touch and tell her where he was. One of the last conversations I had with Lizzie was about Malik. He had contacted her to say he was being put under pressure to stay in India and join his father's firm by his mother as she was dying, he was torn. They had an argument and Lizzie said she didn't put his name on the birth certificate in a fit of anger, which she regretted. She was sure he was coming back to her and a life in Scotland. Sadly, I don't know what happened. He never came back when she died.'

Morgan said: 'Were you told anything when Lizzie died?'

Rosie said: 'Not really, nobody explained what happened. They just said it was an accident and Lizzie had died. We were never told what happened to Sophie.'

Cameron said: 'That's partly why we are here today. It's not public knowledge, and I would ask you to keep this to yourself. But we have confirmed that a young woman found in Galloway is Lizzie's daughter Sophie. She has been living with another family unaware who her real mother was. She is only finding out about her now.'

Rosie said: 'That's amazing. I can't believe that lovely, sweet baby is alive and grown up. I just assumed she'd died in the accident too.'

Tears sprang to her eyes and Morgan realised that she was thinking of her friend who would never know her daughter.

Morgan said: 'What is amazing is that this young girl has a musical talent just like her mother and already plays the violin.'

Cameron said: 'The girl actually enquired about coming here as a student unaware that her real mother had been a student here. You never know, once we get things sorted, she could be a student here.'

Rosie said: 'If I give you all my contacts can you let her know? I would love to help her. If she is as talented as her mother then she will have all the support she needs. I promise.'

Cameron said: 'One more thing. Do you happen to know Malik's second name?'

Rosie said: 'Yes, I do. It was Mittal. Malik Mittal. He'd a flat in the West End if I remember correctly. Lizzie and I went there but it was a bit uncomfortable as his security man had the flat next door. He was always popping in and nosing around. I didn't like it and Lizzie found it uncomfortable.'

Cameron said: 'Thanks Rosie. That's really helpful. Can you remember the name for the security guard or what he looked like? We'll leave now and be in touch when we know more.'

Rosie said: 'Thanks. No, I can't remember his name or really what he looked like. I remember he'd been in the army. Sorry.'

CHAPTER FIFTEEN

In Stranraer Inspector Driver was briefing a team of officers, led by Sergeant Ford. They had been in the village and the surrounding areas for several days trying to find out information about Charlie Trimble.

It was disappointing, Charlie Trimble didn't seem to exist. There were talks of a strange guy walking the cliffs, but nothing concrete.

Then Sergeant Ford managed to get in touch with the lifeboat coxswain Tam Mitchell and struck gold.

Sergeant Ford said: 'It was amazing. The minute I mentioned Charlie Trimble to the coxswain, he told me this was his half brother from Glasgow.

'Let me tell you what he said. Apparently, this is an older half brother. The mother was married to an Irish labourer in Glasgow before she met Tam's father. It seems little Charlie Trimble didn't get on with his step father, it was not a happy homelife.

'Tam says Charlie joined the army at 16 when Tam was around 12. He says he was glad to get him out of the house.'

Inspector Driver said: 'Do we know if Tam kept in touch with him?'

Sergeant Ford nodded to an adjoining room. 'Tam is in giving a statement right now but the gist of it is that Charlie seems to have been in the army for about 12 years. When he came out Tam thinks he got a job in Edinburgh with a company that provided security.

'He wasn't really in touch with Charlie but met him back his mother's house at Christmas. By this time the step father had died and he often spent time with his and Tam's mother in her flat in Glasgow.

'Things seem to have gone wrong about 17 years ago. Tam was on a merchant ship working out of Dover when his mother told him Charlie had lost his job. She said Charlie was in a bad way and she was a bit scared of him.

'Anyway, the next thing Tam knows is he's told his mother is dead, her neck broken after an argument in the Glasgow flat. The police told Tam that Charlie said he was fed up being told he was useless and compared to his feckless father.'

Inspector Driver said: 'So that's the reason Tam moved to the village from Glasgow. No wonder. What happened to the brother?'

Sergeant Ford said: 'It seems he appeared at the High Court in Glasgow. He was sent to a high security health facility without limit of time. He pleaded guilty to culpable homicide due to diminished responsibility. In the State Hospital at Carstairs he was diagnosed with schizophrenia. He was released about a year ago. I don't where he was released to or what happened to him but Tam says he turned up here last summer.

'He's only seen him once, and the meeting didn't go well. Tam says he realised Charlie was drawn to come here as Tam is his only relative but he's not sure he wants anything to do with him.'

Inspector Driver said: 'I think we need to talk to Tam. When this happened, you wonder why he didn't mention his brother? That's strange. I think, now we have briefed the team, you and I need to have a chat with him about where his brother might be. He is a person of interest and, as a priority, we need to find out where he has been living.'

They found Tam sitting in the police canteen with his head in his hands and a cold coffee in front of him.

He looked up when he heard the Inspector say his name.

'You think Charlie's involved in these deaths, don't you?'

The inspector pulled up a chair next to Tam. 'We're not at that stage yet Tam. But your brother's DNA was found at the scene of a murder. Now he could have visited one of the dead men, Quintas MacNeill, as many men seemed to have visited for services in child pornography. Whatever his reason we need to talk to him. Tell me about him, Tam.'

'Well, he was an aggressive wee bugger when we were small. His father left when he was a baby. He worked in the printing industry and a heavy drinker, couldn't handle family life, apparently. My mum met my father, Jimmy, at the bingo near where she lived. He was a hard man but he was hardest on Charlie. As soon as he was 16, Charlie went off to the army. A couple of years later I joined the merchant navy. We never really saw each other for years after that. My father died and Charlie started going home more and more to see my mother.

'When he left the army, he was sort of lost, I think. My mum told me he got a job in Edinburgh working for some big wig doing his security but I never knew much about it.

'That job lasted for a couple of years, this is all about 20 or so years ago. Then around the same time my mum told me he'd lost his job and was coming to live with her. She wasn't happy about that but couldn't say no.

'Anyway, he was only back for a few weeks when I was contacted on my ship to say there been a fight and he'd killed mum in a fit of temper.'

'Did you see your brother then, Tam?' said the Inspector.

'Yeah, I saw him in the prison. He was strange and didn't seem to realise what he'd done? It was the same at the trial, he looked spaced out. He was in Carstairs for about 15 years and when he was released around a year ago, I never heard from him. Then, a few months ago, he turned up and said he'd found a cottage to rent near the village. I've never been to it and I haven't seen him since. He told me he was doing woodwork and a lot of walking. He said he'd money to live on, but I don't know where he got it. There's a lot about his life I don't know.'

Sergeant Ford said: 'Have you any idea where the cottage is?'

Tam nodded: 'I've been thinking and there's a road behind the old lighthouse and up on the moorland. About two miles up that road are some cottages. He's in one of more remote ones and not far from the route of the Southern Upland Way.'

'Thanks Tam. You can leave that with us and get home. But if your brother contacts you encourage him to come and talk to us.' Inspector Driver stood up and made to leave.

They waited till Tam left the building before the Inspector turned to his Sergeant and said: 'Get a team together and start looking for this house. I think you should take an armed response team with you. Once you identify Charlie's house, give me a call and I'll come out. Ok with you?'

It was less than two hours later when Sergeant Ford's name came up on his phone.

'Found it Inspector. He's not here but worth you coming out. I don't think he's been here for a few days. It's got that not lived in feeling and the milk's off. I've left a man outside but I'll wait till you come to look around. Watch the road as there's still some snow up here.'

'I'll be there is 40 minutes,' said the Inspector as he grabbed his coat.

'At last, we're making progress,' he thought aloud.

He drove down the rough road, with snow piled up on either side, to where he saw his sergeant standing outside an old worker's cottage, single storey with two windows at the front.

The Sergeant came to meet him: 'Seems he rented it from the farmer over there. The farmer says he rarely sees him. He's seen him going out with a rucksack early in the morning and coming home late at night, sometimes not even coming home.'

The went inside and looked around the main room. It was furnished with an old couch and a rug. The coal fire was out and the Inspector could not see central heating.

At the back of the lounge was a small kitchen and a back door. To the left a single bedroom, with just an old double bed, a wardrobe and a wooden dressing table in it. The only bathroom was next to the bedroom.

'Pretty sparse living,' said the Inspector.

They both wandered around, checking the small amount of clothes in the wooden wardrobe in the bedroom. They checked the drawers in the small unit.

'Nothing much here, nothing really personal. Nothing that tells us much about Mr Trimble.' said Sergeant Ford.

'We're missing something Sergeant. I can feel it,' said the Inspector looking around the lounge.

'Let's move this couch and see if there's anything underneath.'

That search proved fruitless. They moved into the bedroom. The inspector nodded towards the large heavy wooden wardrobe. They called in a uniformed officer and it took all three to shift it away from the wall.

'Ah, a door,' said the Inspector, panting and red faced. I need to get some exercise in, he thought.

It was locked. After a search they found a key taped under the bed. The inspector opened the door to what was a small room about 4ft by 4ft. He put on the light, the switch just inside the door.

'Oh, my goodness,' said the Inspector as they stood staring at a wall completely covered in guns and militaria carefully positioned on ledges nailed to the wall.

'There's a couple of guns missing,' stated the Sergeant as they both looked at the wall before them.

The Inspector moved into the room to get a better look, closed the door slightly and it was then he saw the back of the door. It was covered in photographs, many of them in black and white. He looked carefully.

'Bloody hell. I think these are photographs of Lizzie Campbell when she was living in Edinburgh. He was obviously following her and photographing her at home and college. It doesn't look as if she was aware.'

The Inspector turned to Sergeant Ford and said: 'Get the team to get all these photographs carefully taken down. We need to see what we're dealing with. He was obviously a bit obsessed with the young Lizzie.

'We need all these guns taken away and tested. I want a team to stay here and keep watch in case Trimble comes back. If he comes back, bring him in. Warn them he could be dangerous and armed. We need to find him.'

The inspector spent another hour at the house, just walking from room to room, checking the outside and trying to get a feel for the man who lived there.

He went outside to give his old schoolfriend Cameron a call to tell they may have had a breakthrough. He stood outside staring at the barren landscape. He wished Cameron hadn't left the police, he knew he had his reasons, but Tom always wished they could work together and hoped Cameron would come back to the "toon." Working on this mystery was the best it could be and he valued his input and experience.

Cameron answered on the first ring. 'Hello Inspector. How are you?'

'Better now Cameron. We've found Trimble's wee house and it's full of surprises. Lots of guns and photographs. They are on their way to forensics and my office to examine but he seems to have been following and taking pictures of Lizzie Campbell for months all those years ago.'

'Bloody hell, that's a shock. If he has all this stuff where's it been while he's been in prison and hospital?'

'Good thinking. I think I'll give his brother Tam a ring and ask if he knows. How are things going in Edinburgh?'

'Sophie's been to the flat she now owns. She looked a bit overwhelmed but she's living quietly at Morgan's flat, and spending time with her uncle. He looks like the cat that's got the cream. We're making good progress on identifying the father. A friend of Lizzie says he was called Malik Mittal from Delhi. We're looking into that.'

The Inspector said: 'Good, let's talk again tomorrow morning and I'll let you know what I find. I feel we are getting closer.'

Cameron turned to Morgan sitting beside him in the coffee shop.

'Interesting. The Inspector says they've found all these photographs of Sophie's mum in this man Trimble's house in Galloway. Plus, a lot of guns. They haven't found him yet.'

Morgan said: 'Poor Sophie. I think she has lot more to find out about her mum. What do we do about her real father?'

Cameron said: 'I think the University will have records and we know the dates almost 20 years ago when Malik was a law student there. We have a surname and hope they have an address in India. I will get onto that tomorrow morning.'

When Morgan got back to the flat about 5p.m. she found Sophie in her room playing the violin. She stopped when she heard Morgan go into the kitchen and came out smiling.

'You look happy Sophie.'

'I am when I'm playing and I sort of escape into my world. But I am feeling better and, I know that, because if feel like playing. I did the right thing going to the funerals. I've been to the church up the road here and said my prayers for everyone. When I was with the Rev I prayed for the family, now I pray for my mum, you and Cameron and my Uncle Dave. The aunts are ok in the hospital, I don't need to worry about them, and I can look after myself. I'm glad I don't ever have to go into that camper van again or visit that creepy farmhouse. Your flat's so light and lovely.'

Morgan said: 'Let's get some dinner on and relax. Cameron is making some investigations so we should hear more tomorrow. What are your plans?'

Sophie said: 'The social worker called today but I said I didn't need an appointment while I was staying with you. My uncle wants me to go to Glasgow for a couple of days, the lawyers need to see me to help me get my formal documents. And some other stuff. I need a bank account the lawyers say they will help with that, and Uncle Dave wants to arrange for me to get a passport in Glasgow. That'll be ok, won't it?'

'I'm sure it will be, but we can check with Cameron and the Inspector tomorrow. Do you need any money just now?'

Sophie laughed: 'No I don't need anything. I've been borrowing your shampoo.'

'Help yourself Sophie. Tomorrow, do you want to go for a walk at the Botanic Garden and have a coffee? The weather looks good.' Sophie nodded.

In Stranraer Sergeant Ford was calling Tam Mitchell.

'Hi Tam. We found your brother's house. He seems to have lots of pictures and stuff from before he was in prison. Do you know where he kept it?'

There was silence for a moment and then Tam said: 'The house in Glasgow was cleared after the murder and Charlie was in prison on remand. But I think he used to have a lock up in Edinburgh where he kept a lot of stuff when he was working. I'm not sure where it was but I think down near Leith. That's all I can tell you. Did you find Charlie?'

Sergeant Ford said: 'No sign of him Tam. You heard anything?'

Tam said: 'Ever since you told me about Charlie, I've been asking around the village. There's been a guy walking the cliffs in all weathers along by the Castle and all along the cliff to the lighthouse. It could be him. He loves walking, could be living rough, he learned that in the army. He used to do that when he lived in Glasgow and would be walking in places like Glencoe, living in a tent for days on end.'

Sergeant Ford said: 'Thanks Tam. Very useful. We'll be in touch. Remember if he contacts you, let us know.'

Sergeant Ford turned to see the Inspector come into the room. They had spent two hours looking at all the photographs taken from the Trimble house. The guns had been removed to undergo examination.

Inspector Driver said: 'I like the way you have put up the photographs just the way they were in the house. Now I look at them in detail I get the strong impression this guy Trimble knew Lizzie Campbell for a length of time before she died. There must be more than 50 photographs. I'm going to call Cameron but I wanted to check you've got the resources from Glasgow to start the search for Charlie Trimble.'

Sergeant Ford nodded: 'Yes got some sniffer dogs and some feet on the ground. We're out near his house just now and then going to move down to the cliff near the lighthouse and walk along the cliff path. Another two guys are checking near the farmhouse and the cliff area there.'

Inspector Driver called Cameron. He answered on the first ring.

'Hi Inspector what's happening?'

'I'm just going to send you a couple of the pictures we found at this guy Charlie Trimble's house. Best you don't show them to Sophie yet. They are of her mother, some of them of her just walking along the street but a couple of her arm and arm with her boyfriend, and, I think it's the elusive Malik almost 20 years ago. It might help identifying him.'

Cameron said: 'We've made some progress on that. The University found us a Malik Mittal, and an address in Edinburgh. Morgan and I have done a bit of research and we seem to have found the flats registered to a business in Delhi called Mittal Holdings. It's still running in Delhi so we're going to contact them to find if Malik is alive and living in India.'

Inspector Driver said: 'That's brilliant work. I think I'll come up to Edinburgh in the next day or so. I had Dave Campbell on the phone wanting to take Sophie on a tour showing her where her mother was brought up and where they went to school. He's also hoping to get her passport in Glasgow. I said I didn't have a problem but want a police escort for Sophie. He accepted but not very happily. It seems she might be away for a few days.'

Cameron said: 'Yes, Morgan said she might be going away with her uncle. She feels Sophie's ok about it as she is keen to find out everything she can about her mother. We've not said anything about our investigations into her real father but I think we may have to tell her something soon.'

Inspector Driver said: 'I should be in Edinburgh in the next two days. The search for Mr Trimble is ongoing but I think I can come to Edinburgh and sit down with Sophie when she gets back. You might know more about her dad by then.

'Another thing, the Sergeant has been back at the farm to accompany the MacNeill family lawyer to try and sort some things out. It seems the debts might wipe out a lot of the value but it will be the wife's family from Skye and the minister's sisters who'll get any money. When he was there some visitors arrived – debt collectors, online gambling people and a couple who didn't stay long enough to speak to him. All very strange. But no sign of Mr Trimble.'

Sophie felt that her new uncle wasn't happy to be accompanied by two police officers as they set off for Glasgow.

They took her first to his flat and Uncle Dave seemed excited to let her see it, his wife Amanda organising coffee and scones in the kitchen of their first floor flat. He explained that they were in Jordanhill.

'What do you want to do now Sophie?'

She thought for a moment and said: 'Could we see the house where you and mum lived with your parents?'

'Yes, of course. I'll ask the police to take us there. I can also show the school we both went to. Then we're meeting the lawyer at lunchtime in the west end. The police say you can stay here tonight and they'll ensure you're fine.'

Sophie spent the next two days being taken around the city. The meeting with the lawyer was just her and the lawyer and they spent two hours setting up a bank account. He transferred £50,000 into her account and made sure she got access to it.

Then she went with Uncle Dave to the passport office and arranged to get one within two weeks. The lawyer told her that her mum's violin had been taken back to the bank for safekeeping but she could get access to it at any time.

After two days of frantic sightseeing and spending time with her uncle and his wife Amanda in their comfortable flat Sophie was ready to get back to Edinburgh. She wanted to see the Inspector and find out if he knew any more about who killed her family.

She found her uncle intense. He seemed nice but it was obvious he didn't like his job as a lawyer very much, talking about all the boring stuff he had to do. He said Lizzie had had a much more exciting life than he had, and he didn't have any musical talent. He sounded quite bitter and Sophie was glad when she left Glasgow, saying goodbye to him at their door.

The police dropped her at Morgan's flat, waiting to see if she was safely inside. When she opened the door to Morgan's flat, she heard talking, putting her small case down she went into the lounge.

The Inspector was sitting with Morgan and Cameron and all three looked up and smiled at her as she entered.

'Hi Sophie,' said the Inspector. 'Hope your trip to Glasgow was ok and the police escort was polite and helpful. Come and sit down and join us.'

Sophie said: 'It was all fine. Uncle Dave and his wife were very kind to me. The lawyer was great and I have my own bank account and some money now, and I'm getting my first passport. I need to register with the health board in Edinburgh, I've never done anything like that before, I was never ill. Why are you here, Inspector?'

'Sophie, we have some possible good news for you,' said the Inspector. 'We're pretty confident that we have tracked down the man your mother was having a relationship with in Edinburgh and who, we believe, could be your father. When I say tracked down, we have managed to contact his family firm in India but we're waiting to hear back from them. He seems to have been the son of the founders of this Indian business but we're not sure he works there. Cameron is hoping to hear from them tomorrow.'

'Does he know about me?' said Sophie.

Cameron shook his head. 'We don't know Sophie. We need to find him first and then speak to him. The inspector and I are prepared to fly anywhere to find him.'

Morgan took Sophie's hand and said: 'This is hopeful news, isn't it? We are getting closer to finding your father. They'll know more tomorrow and you'll be the first to know. Now, I think we should all eat. I made lasagne.'

The next morning Cameron was in his hotel room when the call came back from the Mittal company in Delhi.

'Hi. Is that Mr Cameron Steel? This is Mr Mittal from Delhi calling. I believe you are looking for my cousin Malik?'

'Yes, I am working with the police here in Scotland and his name has come up in an investigation. We are hoping he is the Malik Mittal who was in Edinburgh about 18 years ago studying and may have known a student called Lizzie.'

There was a silence at the end of the telephone and Cameron thought he had lost the link when after what seemed like a few minutes Mr Mittal said: 'Ah that seems such a long time ago. So sad. But Malik has made a new life for himself. Let me explain.'

Cameron sat in silence for almost half an hour listening to the story. When the call ended, he sat looking out of the window. Then he called the Inspector and arranged to meet at the coffee shop outside the hotel in 20 minutes, also calling Morgan and asking her to come, and not to tell Sophie.

Cameron was first to arrive and found a quiet table, ordering a flat white for himself. Morgan and the Inspector came into together.

Cameron could not contain himself: 'I think we've found him, Malik Mittal. He's in New York.'

Inspector Driver smiled and said: 'Start at the beginning Cameron.'

'Of course. I got a call back from the Mittal business in Delhi this morning. Turns out it's Malik's cousin. He now runs the family business and told me Malik has been in America for the last 15 years and built a new life there.

'It seems Malik was the only son of Kumar and Indra and came to Edinburgh to study law before joining the family firm. His cousin says the family accepted when he told them he was in love with a Scottish girl, a musician called Lizzie Campbell. The parents even came to Edinburgh to visit her and meet her parents. The father presented Lizzie with her violin as a sign of his admiration for her talent. The cousin said they were going to marry.

'Then Malik had to come home suddenly when his mother was diagnosed with terminal cancer. He stayed at home for about 6 months but always intended to go back to Scotland. His mother died and he stayed to comfort his father, and help run the business.

'Then his father got a call from a contact in Scotland to say Lizzie and Sophie had been killed in a road accident. Malik couldn't leave to go back as his father became ill as well and he had to stay to help in the business.

'Apparently, there were some arguments as the father wanted him to never leave. The father died pretty soon after the mother and left the business to Malik to run. The cousin says he was heartbroken to lose his parents, the love of his life and his child in the space of a few months.'

Inspector Driver said: 'What happened then?'

'It seems Malik handed over control of the business to his cousin, keeping a share of the business and moved to New York to start afresh. He was able to finish his law degree in America and started his own corporate law business about ten years ago. He still lives there and has never married.'

Morgan said: 'Do you think he's Sophie's father?'

'That sounds pretty certain, it all ties up. But obviously, we need to talk to him face to face and get his DNA,' said Cameron.

Inspector Driver said: 'I would love to go to New York but sadly I need to get back to Stranraer, there's a killer to catch. I think we should tell Sophie that we think we have found her father, but we need to be certain and that means seeing him and getting the evidence. I need to understand why he didn't come back when he was told Lizzie was dead and who told him the baby had died as well, very strange. I think you should go, Cameron. I'm also minded to ask you to go as well Morgan. He might be more open with a woman, and you can tell him about the girl Sophie has grown into. What do you both think?'

Morgan said: 'I'll pay my own way as I can meet a friend, as well as support Cameron. I think we should have a chat with Sophie but not raise her hopes. I also know her uncle wants to take her back to Glasgow to see the grave of her mother. I think as long as the police stay with her, she'll be fine. You should ask her not to say anything to her uncle.'

Inspector Driver said: 'You don't trust her uncle?'

'It's not that. I think Sophie will want to tell him in her own time. Just a thought.'

The Inspector nodded: 'You're right. I keep forgetting she's almost an adult and will be 18 soon, but she's been through a lot. I would like to have gone to New York but

I need to be here, the search for Mr Trimble is not good. They found rabbit remains, as if one had been skinned and eaten and some remains of a fire on the cliffs near the village, but we are no closer to finding him. I'm asking headquarters to send me some reinforcements and the dog squad. I feel we are getting closer to why this has all happened, but I still don't understand the whole story. Perhaps if you find her father, he will be able to fill in some of the blanks. Can we go back to your flat and see Sophie, Morgan?'

The three walked the short distance to the flat, seeing a light in the lounge.

As Morgan walked into the lounge first Sophie looked up from the couch where she had been sitting with a notepad on her lap.

'Hi Sophie, you look busy.'

'Hi everyone. Yes, I didn't want to tell people but you have caught me out. I am writing a new score, calling it Lost.'

'That's a great idea,' said Cameron.

'It was my counsellor who suggested I wrote down all my thoughts and wrote down everything I knew about the people I've lost. I tried writing it but I think I can express it more in music. That's what I'm writing, but it's early days and I have a lot more work to do. I'm writing the Rev and my old mother and my real mother Lizzie into it.'

Morgan put her arm around Sophie and said: 'Beautiful idea Sophie. What a lovely way to remember people who cared and loved you.'

Even the Inspector looked moved as he said: 'Well Sophie, I might have some better news for you, we may have found your father.'

'Really,' said Sophie.

Cameron said: 'Nothing is certain but we have managed to find the fellow student your mother was seeing in the months before she died. We found his family in India and they confirmed that Malik Mittal was involved with Lizzie when he was a student in Edinburgh studying law.

'We can't say yet that he is definitely your father, we'll need DNA to confirm that. That's why I'm going to New York, where we believe Malik is now living and working, and finding out what has happened. Morgan is going to come with me.'

Sophie said: 'I know I can't go but will you call me Morgan when you meet him and tell me what he's like? I'm sure he's my father but I have so many questions for him. Why did he not come back to look for me when my mother died?'

Inspector Driver said: 'Hopefully you can ask him anything when you see him. But his family hinted that he was told you had died in the crash with your mother. Some bad things happened surrounding that accident and I need to find who told him that. He also seems to have been dealing with his own mother's death at the same time.

'I have to go back to Stranraer, Sophie. What are you going to do while Morgan and Cameron are in America? I'm going to leave a policeman with you, if that's ok.'

Sophie said: 'Yes, I'm fine with that. I'm going to work on my music and just relax. I'm going to see Rosie Murray at the music school who knew my mum. I phoned her and she said she would see me. Uncle Dave is coming through to see me as well and take me for lunch.'

Morgan looked at her and said: 'You would say Sophie if you weren't all right? You've been through so much and a lot of change in the last few weeks.'

Sophie said: 'No it's ok. I like my uncle but it feels like he wants me to be just like my mother. He even called me Lizzie before he remembered. I understand but he doesn't seem to realise I have been Rebecca for so long. I mean, I still kneel beside my bed every night to say my prayers. It's not like I can just shed a skin immediately and become Sophie. It will take me time.'

Morgan said: 'I think I understand but none of us know anyone who has had to cope with what you're having to come to terms with. Just give it time and don't do anything you don't want to do. You will have a policeman here if you need him. I'll be back in three of four days. We go tomorrow morning and I'll have my mobile with me. Why don't you and I go for a walk and catch up?'

After they left the flat the Inspector turned to Cameron and said: 'I didn't want to talk about the murder investigation in front of Morgan and Sophie. There's still no sign of Mr Trimble but I managed to get the search warrant extended to include his bank records and his electronic devices. We managed to find a laptop hidden under floor boards in the house and they are just going through it.

'It seems he has a fair amount of money and some payments dating back a few years from a company called Elite Security, which is now defunct. It seems they did high end security for visiting dignitaries. I think if you get to see Malik you can ask if he knows this name. I'm also going to try and find out who ran and owned this Elite Security business.'

'Absolutely. I have Malik's business address. We fly tomorrow morning so I hope to see him at his office the following morning. His family in India have informed him that we are investigating the death of Lizzie Campbell and want to talk to him. That's all he is aware of, and we haven't said anything about Sophie. Best to do that face to face.'

'Cameron, I wish you would come back into the police. I know the firearms unit was very stressful. But you could consider coming back into the Scottish force. We need people like you.'

'Tom that's very nice of you to say. I've been thinking about it as I have enjoyed being involved in an investigation. But I need to give it further thought. I've been drawn into the private side of security advice and I might develop that, I have to do something. Also, it would be good to be closer to my sister and family in Stranraer but I'm not going back there to live. I like the look of Edinburgh actually. It's changed since I was last here.'

Inspector Driver said: 'Take your time. Now I'm away to Stranraer later today to try and find this man. Text me when you arrive in New York tomorrow and we can talk. Safe journey.'

CHAPTER SIXTEEN

Morgan found the flight to New York passed quickly with Cameron easy to chat to and she managed a couple of hours sleep. They arrived lunchtime New York time and got a taxi to their hotel on the upper west side. It was close to Malik's office, Cameron said.

Morgan planned to meet Max but didn't want to mention it to Cameron, it was part of her life she didn't want to discuss with anyone. They agreed to meet for dinner about 9p.m at a restaurant near the hotel, but she had the afternoon free and they agreed to have a sandwich together before going their separate ways for the afternoon.

She was keen to see Max and put the past behind them and get back the friendship she had missed in the last few weeks. She felt strangely excited to see him.

Morgan settled into her room. Cameron was next door on the fifth floor and they were meeting in the hotel cafe for a sandwich in 20 minutes. She'd managed to get into her computer and was pleased to see an email from Max.

It said: 'What a lovely surprise Morgan. Love to see you. I can meet you at 6pm at the museum and we can go for a drink. I am settling in here but I don't know many people yet so seeing you will cheer me up.'

Morgan replied: 'I'm not sure I can cheer you up but see you at 6.'

After meeting Cameron for coffee and sandwiches Morgan said: 'I'm going to try and sleep for an hour or so before I go and meet a friend. I'll see you at the restaurant later.'

'Yes, good idea. I'm having a wee sleep too and will check in with the Inspector before I fall asleep. I will see you later and we're not seeing Mr Mittal till 10a.m, tomorrow. I checked and his office is just a short walk from here so we can have a lie in tomorrow and take it easy.'

Morgan walked the few blocks to where she was meeting Max. He was waiting at the door of an impressive museum entrance when Morgan arrived, looking happy to see her and rushing to envelop her in a big hug.

'Morgan, it's so good to see you and have you in my arms again. I can't tell you how much I have missed just hugging you.' Morgan found herself speechless as this was a much more effusive Max than she was used to. 'There's a cocktail bar near here that's always busy but we can find a quiet booth. I've been with a couple of colleagues.'

Morgan said: 'It's been a long day and I just feel like a glass of wine and a relaxing time. How are you anyway Max? You look good.'

Max said: 'Morgan, first let me say I know how stupid I've been and how much it must have hurt you. But coming here made me realise the rut I was in. I don't mean a rut with you but with the university. I know that's no excuse and I know what happened will haunt me for the rest of my life in the UK but here no-one cares. They just want me to do my job. It's exciting.'

Morgan said: 'Max the last few weeks have made me understand how unimportant so many petty things are. We all make mistakes but only a few of us are found out. You were just unlucky and I feel sorry for you and the girl involved. It's sad she got involved with such a nasty controlling boyfriend and what he did was cruel.

'I think you did the right thing coming here. I want to thank you for your gesture of making sure I can stay in the flat. It seems a bit over the top to give me joint ownership but we can discuss that again. It means I don't have to move which is great even if our neighbour Barry is still as nosy.

'What about the job? It sounds great.'

Max spent the next hour explaining about his new role in ancient artefacts and his plan to do exhibitions. He seemed genuinely enthused and Morgan thought she'd not seen that interested expression on his face for several years.

Eventually he stopped talking and said: 'What are you doing here anyway and who are you with? Is it a work trip?'

Morgan said: 'It's a long and strange story and very different from my normal day to day job Max. When I left the flat just a few weeks ago I basically ran away to that village in Dumfries and Galloway. Well, it snowed and snowed and bloody snowed. I was in a bed and breakfast in a small village and there was a policeman there from London.

'It turns out there was a cold case and a baby that went missing about 17 years ago. Anyway, while we were down there three people were killed and it turns out they had been raising that missing baby as their own, a girl of nearly 18 now.'

'Amazing,' said Max. 'You never think that sort of thing happens. Mind you I never thought someone would video me with a woman.'

Morgan ignored his comment and continued: 'Well now, it seems her father, who she has never met, may be living in New York and we're here to meet him. I've built up a close relationship with the girl and the police want me around. I'm just helping and it's all above board. I suppose I was just there when they needed someone. The village was cut off with no power or mobiles. I helped out and then they arranged this trip at short notice and I agreed to help. I'm here for a few days and then back to Edinburgh.'

Morgan spent just over two hours with Max and it was like the old days. He seemed like the old Max with his enthusiasm for his new job. They left the cocktail bar just before nine and Morgan felt awkward when Max lent in to kiss her. She turned her head and the kiss landed on her cheek.

But they promised to try and see each other before she flew back. He gave her a big hug and gave directions to the restaurant. It was a few blocks more than she realised and she was running a few minutes late when she opened the door of the Italian and was met with a wall of noise and heat.

She looked around and finally spotted Cameron at a small table at the back.

'My God I'd forgotten how many people live here and how they seem to go out for dinner all the time. I would love to go back down to Greenwich Village. I seem to remember lovely restaurants and shops down there. I know it's not a holiday but it seems a long way to come and not see something of the city.'

Cameron said: 'I agree, but best see what we find tomorrow. The Inspector called and said he might have some new information. It will be interesting if this is the right person. He seemed to confirm a relationship with Lizzie Campbell, unless of course, she was seeing someone else as well and we don't know about that. Her brother seems to know remarkably little about his sister's life.'

Morgan said: 'That's a bit unfair. They were siblings but with different lives. He was in Glasgow doing law and she was a developing star in music. I think that is quite common among families.'

Cameron said: 'Is that polite way of saying that all families are fucked up?'

'No. I'm just saying we shouldn't judge people too much.'

They stopped talking when the waiter turned up. Morgan decided to have a plate of pasta and a glass of red wine. She still felt a bit spaced out and weary.

By the time they got back to the hotel she could barely keep her eyes open. She said good night and arranged to meet at 8a.m. for breakfast.

Morgan must have slept for a full nine hours and when she awoke, she felt ready for the day ahead. I hope it is him, she thought, and can answer a few questions. Like where he has been for the last 18 years.

Just before 10 am they walked up Fifth avenue towards the office where they were due to meet Malik Mittal. As they came to the number of a plush office block just opposite the main gate at Central Park, Morgan looked at the giant brass name plate and said: 'My God he owns the company.'

It read – Mittal Associates, Corporate Law.

They were met by a concierge and when they gave their names he said: 'Please take the lift to the second floor and Mr Mittal's personal assistant will meet you.'

A young beautiful girl was waiting at the lift. 'Follow me,' she said 'Mr Mittal is in the board room. Can I bring you coffee or tea?'

She led them into a large room with windows showing Central Park in all its Spring glory. Morgan thought she had never been in a more beautiful room. The sun was shining in the windows and it took her a minute to see a tall handsome man get up out of his chair and come towards them with his hand outstretched. Morgan looked closely.

He looked about 40 with big brown eyes and a touch of grey at his temples. She couldn't see a wedding ring.

He spoke first. 'Welcome to New York Mr Mackenzie and Ms Cooper. I hope you had a good flight?'

Cameron said: 'Thank you so much for agreeing to see us and giving us your time. This is a long story and one that reaches back in time. We are sincerely hoping we've found the right person.

'This is a very delicate situation. I believe you confirmed to the policeman who called you that you were involved with a Lizzie Campbell in Edinburgh almost twenty years ago?'

Mr Mittal said: 'First things first please, call me Malik. I must be completely honest with you. Since that policeman called and mentioned the name of a woman who meant a great deal to me my mind has been in turmoil. When my cousin called me from India and said someone from Scotland had been asking for me, I wondered what was going on. I was immediately transported back to another time and another life. Then when that policeman called, I could hardly take it in, it took my breath away. I know Lizzie and our baby died in a car crash so I am fascinated why this case has been re-opened. I have been grieving for nearly 20 years so you can imagine how that call turned my life upside down.'

Cameron said: 'The case involving Lizzie Campbell has been re-opened due to new evidence, having a fresh look at the accident all those years ago.'

Malik looked shaken and said: 'What new evidence?'

Cameron said: 'First, let me explain how I, a policeman from London and Morgan who lives in Edinburgh have been asked by the police to come here.'

He started to tell Malik of the meeting in the bed and breakfast, the snow and the sightings of a young girl he seemed to become very excited.

He said: 'Is this young girl connected to Lizzie?'

Cameron said: 'I can confirm that a young woman, aged 17, who was found in the south west of Scotland only a few weeks ago is the daughter of Lizzie Campbell. DNA has confirmed this. She had been living with another family and how she came to be with them is being investigated.'

There was a stunned silence. As they looked at Malik, they saw tears starting to fall down his face.

'I apologise but this is too much to take in. I have blocked this out of my mind for so many years. I assume you think that this girl is my daughter, that she didn't die in the crash? I cannot believe that, for all these years I believed both Lizzie and my daughter, and again I say my daughter, were dead. Excuse me but I need to get some fresh air.'

He got up and left the room leaving Morgan and Cameron stunned.

Morgan said: 'He seems genuine enough. What happens now?'

Cameron said: 'The Inspector said they can arrange a DNA test here if we need it. I think that would be a good idea before we suggest he comes back to Scotland. Mind you we might not be able to stop him if he thinks for one minute that his daughter is alive.'

At that point Malik came into the room and seemed to have regained his composure.

He said: 'I have cleared my diary for the rest of the day. I am not sure I can work after what I believe I heard.'

Cameron said: 'Perhaps you could tell us about your relationship with Lizzie Campbell.'

Malik said: 'Lizzie was, and still is, the love of my life. I was sent to Edinburgh by my father to get a law degree. We were both young and met at a concert at the music school and then I saw her in a coffee shop. I was brave and sat down beside her and we chatted for more than an hour. She invited me to meet her at the music school the next day.

'My father had bought me a flat to live in, while I was at university. He also bought a second flat next door to mine, hired a security person to make sure I stayed on the straight and narrow and ensure I didn't go drinking and meeting any strange women. My parents had big plans for me.

'I used to meet Lizzie at the music school and watch her studying with a concentrated expression on her face. She bit her lower lip when she was thinking. I could not take my eyes off her. I was, as you say in Scotland, smitten.

'After that we were never apart, although sometimes it was difficult with studying and the security ring around me. We often met at her flat.'

Cameron said: 'I assume you were her only boyfriend. Did she tell you when she fell pregnant?'

Malik seemed reticent to answer the questions sensing there was some hidden criticism of him.

He sounded defensive when he said: 'I was her only boyfriend. We were committed to each other. Family tore us apart and for that I will always regret having to go home.'

Morgan said: 'What happened?'

He said: 'Lizzie and I were getting to know each other when she fell pregnant. But we were determined to be together and bring up the child. Then my father contacted me to say my mother was seriously ill with cancer and might not survive. He ordered me home and the security man was no longer in his employ. He was sacked, the flats were sold. I had to go for two reasons – I had no money of my own and my mother needed me. Also in my family you did what your parents asked. I flew home to Delhi when Lizzie was about 7 months pregnant with our child.

'I promised her I would come back when I could. I told her I would write every week. I had no mobile phone in those days. Then my mother died and we went into a period of mourning.'

Cameron said: 'Did you say you wrote to Lizzie every week?'

'Yes, every week but I never got any letters back.

'Then my father told me that Lizzie and our baby had been killed in a road traffic accident. I could do nothing about getting back to Scotland and I was trapped in India. I had no money of my own and my father would not fund me to leave. He and my mother had liked Lizzie and had given us their blessing but the death of my mother changed everything. This all happened around the time my mother died.'

Morgan looked at him and asked: 'Was Lizzie aware that you still loved her and were committed to her? It seems, from a distance, that you just left and abandoned her when you went back to India.'

'I know how that must look but it's not true,' he said. 'I had asked her to marry me and my parents had given me my grandmother's diamond engagement ring to present to her. I gave her that ring before I left for India. She knew I would be back. I loved her and we were going to be married when I got back.'

Cameron said: 'No-one ever mentioned an engagement ring being found in the accident or in her flat and possessions. Another thing, why was your name not put on the birth certificate as father?'

Malik said: 'Lizzie had been getting very nasty letters about our relationship. When I had to go back to India, we felt it best if we pretended that I was not coming back. The letters seemed to stop after that. But she knew I was coming back as soon I could. I had to deal with the grief of the family after my mother's death and the way it affected my father. I am an only son and a lot was expected of me.'

Cameron made his excuses and left the room.

Malik looked at Morgan and said: 'What is she like, my daughter?'

'She's beautiful and talented, just like her mother. She's also very mature for her age but has had a lot to take in these last few weeks. She's a lovely girl.'

'Where has she been all these years? Why did no one find her before now?'

'She's been with a family but kept under the radar. I'm sure the police will be able to give you all that information. I think Cameron is away contacting them to see what they want to do.'

Just then Cameron came back into the room. He looked at Malik and said: 'Thanks to your helpful assistant I was able to get in touch with our Inspector in Scotland. He has arranged for a private company to come here within the next hour and take a DNA sample which we can compare to Sophie's. But he has suggested you think about making arrangements to come to Scotland as soon as possible.'

'Of course I'm coming to Scotland. Nothing will keep me from my daughter.'

Cameron said: 'While we're waiting for the medical team can you tell me more about the security man you had while you were in Edinburgh?'

Malik laughed: 'Gosh you are asking me to think back nearly 20 years. It was another life. My father hired a security company when I got a place at Edinburgh University to study law. He was very scared I was going to be kidnapped or fall into bad company, I think. All I can remember is the company was called Elite Security and the man who was with me for a couple of years was just known as

Charlie. He lived in a flat, bought by my father, next door to mine and basically came with me to university and checked out visitors.

'When I met Lizzie, it was very difficult. He was always around and we struggled to find time alone. I used to escape and meet at Lizzie's flat. Listen, I know I sound calm but inside my whole body is on fire. I spent many years grieving for Lizzie and our baby. I have never met anyone who matched Lizzie and she still lives in my heart. I will never forget her. On top of that was the guilt that I could not be there with her. She might not have died if I had been with her.

'I also feel guilt that I could not come to Scotland when I was told she was gone. I liked her parents but things were too difficult for me in India, that will always be a regret. But now it seems I have been given another chance and I have a daughter. The person who sent me the photograph of Lizzie lying dead in her car really affected me. It was all so cruel and I could not face travelling to Scotland when I was told there was no hope.'

Just then the door to the office opened and the personal assistance came in to say the medical team were in the adjoining office waiting for Malik.

When he left Cameron turned to Morgan and said: 'I wonder who sent him that picture? There would only be police pictures unless it was sent by a person who was actually at the accident. Very interesting. I spoke to the Inspector. He thinks we should all get back to Scotland tomorrow or the next day. He should get the DNA results tomorrow. What do you think of Malik, Morgan?'

'I think he's pretty genuine. Everything he said seemed to me to be true. The proof will be if he is Sophie's real dad, what sort of father will he be?'

Just then her mobile rang. It was a UK number but she didn't recognise the number. She answered it.

'Hi, Morgan Cooper here, who's calling?'

'It's me, Sophie. This is my new phone. I just couldn't resist calling to see how you are? Really, I want to know if you've found my dad. I keep thinking about him.'

'I understand that Sophie and we hope to be back tomorrow in Edinburgh and can tell you more. The Inspector will tell you more. How are you anyway? What have you been doing?'

'I am not a child, Morgan. I can take bad news if this man you are seeing in America is not my father but I need to know.'

Morgan handed her mobile to Cameron.

He said: 'Sophie it's Cameron here. There's not a lot Morgan can say just now. But I can tell you we have found the man who was your mother's boyfriend and he's coming back to Scotland with us. But we need his DNA to be sure it's the right person and you need to be patient. None of us are treating you like a child but we don't want to raise your hopes until we know for certain. The Inspector will tell you when we are home. I'm putting you back to Morgan now.'

When Morgan took the phone back there was silence at the other end.

'Sophie are you still there?'

'I'm sorry, she said. 'I've just been sitting here in the flat thinking the worst. I went to see the teacher Rosie at the music school. She was lovely and talked about mum a lot. She showed me some pictures of my mum playing her violin at the school.

'Today I'm getting my mum's violin out of the bank and will bring it back here. I just play my old violin but I like to look at my mum's.'

'Are you ok by yourself in the flat? Are you not going out to do some shopping for yourself?'

Sophie laughed: 'No I was brought up to believe shopping was bad for the environment. I was told not to buy anything unless I needed it. I don't need anything.'

'Ok that's me told,' said Morgan. 'But I will bring you back a present.'

'Bring me back a father,' said Sophie.

When the call ended Morgan turned to Cameron and said: 'When will we get the result of the DNA test?'

Cameron said: 'I'm going to call the Inspector now.'

Inspector Driver answered on the first ring. 'Hi Cameron. How's things?'

'Well Malik is with the medical team just now giving his DNA sample. He seems a pretty genuine guy. We're just checking what you want us to do.'

'I think you all get on a flight tomorrow morning. The medical outfit have assured me that the results will be emailed by tomorrow morning so by the time you get here we should know if he is Sophie's dad. But anyway, if he's happy to come to Edinburgh I want to talk to him about Lizzie and the time they spent together. I'm back in Edinburgh now.'

Cameron said: 'Any luck finding Mr Trimble?'

'No luck yet. We have found his Range Rover in a car park in the New Galloway Forest. We think he may have had a motorbike so he could be anywhere hiding out. One strange development was we got another anonymous message. I think from him and from an email address we cannot trace. It was another picture, pretty faded, but definitely the moment Sophie was taken from the crashed car where her mother lay dying. It shows the Rev in his motor home and the wife carrying the baby seat. It's very disturbing but it proves whoever took the picture, and I think it was Trimble, was there at the scene, watching it all. I'm obviously not showing this to Sophie or anyone.

'But it's evidence now. It also had a message that said "they took her" and that was all.'

Cameron said: 'It must be from Trimble. Malik says he got sent a picture of Lizzie in the crash. That must have been Trimble surely?'

Inspector Driver said: 'It looks that way. We still have a lot to find out. Can Malik remember much about the security people his father hired to look after him in Edinburgh?'

'Yes, I think it's the same bunch and the guy was called Charlie. I think he's blocked a lot out of his mind about that time with the trauma of losing Lizzie, the child he had never seen and his mother. He looks a bit shell shocked but determined to come to Scotland.'

'Good,' said the Inspector. 'Get the flights arranged today and I'll see you in Edinburgh tomorrow. Hopefully we will know more by then. I want to go back and have another chat with the lawyers in Ayr so I'll update you.'

Just then the door opened and Malik came back into the room.

He said: 'I've just made arrangements for all my meetings to be cancelled or rearranged and other people to take over my work. My diary is clear for two weeks and I'm going home to pack. I assume we are all flying together tomorrow morning. I wonder if I can take you both to dinner tonight? I know a good place that's quiet and good food. My assistant is booking the flights for us all so you don't need to do anything. I'll arrange my car, to take us to the airport in the morning.'

Morgan said: 'I love a night out in New York. I have to go somewhere first so if you tell me where I can meet you. I'm packed, in fact I never really unpacked, so I can leave anytime tomorrow.'

She left Malik and Cameron chatting over coffee and made her way back to their hotel. She texted Max and suggested they meet again at around 6p.m.

He came back and told her to come to his office at the Museum so he could show her where he worked.

She lay down on her bed ostensibly to rest her eyes and woke up an hour later, deciding to get ready and leave an hour early, to have a look at the shops on the way and buy a present for Sophie.

She had a successful shopping trip, buying jewellery from one of the top shops on Fifth Avenue for Sophie and arriving at Max's workplace at 5.30pm, to find him waiting in reception, ushering her through security to his office on the second floor. He seemed at ease and everyone seemed to know him.

He was in an office at the front with a view of Central Park.

'Wow,' said Morgan. 'You've landed on your feet here Max. No wonder you like this job.'

'Yes, it's great, so far. Would you not come out here and work Morgan? I would like that, we get on, it's exciting here.'

'Hold on Max. I think it best if you find your feet here for a while and we keep in touch. This is your new start, right?'

Max did what he always did when he was embarrassed. He laughed and said: 'Just joking. I know you have your life in Edinburgh. But I still miss us, Morgan.'

Morgan felt nothing when he said that but took his hand in hers and said: 'It's too soon, or perhaps it's never going to happen Max. Too much has happened and we both need some space. Perhaps it was the end of the relationship. It can't have been right for you to do that.' She could not even bring herself to say anything more.

'Let's chat about something else and then you can walk me to my restaurant. We'll stay in touch and, I promise,

I'll come out for a holiday but we both just need to get on with our lives.'

It was just before 8p.m. when Max left her close to the restaurant where Malik and Cameron were waiting.

They were in the bar area and before she even had time to say anything a smartly dressed waiter was at their side to escort them to their table.

Everybody seemed to know Malik and he was greeted warmly at almost every table before they finally came to private booth at the back of the restaurant.

'This looks lovely Malik. Is this a regular haunt of yours?'

'I eat out a lot for business and this a good private place where you can talk. I know you want to ask me questions so I chose here.'

Cameron said: 'Let's order and then why don't you just tell us about you and Lizzie and what it was like in Edinburgh.'

They sat in silence for a few minutes scanning the menu and the waiter appeared at just the right moment to take the order.

Then Malik opened his briefcase and brought out a number of slightly faded photographs.

'These might illustrate how happy Lizzie and I were and in love.'

He handed them first to Morgan and she looked at a picture of a younger Malik with a beautiful blonde smiling woman on his arm walking along a beach at what looked like Portobello.

Morgan didn't say anything as she looked at the picture of the two of them outside a museum, on a train, up a mountain, sitting in front of big fire and then she saw a picture of them both close up and Lizzie wearing an emerald ring with large diamonds on either side.

'What's this picture Malik?' she said, handing the pictures to Cameron to look at.

'That's the day she accepted my marriage proposal. That was my grandmother's engagement ring. My parents gave it to me to give to Lizzie. That was when we were full of hope for the future, of a future with both of us in it. We were so happy.'

Cameron nodded: 'You look happy. What happened after that?'

'We were happy. Not long after we got engaged my parents came over to meet Lizzie. They met her parents and everyone got on well. My parents had accepted that Lizzie was my choice for a wife and they knew I was determined. My father even bought the violin for Lizzie.

'Then when my mother went back to India and found that a sore stomach was stage four cancer, my father ordered me to come home, you could do that in those days, and sold the flats, dismissed the security and got me on a flight home. I only had time to see Lizzie once more and promised her that I would be back as soon as I knew what was happening.

'I kept in touch with her but my mother lived for several months and I was not able to get back to Scotland for the birth. Lizzie understood. My mother died just a week before Lizzie and I was coping with that, my heartbroken father and the news from my father that Lizzie and my daughter had died in a road accident left me heartbroken. I had my mother's funeral and I had to help my father with his business. I never made it to Scotland for Lizzie's funeral and that has lived me for almost 18 years.'

'What a tragedy Malik,' said Morgan. 'Did you know Lizzie was going up north that time?'

'Yes, I knew. I knew she wanted to get away from Edinburgh for a few days. Lizzie was so happy about the baby, happy with her studies but she kept getting these strange letters. Two lots really, one nasty lot that said she was talentless, stupid and ugly, and another lot which said she was the most beautiful woman in the world. She tried to pretend she wasn't bothered by any of the letters but I persuaded her to go to the police. I could tell she was worried.'

Cameron said: 'The police have only found a couple of the nasty letters. The rest must be destroyed. The violin is safe and, in a bank, but left to Sophie. The engagement ring has never been mentioned and it's not in the police report that she was wearing it.'

Malik said: 'Whoever took Sophie from the car perhaps took the ring too?'

Cameron shook his head. 'No, they didn't look the sort to take jewellery. They seem to have just wanted a child for themselves, and they took Sophie. They looked after her well and you will find a lovely girl. If she is your daughter, you will be very proud of her.'

Malik looked up and said: 'I feel it is my daughter and I am very much looking forward to going to Edinburgh. Our flight is at 11a.m. I will come with my driver to pick you up at 7a.m from your hotel.'

Cameron said: 'Can I keep these photographs for a few days? I'll make sure you get them back in a good state.' Malik nodded.

Morgan was enjoying her food and turned the conversation to living in New York.

'What's it like to live here?' she asked.

'Very expensive,' said Malik 'but exciting as well. I've been here about 15 years now and live a low key life. I have a flat in town but I mainly work. My father's business was handed over to my cousin who runs the it now, although I still have a share in it and that takes up some of my time.'

Cameron said: 'I think I talked to your cousin when we were looking for you. What sort of business is it?'

Malik said: 'It's changed since my father and grandfather started it. Then it was steel and coal. Now its communications and digital. The only way to survive in business is to evolve with the changes in the world. My cousin told me you called and I was fascinated. I had no idea it might be about my daughter Sophie. I accepted a long time ago that she was dead.'

Morgan said: 'Her brother never contacted you or her parents to say she was missing?'

'No, I didn't really know her brother. But we had few mobiles in those days. Her parents probably didn't want to worry me, or wondered why I hadn't come back. It's too late to explain to them now isn't it.'

Cameron said: 'I think we should get an early night. That was a lovely meal, Malik. Thankyou.'

When they left the restaurant Malik's driver was already there and opened the door for Morgan and Cameron.

As Morgan and Cameron entered the hotel his mobile rang. It was the Inspector.

'Tom, what's the problem?' said Cameron.

'No problem just wanted to update you. We should have the results of the DNA by the time you get back tomorrow. I also wanted you to give you some new information. We've looked at these pictures and if they are from Trimble then he must have taken them from a viewpoint above the accident all those years ago. It means he was there, watching. We still haven't found him but we have had reports of fires in the Galloway Forest and a holiday home broken into. We're looking for fingerprints.'

'Ok Tom, I'll let you know when we get back tomorrow. Is Sophie all right?'

'Yeah, I had her uncle complaining she was too busy to see him. She seems to have been back at her mother's flat and calling her lawyers. She's also been at the music school talking about her mother with that old friend of her mum. The girl's ok and pretty clued up. She's obviously wanting to know about her father. I'm pretty sure it's Malik but we need to be certain. There's so much I don't know about this case but the science is one thing I can be confident about. Safe travels.'

The flight home was as comfortable as it could be. Morgan liked the driver who picked them up at the hotel and dropped them in comfort at the airport. It was pretty straightforward and they all slept a lot. She watched Malik, his face giving nothing away but she could sense the turmoil in his body language. Cameron, on the other hand, looked relaxed and just slept.

They landed at Edinburgh where waiting for them was the Inspector. He welcomed Malik and said he was taking him to the station immediately.

Malik seemed relaxed and happy to agree with anything and they left together in a police car.

The Inspector turned and waved to Morgan and Cameron that he would be in touch.

Morgan suggested Cameron came back to the flat with her to have a coffee and catch up. They grabbed a taxi and were back in the West End in about fifteen minutes. When Morgan opened the door, she was surprised to find no-one there.

'I wonder if Sophie has gone to the police station?'

Cameron nodded: 'I would think so,' he said as he sank into the couch and cushions.

Morgan laughed at his relaxed stance: 'Ok I'm sure you're right. I'm just over protective and like to know she's safe. I'll make coffee before I even think of doing anything else.'

They were sitting, not talking, but just relaxing after the flight when Cameron's phone rang.

It was the Inspector.

'Hi Tom. How's things? Morgan wants to know if Sophie's at the police station?'

'Yeah, she's here and I called to let you know we have confirmed Malik is her father. They're together just now in one of the rooms. I wonder if you and Morgan can come down to the police station? I'm staying in Edinburgh for another couple of days but need to get back to Galloway at some point. I've left the Sergeant in charge of the search for Trimble but no luck yet. Mr Mittal has indicated he intends to stay in Edinburgh for as long as he needs. He's booked a hotel in the west end. I need a word with you Cameron about another development when you get here.'

Cameron said: 'Morgan and I will be there as soon as possible.'

Morgan said: 'Give me five minutes. I want to change and freshen up. You're welcome to a shower here if you need to do the same.'

It was 20 minutes later when they both left the flat. Morgan was driving and they were at the police station in a few minutes.

As they walked into the station Morgan could see a beaming Sophie coming towards her, dragging Malik behind her.

'You've heard the good news, haven't you,' she said.

'Yes, I heard Sophie. That's such good news. It's amazing that you have found each other.'

'Yes,' said Malik, 'and I'm never letting her go.'

'Dad, can you say that again? It was Morgan who helped me at the farm when everyone was killed and has been my friend. I'm staying in her home and I feel very safe there.'

Malik said: 'Ms Cooper, Morgan. I can't thank you and Cameron enough for all you have done for Sophie. Cameron said he had to go a meeting but I wonder if you would join Sophie and me for something to eat. We can walk to a good restaurant from here.'

Morgan said: If that's ok with the police then I'm happy to join you.'

Malik nodded and the three of them walked the short distance to an all day Italian. A table for three was found.

Back at the station the Inspector was busy briefing Cameron.

'Cameron can you be here later today? I don't need to see Malik, his daughter or her uncle for a day. I had the uncle here all morning but persuaded him to go back to Glasgow for a few days and allow Malik to establish a relationship with his daughter. He didn't seem very pleased and was even less happy when Sophie said she wanted to be alone with her dad.

'Anyway, the lawyer for the family, the father, has asked to come and see us here. He wanted us to go to Ayr but I said we couldn't. He says he has remembered something that might help the investigation. He should be here about 4p.m. so we have time for a coffee and snack.'

'Interesting,' said Cameron. 'Will be glad to hear what he has to say.'

Charles Robertson turned up right on time, habits of a lifetime and dressed in a dark suit and white shirt with a new tie. Old habits die hard, thought Cameron.

They ushered him into a private meeting room and he thanked them for their time and said he wasn't sure the information was any good to the investigation.

'Let us be the judge and if you think it might be important, then I want to hear it and so will Cameron,' said the Inspector.

'Well,' said the lawyer, 'I don't like to spread gossip but the parents are gone so I suppose it's all right. Dave Campbell was three years older than Lizzie. I don't know if you have heard this but he was adopted. The Campbells didn't think they could have children and searched for a child for a long time. He was found in Glasgow, the result of a couple with serious drug problems, and he'd been removed from the family home. The Campbells took him home. Then amazingly when the Campbells had given up the hope of having a child naturally, Lizzie came along. She was a little miracle, her mother said. A good child as well.'

Inspector Drover said: 'This is important Mr Robertson. How did the boy deal with a little sister?'

'For the first few years they got on remarkably well, it seems. He was glad of someone to play with and Lizzie had a sunny personality that meant she got on with everyone.'

Inspector Driver said: 'What about when they got older?'

The lawyer seemed to hesitate and spoke slowly: 'I am trying to remember what the father told me. It seems when the boy was about fifteen and Lizzie, around twelve, they noticed a change of behaviour.

'He seemed very interested in Lizzie as a girl, put it that way.

'Her father told me that Lizzie became rather fearful of him and, at her instigation, a lock was put on her bedroom door. I am certain that's one reason that he bought David a flat in Glasgow when he left to study law.'

Cameron said: 'What about once they both left home, did they see much of each other?'

'I don't know anything about that. The only thing I remember was seeing Lizzie at a concert in Edinburgh and her parents were there, but not the brother. She told me she didn't see much of him except at her parents at things like Christmas. I put it down to different interests. That's all I can tell you. In their will, the parents left everything equally to both Dave and Lizzie. They were very fair, but they couldn't hide their pride and love for Lizzie. She was a lovely girl and a big loss.'

CHAPTER SEVENTEEN

Sophie could not stop holding her father's hand as they sat in a coffee shop in Edinburgh. She had felt a connection to him the moment she'd met him. It didn't even need the policeman confirming that he was her father.

She listened as he explained how he believed she had died in the car with her mother. How he was trapped in India dealing with his own mother's death, his father's grief and a business to run. He apologised for not coming to look for her.

She told him that was not important now, they had a future together to look forward to.

Malik said: 'It's amazing, you have the same sweet nature as your mother. I feel very close to your mother sitting here in the city where we met all those years ago. It seems like yesterday. I have never met anyone I loved as much as your mother, Sophie. We chose your name together when we knew you were going to be a girl.'

Sophie said: 'I can take you to my mother's grave. She's buried near Glasgow and close to her parents. I also want to show where I lived in Galloway some of the time.'

Malik had said: 'What these people did was wrong Sophie. They took you away from your mother and your family. But they seem to have loved you and looked after you. They didn't deserve to die like that. We need to leave it to the police and concentrate on getting to know each other.'

Sophie felt at peace sitting with Malik. She had told her uncle she couldn't see him for a few days. She wanted to spent time with the man she now knew was her father.

She took him to the flat her mother had left her. He said he had been before with her mother when she viewed the flat to buy. When they walked into the lounge, she could see tears in his eyes and he said: 'I feel Lizzie here.'

Sophie said: 'This is the violin she left me. It's been in a bank but I got it out to show you and to try and play it.'

Malik said: 'Amazing. That's the violin my father and mother gave Lizzie as a present when they came over. I can't believe you still have it.'

'Yes, it was kept safe by her parents. They apparently always believed I would be found and kept this flat and violin for me. They must have been nice people.'

Malik said: 'Yes, they were. Can you play something for me?'

Sophie picked up the violin and prepared to play. When she started a strange sound came out of the violin.

'There's something wrong with it. I've never tried to play it before,' said Sophie as she put it on the ground and bent down to have a look inside.

'Look there's a small brown envelope taped to the inside. Do you think this was put there by my mother?'

Malik said: 'It must have been.'

Sophie pulled the small package out and laid it on the floor. They both looked at it and then Malik picked it up and opened it. There was no message and only a small key fell out.

Malik said: 'I think we need to take this to the police. Why would your mother hide a key? The police said she didn't take the violin with her when she went north on her trip. So, she must have put this key inside before she left and hidden it for safekeeping. There's nothing in the flat that it could open. It's been lying in this violin all this time.'

They left the flat with the key, and the envelope, safely tucked in Malik's jacket, making their way to the police station.

As they walked Malik said: 'I want to take Morgan and Cameron out for dinner tonight to thank them. What do you think?'

Sophie nodded and said: 'I would love that. They have been such good friends. Having Morgan is like having a big sister.'

She immediately called Morgan. 'Hi, It's Sophie, Dad wants to take us all out for dinner tonight to a lovely fish restaurant. Are you ok with that and we want Cameron to come as well?'

Morgan was in the flat and said she would go. 'Cameron is at the police station. So, you need to call him.'

Sophie said: 'Dad and I are on the way there. Guess what happened? I'd never tried to play the violin before and when Dad asked me to play, a strange sound came out. So, I put it down and looked inside in case dust had settled in it. I found an envelope with a key inside and I think my Mum hid it in there, it was taped to the side of the violin. We're off to see the police now to try and find what it's for. It doesn't fit any door in the flat. It looks more like a bank key, Dad says.'

'Sounds interesting,' said Morgan. 'See what the police make of it and perhaps take a picture of it and we can discuss tonight.'

Morgan and Cameron were already in the restaurant sipping a glass of champagne that the waiter said Mr Mittal had ordered when they saw Sophie come in with her dad.

Morgan thought it was first time she had seen real happiness on the young woman's face. She was staying close to Malik and there was no awkwardness between them. They looked comfortable together even after such a short time.

Morgan and Cameron stood up as they came towards the table. It was Malik who spoke first.

'Thanks for agreeing to join us for this dinner. We want to thank you both for being such a support to Sophie. We hope you become our friends for life. Oh, and thank you for finding me and bringing me such joy.'

'Let's order and then we can talk,' said Cameron.

Morgan followed everyone else and ordered fresh fish and then turned to Sophie and said: 'So you've been so busy. I've hardly seen you in the flat. What have you been up to?'

'Well, tomorrow Dad and I are going to Glasgow to meet my uncle for lunch. Uncle Dave is keen for me to stay in Scotland and go to music college in Edinburgh. I like the idea as it's what my mum did but Dad is talking about going to live with him in New York, getting private tuition for my music and school work. Part of me wants to leave Scotland for a while and it would be good to get to know Dad.'

Malik said: 'I'm not putting any pressure on her and, if it came to it, and she wanted to stay in Scotland, I can work from here. But too many things, bad things, have happened here and I think a change of scene might be good for her. Ultimately, it will be her decision.'

Sophie smiled and said: 'I need to get everything sorted here and then think about my future.'

Just then the main courses arrived and everyone was silent as they enjoyed the food. Morgan thought Malik looked ten years younger when he was with Sophie and they chatted like they had known each other for years.

Malik sat back and looked at Sophie he said: 'Of course, I want Sophie to come and meet her relatives in India. I don't have any brothers or sisters but I have a few cousins. I think you spoke to one of them who runs the family business now. Well, they have many children and they all knew about Lizzie and my love for her so they will be wanting to meet our daughter. She needs to understand her heritage – Scottish and Indian.'

Morgan said: 'Malik how do you like living in New York and America?'

He laughed and said: 'America has been good for me. When I needed a new challenge and decided to leave India and the family business it welcomed me with open arms. I've built a good business in corporate law and I like my life there.'

Cameron said: 'Listen this has been a lovely meal but back to work. Do you have a picture of the key you found? I assume the police have no idea what it's for?'

'They're checking all the banks for safe deposit boxes. The problem they said is that it could have been there since before my mum died,' said Sophie.

She brought out a picture and Cameron looked at first for several minutes, then he passed it to Morgan. She stared at the picture and then looked more closely at the key.

'Something about this seems familiar to me,' she said. 'Let me explain. When my mum died, I took out a security box in Edinburgh to store her jewellery. It looks very like the key I have for that. Let's go back to my flat and look for it and compare. I recognise the strange little, almost horns, on the top of the key. I could be wrong but my storage box is with private fund managers in Charlotte Square.'

They left and were back at Morgan and Sophie's flat in ten minutes. Morgan made them all coffee while she went to a box under her bed where her important documents were stored. It took her about 20 minutes before she found the box and the key inside.

'We need to take this to the police station to compare but it looks like the same key. What do you think Cameron?'

'Yeah, very similar. Will I meet you at the police station tomorrow morning? I'll ring the Inspector now and ask him to meet us. You can bring all the details of where your storage box is and we can check.'

When Malik and Cameron left Sophie was sitting on the couch obviously eager to chat.

'I meant to tell you that my aunt in Kyle of Lochalsh has been in touch. The family lawyers of the Reverand called her and told her the farm is ready for sale. Apparently, there was a lot of debt. I told them I don't want anything from the sale of the farm. They left the farm mostly to me but now it is proved I am not their child I don't where it leaves everything. So, I just said I want my aunts looked after in the care home they are in near Dumfries and any money left to go the family in the north who were so kind to me growing up. In fact, my aunt is going to the farm next week and wants me to be there. I've asked Dad to come down and see the beauty of the area and support me and meet my other relatives but I would really like you and Cameron to come too.'

Morgan laughed: 'I'm happy to go as long as there's no more snow. I would like to see the area in Spring, without the snowdrifts, but with daffodils and flowers growing on the cliff walk.'

'That's settled then, I'm going to bed to think about my future.' said Sophie.

'Don't think too much Sophie. It will all work out for the best and you will know what to do when the time is right. There is still too much going on. Just take care.'

Once Sophie had gone to her room Morgan decided to catch up on emails. Funny, she thought, fewer and fewer people are using them these days and she gets most of her news from WhatsApp.

Once she got through some of the retail shops offering new summer styles, she found one from Max.

It said: 'Settling in and got my own apartment and loving the job. Would you come back out for a few days and we could go sightseeing together. You don't need to stay with me but I have a spare couch.'

Then the next email was from her boss Mr Stevens at her work. It was not what she expected.

'Morgan, I know you are a bit bored and thinking about a change. I don't want to lose you. I have an opportunity in New York and Washington coming up. We need someone like you to help with the setting up of our office and give reputational advice on how we can work with Congress and the Senators. Have a think about it and we can chat when you get back. It would be a year contract and your job would be open here when you get back. The experience would be good for you and a break from here.'

Morgan sat stunned and went to make a cup of tea. She sat for almost an hour thinking about her future and then decided bed was the best thing for her. A good sleep and she would be able to think clearly.

The next morning, she must have slept in as her phone rang just after 9a.m. It was Cameron.

'Hi, ok if I pick you up at 10 to go to the police station? Bring your key and we can compare it with the one at the station.'

'Yes, I'll be ready,' said Morgan. She went to the kitchen and found a note from Sophie saying she had left early to go Glasgow, saying she would call later.

Morgan was glad to be on her own to think and was organised when she saw Cameron outside in a taxi.

The meeting at the police station lasted just a few minutes. Inspector Driver took one look at Morgan's key and compared it to the one found in the violin. 'They look the same to me,' said the Inspector.

Morgan said she could take them to the private fund company in the city's Charlotte Square where she had a security box.

When they arrived at the office they were met by a senior director. Morgan realised the police had phoned ahead.

The director introduced himself as a Mr Thompson and said: 'We have checked and we do have a box registered to a Ms Lizzie Campbell. I have brought it to a room for you. Do you want me to open it for you?'

Morgan was the first to reply: 'Should Sophie not be here?'

Inspector Driver said: 'I hear what you're saying but we need to see if there is anything in this that would aid the investigation.'

Cameron added: 'I agree with Morgan. Surely it can wait till tomorrow morning. I think Morgan said she would be back tonight. We could do first thing tomorrow?'

Tom Driver shook his head, turned to the bank official and said: 'Sir, could we do this tonight? I will make sure the daughter of Lizzie Campbell is here. Everyone fine with that? Morgan, can you give her a ring and make sure she's back at teatime? We can come here about seven, Ok with everyone?' The director of the company nodded in agreement.

Morgan got Sophie on the first ring of the phone. 'Hi Sophie, it's me. Are you ok and enjoying your day in Glasgow?'

'Yes, it's good. In a restaurant with Dad and Uncle Dave. Any news on the key?'

‘Found it Sophie. We didn’t want to open the box without you there. Can you be back in time for us to get the bank for 7p.m and meet the Inspector there.’

‘Yes, I’ll be back at the flat about 5p.m. How exciting but scary too. I wonder what we will find?’

They met at the flat and Morgan was surprised when both her father and uncle arrived with Sophie and said they were coming to the bank. At just after 7p.m they were all sitting in a conference room with the Inspector and Cameron.

Sophie said: ‘They heard me talking to you and both wanted to see what Mum had left.’

The director of the bank brought the box into the room. There was a strange atmosphere as they all stared at the box. The director said: ‘This box has not been opened for more than 18 years.’

The silence was broken by the Inspector. ‘I want the director to open the box but I would ask everyone not to touch anything inside at the moment while we assess what is there and if it’s relevant to my ongoing investigations. Is that ok with everyone?’

Everyone nodded. Sophie stepped forward with the Inspector as the lid was lifted. It was not full of money or jewels. It showed a tied package of letters, a single envelope addressed to ‘Sophie’ and a small beautiful jewellery box.

Malik said: ‘That’s the box the engagement ring was in when I gave it to Lizzie all those years ago.’

Inspector Driver said: ‘While I understand everyone wants to look more closely at what is inside I want to take this to our office, let our forensic team look at the items and we can then share with people. I believe this box was last touched by Lizzie Campbell days before she died. Is everyone ok?’

Everyone nodded their head in agreement. Sophie looked pale and turned to her father and asked him to take her outside for some fresh air.

'Mum wrote me a letter. Did she know she was going to die Dad?'

Malik hugged her close and said: 'I just don't know. I know she was scared of something and she must have done this before she went north on the trip. We will know more when we get to read it. It's understandable that the police want to examine them first but we really need to see what she left. I'm sure that's her engagement ring and it wasn't found on her when the car crashed. I think they thought it had been stolen, but perhaps she never had it on.'

Just then they were approached by Uncle Dave. He looked angry.

'This is ridiculous. That's my sister's box and we should be allowed to examine what's in it. They have no right to take it away.'

It was Sophie who replied: 'Uncle, they must be doing the right thing. I'm sure we'll see the stuff soon enough. I hope they find something that explains my mother's death to me and the killing of the people who looked after me for all those years.'

'You're right Sophie. I just found it very emotional. I felt like Lizzie was in the room watching. I just want to know why she locked it all away. She could have left it in a security box at her flat.'

Sophie said: 'We don't what she was feeling or if she was scared of someone. Perhaps she felt it was only safe in a bank.'

Just then the Inspector approached them. 'It's late tonight. I'll be in touch with you all in the morning. I'm going back to the police station now and Cameron will accompany me.'

Morgan smiled at the others and said: 'Why don't we go back to my flat, all welcome, and order a takeaway and open some wine?'

'Sounds like a good idea Morgan. Thank you very much,' said Malik moving to leave the room.

Uncle Dave said: 'Do you mind if I come back as well? Not sure I fancy going back to Glasgow with all this is going on.'

Just as they were leaving a bank official came in and asked to speak to Malik.

They waited outside till he came out. 'Sorry, had to sort out something with the bank. Apparently, Lizzie paid for a ten-year term, the normal term, and they don't understand why the box wasn't dealt with when that term was up. But it wasn't and now they want me to pay for the missing time. I said I would sort it out tomorrow. They were ok with that.'

'That's very good of you Malik,' said Dave Campbell. 'I wonder what the police will find in those letters and her letter to you Soph?'

'We just have to be patient,' Sophie told him.

Uncle Dave didn't mention it again and the atmosphere in the flat was almost normal as they tucked into a takeaway and chatted about everything except the investigation and the box.

They had just finished the meal and Morgan left Sophie chatting to her dad and uncle, her new family. It all sounded pretty relaxed and she went into the kitchen to make a cup of tea.

Her mobile rang. It was Cameron.

'Can you talk?' he said in a very quiet voice.

'Sounds mysterious Cameron. I'm in the kitchen so talk away,' said a bemused Morgan.

'We've gone through the box and the letters are a bit disturbing but we haven't looked at the letter to Sophie from her mother. The inspector thinks she should do that. He wonders if you can bring her early tomorrow morning at the station and we will meet you both there. I think it's best you tell her alone.'

Morgan found herself lowering her voice: 'I'll speak to her later when the other two have gone. I don't like the sound of these letters. What do you mean disturbing?'

'Filled with hate, calling Lizzie a whore and of sleeping around,' Cameron sounded angry. 'We can explain more tomorrow. They've gone to forensics to see if we can find who sent them. They're unsigned. So will we see you both about 8a.m?'

Morgan agreed and said goodnight to Cameron, ending the call.

As she went back into the lounge she saw Sophie, her uncle and her father sitting relaxing around the table. She walked in just as Sophie said: 'This is lovely but there is someone missing, my mother. I would love to just sit here with her chatting and drinking a glass of wine, if she would let me. I'm also missing the Rev and my other mother. Sometimes I feel so lonely and it's so good to have you all around me.' As she said that she looked at Morgan and smiled, a sad smile.

Morgan said: 'Think it's time we all turned in. It's been a long day.'

Dave Campbell said: 'Yeah, you're right. It's been good spending time with you all. You know Sophie we all care for you and want the best for you. I have to go back to my office and home tonight but can you keep me up to date with what's happening?'

Sophie said: 'Thanks Uncle Dave, I'm sure the police will keep us informed.'

When they both left Morgan told Sophie about the police wanting to see her in the morning early, so she could read the letter from her mother in privacy.

'So, I said we would be there before 8.m. They want you to read it and then they will take it away for examination. I'm going to suggest they give you a copy to keep just now. Ok.'

Sophie looked tearful and said: 'That'll be so strange to read a letter written all those years ago. I want you to be there as well Morgan. Should my dad be there?'

Morgan said nothing and Sophie then said: 'No I want to be there alone to read it. I can share it with Dad and Uncle Dave after.'

Morgan said: 'I think that's the right decision. You want to see what she says first as it is just addressed to you. It's her letter to you.'

The next day they arrived at the police station a few minutes early. Cameron was waiting at reception.

'Hi Sophie and Morgan. We're in the Inspector's office and everything's ready. We've arranged coffee.'

They followed him to a large office on the first floor. The Inspector was at his desk and on the table was the box, empty now but with the ring box and a single letter lying beside it.

Inspector Driver said: 'Sophie, I want you to have some privacy to read your mother's letter. This, I assume is your mother's engagement ring. I am happy for you to take that away.'

Morgan said: 'I know she can't take away the letter but can you give her a copy?'

Inspector Driver nodded.

The Inspector first asked Sophie to put on some gloves. Then he handed her the letter which was faded white with just the name 'Sophie' on the front. He helped her put a small letter opener through the top and allowed her to pull out the letter.

It was one page, and as Sophie started reading it Morgan

watched the level of concentration on her face. They then left the room, leaving Sophie with the letter from the past.

Sophie read the page in silence. Then she looked out of the room and indicated for Morgan and the other two men to come back in.

Then she said: 'I don't mind you hearing it, Morgan. It's so sad. It's as if she knew she was going to die.'

She started reading: 'Sophie if you are reading this letter then I am no longer able to be with you. I'm so sorry I could not stay with you.' She took a gulp of air.

'I want you to know how much you were loved by both your father and me. We made a commitment to be a family and our love will sustain you. I met your father at university and I loved him from the start. He was so kind and gentle and I felt safe with him.

'I hadn't felt safe for so long. I always felt someone hated me and I feared for my safety.

'Someone was following me, letters started to arrive and when Malik had to go back to India to be with his mother and father, I felt so alone.

'I feel I'm being paranoid and I hope I'm wrong but Edinburgh is starting to close in on me.

'I decided to go away for a few days as it was becoming too intense. If you are reading this letter then I never came back from that trip. Goodbye my sweet. I loved you from the moment I saw you.'

Sophie just sat in the chair, holding the letter in her hand. It was the Inspector who leaned over and asked her gently: 'You ok Sophie? Let me take that letter, get it photocopied and then you can take it with you.'

He turned to Cameron and said: 'This helps me understand a bit better what happened all those years ago.'

Morgan said: 'Sophie, let's get the letter and go and have a coffee. Then you can decide what you want to do.'

This seemed to rouse Sophie. She looked at Morgan and said: 'Can I take Mum's ring? I want to wear it.'

Morgan turned to the Inspector and Cameron and they both nodded.

'I'm sure that will be all right,' said Morgan. 'It belongs to you now and your father will want to see it again.'

Sophie slipped the emerald and diamond ring on her left-hand ring finger. It fitted perfectly.

'It's funny,' she said 'but I feel closer to my mother more than ever. She must have been so scared all on her own.'

Turning to the Inspector she said: 'What do think really happened to her? 'Was it just an accident?'

'That's what I'm going to find out, Sophie. This letter and the other letters might help with that and help us understand what was going in Edinburgh all those years ago. I promise you I will get to the bottom of this. Now go and get your coffee.'

Morgan got them both a flat white at a coffee place close to the police station. She didn't speak as they sat at the table until Sophie looked up and said sheepishly: 'Sorry, been lost in thought.'

'No wonder,' said Morgan. 'That was very emotional. Your mother sounds a lovely woman and very wise. She made sure something was left for you no matter what happened. She put her letter, her engagement ring and some other documents and left them safe for you for almost 20 years.'

Sophie said: 'She must have been scared something bad was going to happen, and it did. I hope the police can find out what really happened to her. She should have been safe and been my mum all these years. I've missed out on so much. I need to call my dad. Is it ok if he comes over to the flat?'

'Absolutely,' said Morgan getting her coat and bag ready to leave the café.

Morgan heard her phone ping as they left. It was Cameron asking her to go back to the police station. She turned to Sophie and said: 'Can you just go back yourself and meet your dad there? I have to go somewhere first. I'll be back soon and get some food organised.'

'Sure, I've already called dad and he's meeting me at the flat. See you later. I need to chat to you about something else anyway.'

Cameron was waiting at the reception for Morgan when she returned, he said the inspector was in his office.

Morgan thought Inspector Driver looked exhausted when she saw him. In fact, both him and Cameron had big shadows under their eyes, lack of sleep, she thought.

The Inspector spoke first: 'Morgan, just wanted to make you aware of what we found in the box. The ring you saw us give to Sophie and the letter which was sad and disturbing to say the least, as if the girl knew something bad was going to happen to her. I wanted to update you on the letters Lizzie had carefully kept in that box. It gives us a picture of what that young woman was going through all those years ago. We knew about the letters from the admirer and they are in police files. Thank goodness it was before social media but today that we would be classed as stalking.

'It's these new letters that she kept that I find more distasteful. They are nasty – you know the sort of thing, language designed to knock your confidence. It was obviously someone who didn't like the fact that she was seeing an Indian student, that she was pregnant and that her career was taking off. I suspect Lizzie had an idea who was sending them and that's why she kept them. The smart thing she did was keep the envelopes and I have now the letters with our forensic and DNA specialist to see we can find some DNA on the envelopes. Let's hope they licked them. It will take them some time to see if they find anything.'

Morgan said: 'That's horrible. A new mother getting creepy letters from an admirer and nasty letters from someone who wanted to do her down. No wonder she went away for a few days to breathe. She must have felt suffocated and so alone, and worried about her own safety and that of her new baby. It makes me wonder that if the Rev and his wife had not stopped that morning and taken Sophie she would have been safe. If someone tampered with that car, how could they be so sure that the baby wouldn't be hurt or killed?'

Cameron said: 'I think it makes us all wonder if either of these people, and there must have been two, wanted something bad to happen to Lizzie. Did they have anything to do with her accident?'

Inspector Driver continued: 'I wanted to make sure you and Cameron were on the same page when Sophie asks about the letters. I think you just say they're being examined to see who sent them and they are pretty nasty. I wouldn't divulge what is in them yet.

'Now I need to get back to Stranraer. The net is closing on Charlie Trimble. Sergeant Ford has been out in the Galloway Forest and they've found a sort of shelter and evidence of someone lighting fires to keep warm. We think that's where Trimble's been hiding out, a search is ongoing now. We're also checking his DNA for both lots of letters in case he sent some of them.

'Cameron, I want you to speak to Malik and see what he remembers about the security man when he was hired to look after his security in Edinburgh. I feel we're getting somewhere now.'

Morgan was deep in thought when she left the police station and drove back to the flat. She didn't hear her phone ringing until about the tenth ring and looked at who was calling. It was Max.

'Hi Max, is everything all right?'

He laughed: 'Yes Morgan everything's great. I'm calling to tell you I'm coming back to Edinburgh for a few days and hope we can meet. The procurator fiscal wants to interview me. It looks like there will be a trial in a few months.'

'That's great Max. Just text and we can meet for dinner. Do you want to stay at the flat?'

'No, I've booked a hotel at the west end for three days. I don't want to intrude on your new life. It'll just be good to see you.'

'Don't feel you have to stay in a hotel. I'll be good to catch up. I have lots to tell you. I have to go Max. I've got to get home,' said Morgan.

With that Max rang off.

When Morgan let herself into the flat there was silence and, for a minute, she thought no one was in. Then she looked in the lounge and saw Sophie and her dad hugging each other closely, the copy of her mother's letter on Sophie's lap, both of them looking like they had been crying.

'I'll make coffee and some breakfast,' she said: 'I'll be in the kitchen.'

Sophie came through and gave Morgan a hug. 'Thanks Morgan. I have a couple of other things to ask. I called Uncle Dave and he asked if he could come through and see the letter. I said 'Yes of course. Is that ok? Dad suggested we chat to him here and then go for a walk and some lunch together to discuss everything.

'Also, my aunt from Skye called to say they are sorting the farm and it seems once Quintas' debts are all paid off then the farm and land will be sold and shared between her and Quintas' sisters, to help with their care. She wants to meet us at the farm later this week. I thought Dad and I could go so I could show him the farm and he can meet some of the family. We planned to leave tomorrow morning.

'I've lost track of days but I'm hoping you'll come to Galloway too.'

Morgan laughed: 'Gosh that's a lot to take in. Of course, your uncle can come here. I'll stay out of the way, as I have some things to check on, emails to catch up on.'

Morgan heard the doorbell about an hour later but she stayed away from the kitchen and the lounge. She heard Sophie boiling the kettle, and chat in the lounge. It was past 11 when she heard them all leave.

CHAPTER EIGHTEEN

The next morning Cameron was meeting the Inspector at police headquarters for a briefing before he drove back to Stranraer.

When he walked into the police station just after 8a.m. he saw a very tired Inspector sitting hunched over a coffee in his office, staring into space.

'You look exhausted.'

'I am,' said the Inspector. 'I've been up all night, better update you. The Sergeant contacted me last night to say they'd a definite sighting of Trimble, spotted going into an internet café in Castle Douglas. Apparently, he was looking pretty rough and a bit smelly which made people think something was wrong, someone called us, we had a team nearby but he managed to slip past them. We know he's in the area and trying to use the internet, he doesn't seem to have a phone registered to him. It ties with our belief that he's been living in the Galloway Forest. His brother thinks he was always going up there to walk so he may have a hideout. We just haven't found him yet. I'm going to send a drone up to look for him.'

'Are you going back to Stranraer today?' asked Cameron.

'Yes, I think we're close to finding Mr Trimble and some answers. Sophie seems all right and has her dad and uncle to look after her, Morgan and you as well.'

'Yes, she was a bit shaken after reading the letter from her mum. But she spent last night with her father and uncle. She's apparently planning to go back to Galloway to meet up with her aunt from Skye and the lawyers about the farm. Her father is going with her to see where she lived and she's asked Morgan to go. I think they might be leaving today as well.'

The Inspector looked surprised. 'I think if that's the case you should go as well and keep an eye on her. We've had forensics take another look at these letters Lizzie had from an admirer. The DNA on the envelopes is too degraded to find anything but I am convinced that Mr Trimble was her admirer.

'I called Malik and he remembers Mr Trimble always being around when he went to meet Lizzie. In fact, they seem to have played cat and mouse with him and he often just turned up at their door when they were together. He never really thought anything about it as his father had hired him from a good company to provide protection for him. He thought Trimble was just been over cautious. Now he thinks he must have had a "thing" for Lizzie. He knows that when he went back to India and the security contract was cancelled, Lizzie said she still saw Trimble following her. They laughed it off at that time.'

Cameron said: 'What does that mean though? Do you suspect he's the person who sent those pictures from the crash and was actually there watching the crash and the MacNeills taking the child? If he was there then how did he know where Lizzie would be? I don't think she would have told him about her trip. I think the only people she told were her parents and the girl she was visiting, and none of them would tell Trimble or anyone else.'

'That's my guess and that ties him to the deaths of those three people, payback time for taking the child? He's a dangerous man and I am worried about Sophie being down there. We will have a presence but it would be good if you were there.'

'Of course, I'll be at her side and Morgan's there as well. I assume you are leaving soon but have you managed to pull together a timeline for his movements over the last 20 years. Where's he been and what's he been doing?'

'Well, we don't have all the details but we believe he left the army – I'm still waiting for them coming back with dates of service, around 25 years ago. Then he seems to have got a job with this security company, Elite, and got the gig protecting Malik while he attended University in Edinburgh.

'It was through this security job that he met Lizzie. What happened then is known only to Lizzie and Mr Trimble but I suspect he became a bit fixated on her.

'We think he was the one who sent the flowers and the letters. What we do know is that when Malik was ordered back to India the contract with Elite Security was cancelled and Trimble was out of a job.'

'But that's months before Lizzie's car crash. What do you think he was doing after he got sacked and, if you're right, found himself watching the car crash in the north of Scotland?' said Cameron looking intently at the Inspector.

'We don't know yet. The security company came back to say he did no more work from them after the Malik contract. There is a gap of about six months before the crash. I'm beginning to get a picture of a young woman, trying to work, and pregnant who gets flowers and letters at home from a so called admirer, and then letters delivered to her house from someone who says she is stupid, talentless and a tart. We would look at that sort of behaviour differently nowadays, thankfully, but I'm not sure how seriously they took it 20 years ago or so.'

The Inspector stopped and started looking through his notes.

'We think that after the Lizzie's crash Trimble went back to Glasgow to live with his mother. It was soon after he got back and out of work there was the argument and he killed her. He then spent about 12 years in Carstairs and prison before being released and coming down to Galloway to live.

'We're not sure what he was doing down here but he seems to have been living mostly under the radar, even his half-brother hardly saw him. We don't know if was ever around the farm where the MacNeills lived.

'Talking of that farm. There were still people coming to the farm this week. The Sergeant kept a presence in case Trimble came by but it seems Mr Quintas MacNeill had clients calling looking for his services in pornography. They hot footed out of there as soon as they knew he was dead and they were talking to a policeman. We've got their car numbers and names and addresses, to follow up. It was so busy one day at the farm there was no way Trimble was going to be there.

'Then, there have been the gambling companies looking for the brother. Letters arriving still from the National Lottery saying they are suspending his account. The lawyers acting for the family say he had the farm in debt to a figure of around £100,000. It seems it now belongs to Mrs MacNeill's family in Skye. I'm not sure what's left but there are about 200 acres of land.'

Cameron nodded: 'I don't think Sophie wants anything to do with the farm.'

The Inspector moved closer to Cameron and said in a softer tone: 'What about you Cameron? You made any decisions? The three months with us will be finished in a few weeks. Do you fancy joining the police again? We could do with you in Galloway.'

Cameron laughed: 'Not sure Galloway, much as I love it, is the place for me to work. I'm not sure yet. Malik mentioned something the other night that was interesting. I don't think he's discussed it with Sophie yet but he talked about her going back to America with him to study, get her qualifications and get the best musical tuition. He also suggested he was worried about her safety and wondered if I would go out for a year. I must say a year in New York, in a well- paid job, with people I like, sounds very attractive. I said I would think about it after he discussed it with Sophie.'

The inspector said: 'I don't think her uncle would be too happy about that. He's been talking about her studying in Edinburgh at the music school. He seems to want her around. I hear he's going to Galloway as well but not sure why.'

Cameron looked a bit taken aback: 'I didn't know that. Morgan's leaving with Sophie and her dad at lunchtime. They're booked into a hotel in Stranraer, I'm going to meet them later for a meal. They plan to go to the farmhouse tomorrow.'

Inspector Driver said: 'I'm driving back this afternoon too. I might try to meet you at the hotel but my wife might have other plans. I seem to have been away for weeks. This job takes its toll on family life and I've never had such a complex murder investigation and complication of finding a lost child at the centre of everything. I've been so grateful for your help and Morgan has been a star.'

Cameron, smiled and said: 'I've been happy to get involved. I felt so sorry for that young girl we found at the farm and finding her father has been one of the highlights of my career. It's not over yet, we've still to find Trimble and get to the bottom of what started this. I still don't think that crash was an accident. There were too many people there with something to gain, the MacNeills who got a child, Trimble who was recording it. It all seems too organised.'

The Inspector nodded: 'Yes, I agree. But until we can talk to Trimble we might never know. I know Malik thinks that after Trimble lost his job, Lizzie was sure he was still following her. Whether that was off his own bat or he was working for someone else keen to know what she was doing every day.

'Listen, I think we need to get on the road. We can chat more over dinner in the town,' said the inspector as he tied up his papers and packed his briefcase.

CHAPTER NINETEEN

Morgan was enjoying the drive down to Galloway. The sun was shining and Ailsa Craig was looking almost ethereal in the mist. Malik, sitting in the front, was enthusing about the colour of the sea and the extensive bird and sea life on the rocks, pointing out seals to Sophie in the back seat. They stopped for coffee at a farm shop and it was warm enough to sit outside and look at the view. They passed Turnberry Hotel and had just over an hour to travel.

Malik said: 'This is beautiful. I never had a chance to see this coastline when I was studying in Scotland.'

Morgan laughed: 'It's looking a lot better than the last time I was down here. It was fine driving down and then the dark clouds full of snow descended. I'm glad to be seeing it now Spring is coming. It's a time for hope.'

Malik smiled: 'Yes, I'm feeling full of hope now I have found my daughter. I'm praying she will come with me to New York to continue her studies and allow us to get to know each other.'

'How do you feel about that Sophie?' said Morgan turning to the young woman looking wistfully at the sea.

'I'm still thinking about it but I think it might be a good idea. I want to study music and the people at the music school in Edinburgh are keen for me to go but I need to get some qualifications. In New York I can go to school and get music tuition. And, I get to live with my dad,' she said shyly.

Then she added: 'I haven't said anything to Uncle Dave yet. But I know he will want me to do what's best for me. He'll understand.'

Morgan thought she sounded a bit unsure but let it pass.

Then Sophie added: 'Actually, I'll miss you, Morgan. You've been a good friend and support. I hope you'll visit if I move.'

Malik looked at Morgan, speaking softly he said: 'Morgan, I too want to thank you for your care of Sophie. I have told Sophie how guilty I feel for leaving her mother to go home when she was pregnant with our child. I was a young man and, like many young men in my culture, I did what my parents asked. It was a necessity for my father, and I know now, for me, that I went home to spend the last few weeks with my mother. I was torn but Lizzie knew I was coming back. My guilt is that, at the time, we were young and found the attentions of an admirer for Lizzie as fun to talk about. I know, when I left, she treated the horrible letters delivered to her house with more seriousness and thankfully took them to the police. I have dreams that she was scared and alone when she took that fateful trip north.'

They were back in the car and driving towards Girvan when Morgan saw Sophie lean forward to touch her father's shoulder.

'Dad, I've been thinking about what you said about feeling guilty. You've told me to look forward not back. We will never forget mum but we can remember her and I think about her every time I play on her violin. I know she had a lonely time for the last few months of her life.'

Malik turned round to look at Sophie and said: 'You're right. I think I just feel so guilty leaving her to deal with all these things by herself. She obviously didn't feel her brother could support her much. He told me he didn't know about all the things going on with Lizzie, the letters and such as he was in Glasgow and at university. They didn't see much of each other, except at the family home at special meals and Christmas. He said the last time he saw her and you, Sophie, was when you were at the family home for your first Christmas with your grandparents.'

Morgan said: 'We're nearly at the hotel. It's been a good journey and we've time to settle into our rooms at the hotel before dinner at a local restaurant in Stranraer. Cameron is joining us and Uncle Dave. I'm not sure where he's staying but he said he would be there.'

CHAPTER TWENTY – SEVENTEEN YEARS BEFORE

Lizzie Campbell was just glad to be getting out of Edinburgh, her mind in turmoil.

The last letter had come though her door yesterday, she hesitated in opening it, but despite her reluctance, slit it open with a knife. The letter was just like the others, telling her she was useless, a nasty little whore and a bad mother. It ended by saying even her boyfriend had left her, it was someone who knew too much about her.

It was so nasty she found herself not worrying about the other person who was sending her love letters and flowers and, she suspected, was following her. In among the doting letters were pictures of her walking around with Sophie in her pram, playing at the music school and sitting in a coffee shop. She knew someone was watching her.

This time she went to the police station, holding Sophie in her arms, and explained that she was being followed and being sent strange, nasty letters and fawning letters and flowers, but she felt the policeman just found it funny. He asked if she was not flattered that someone was sending her flowers. Thankfully, they took the nasty letters a bit more seriously and he said a senior policeman would be in touch. She went away disheartened.

At home she tried to phone Malik, desperately needing to talk to him, but the phone was answered by a maid in the family house in Delhi and she was told he wasn't available.

She made the decision to get away and called her old schoolfriend Polly in Wick. She told her she had booked into a small hotel close to her house and would be able to see her and introduce Sophie. Polly was so happy that she was coming north to meet up with her that Lizzie didn't have the heart to tell her she was running away from Edinburgh. She called her parents and asked if she could bring Sophie to visit after her trip north. They sounded so pleased it cheered her up, looking forward to being with people who cared about her.

She packed her car and with Sophie safely in the baby seat in the back, set off. Driving over the Forth Road Bridge her thoughts went to Malik, meeting him the best thing that had ever happened to her. He loved her and wanted a future, supporting her ambitions. She knew that now. When he told her, when she was seven months pregnant with their child, that he had to return to India as his mother was dying, she understood. But when she didn't hear from him till just before Sophie was born, she wondered what had happened. She knows she was angry and that was why she hadn't put his name on the birth certificate. She's been influenced by her brother who kept telling her Malik wasn't coming back. But he got back in touch just after Sophie was born and she was able to send him pictures. She didn't tell him about the birth certificate but she knew he'd understand. She hadn't told him about the letters still coming through the front door. The fawning nice letters and flowers only started after Malik left and Lizzie always felt someone knew too much about her and where she went.

She was sure she was being followed. She didn't want to worry her parents: her brother would have told she was paranoid and Malik had too much on his plate with his family, and was too far away, to worry him. She felt very alone sitting in the flat at night with Sophie but she was a good baby and had started to sleep for six hours at a time, but Lizzie still woke up every hour to check on her sleeping in the cot beside her bed.

She realised she had kept too much from Malik and made a decision to tell him everything when she saw him, including the nasty letters. She was determined to go back to the police and insist on an investigation. She just needed to get away for a few days to think clearly.

The letters had cast a shadow over her happiness with how her career was going. The two solo concerts done while pregnant had been well received and she'd been approached by an orchestra.

That and knowing Malik was coming home to be with her made Lizzie feel happy and light. She held onto that happiness as she drove out of Edinburgh, opening the window of the car to feel the fresh air on her face. Just getting away from the city and the sinking feeling when she saw the envelopes, some of them shoved under the door, noone there when she opened it, or posted, land on her mat in the flat, gave her a lighter feeling. She felt stronger somehow.

She made good time on the A9 and stopped for a cup of tea at a roadside café, busy with tourists already. It was only when she was sitting in the café with Sophie on her lap that she felt she was being watched. She looked around. It was busy with a bus party and lots of grey-haired ladies drinking coffee. She saw two young men but they had jackets pulled up around their faces and she could not see anyone she knew, but she couldn't shake the feeling.

She didn't waste time and packed up the car and Sophie,

determined not to stop till she reached Wick. Her friend Polly was waiting at her front door when she heard the car pull up five hours later. Polly had been her best friend through music school but moved to Wick after marrying her schoolboy sweetheart and supporting him as he tried to make a living as an artist.

'You must be exhausted Lizzie,' she said 'come away in and have a cup of tea.' It was just what Lizzie needed – to be wrapped in the arms of an old and valued friend.

'I've missed you in Edinburgh Polly,' said Lizzie with tears in her eyes.

'Come on Lizzie, what's wrong?'

'Nothing really, life is going well. I have Sophie who is just so sweet and the love I feel for her is so overwhelming sometimes. I just look at her and cannot imagine being apart. Malik is coming back and I realise he always loved me although I was a bit unsure when he left me pregnant and alone in Edinburgh. But he's coming back and we're going to marry. He's the love of my life and I trust him. It's just I've been getting all these letters, one lot nasty and the other lot a bit creepy.'

Polly looked shocked and took Lizzie's hand. 'Did you share this with Malik or tell your brother?'

'No, I didn't want to worry Malik and my brother isn't really interested. He has his own life and I hardly see him. Funny a friend said they saw him in Edinburgh last week but he never contacted me. I went to the police about the nasty ones but they didn't seem that concerned.'

Lizzie went into her bag and pulled out two letters. She handed them to Polly.

'I brought you one of the nasty ones and one of the sickening ones to read. I've put some of those nasty letters in a bank vault in case something happens to me and they need to find them.'

'Don't talk like that,' said a shocked Polly. 'Nothing is going to happen to you. It's depressing getting unsigned letters from people and you don't know what they are trying to do. I think the nasty one is trying to destroy your confidence. It could be someone jealous of your talent, and basically, just jealous of you.

'The other ones are a bit more worrying. It feels like someone is obsessed with you. Listen let's discuss this when you have had a rest after the long drive. You can book into your hotel and come back here tonight for dinner with us. Tomorrow, I thought we could take a long walk on the beach with the dog. I think we're going to try a barbecue in the garden tonight but wrap up well. It's always colder up here.'

The friends spent three days chatting and walking in between sitting drinking coffee and catching up. When the time came for Lizzie to leave, she felt refreshed and able to take on the world and the two letter writers.

As she left, with Sophie safely in the back in the best baby seat she could buy, Lizzie said: 'Thanks Polly, hopefully I'll see you at the wedding and, I want you to be my bridesmaid.'

Suzy said: 'Of course I would love to. Let's plan for me to come down to Edinburgh to see you this summer. Let's catch up then and plan.'

Lizzie left Wick feeling happy and looking forward to seeing her parents. Sophie was awake but quiet in the back as she hit the road, early in the morning. Her plan was to drive down to Inverness, stop there and work out the best way to cut across to the west and get to Glasgow.

She had only been left Wick an hour when she felt the car veering to the left. It kept wanting to swerve and she thought she would stop at the next petrol station and call the emergency services when it gave a sudden jerk and veered sharply, Lizzie desperately trying to steer it back onto the road. She saw the tree coming towards her, but had no time to do anything. She tried to brake but nothing worked. Then a terrifying sound came to her ears and darkness, darkness, darkness, the sound of Sophie crying, the last thing she heard.

CHAPTER TWENTY-ONE

Morgan, Sophie and Cameron were at the restaurant in Stranraer just before seven that evening, waiting in the bar for Sophie's Uncle Dave to arrive. They waited and waited and apologised when the waiter said their table was ready. After an hour, Cameron asked Sophie if she had Dave's mobile. Sophie showed it to Cameron and he called it. It went immediately to messages and he left a message: 'Cameron here David, just wondering where you are. Call me back if a problem.'

Morgan said: 'I think we should just go ahead without him. I'm starving after that journey and we all need to eat. We've got a big day tomorrow back at the farm.'

Sophie said: 'Where is he though? Is he all right? Uncle Dave promised me he would be here. We wanted to talk to him about New York.'

'Does that mean you've made up your mind about New York Sophie?' Morgan asked.

Sophie nodded and looked at her dad. '90 per cent certain. Dad needs to get back to his business and I don't want to be here without him. I want to get to know him and New York sounds like a good place to get my qualifications and progress my music. I've spoken to the music school here and they will hold a place for me for a year or two. Mum's friend Rosie has been so helpful and encouraging. Also, I want to get away from Scotland for a wee while.'

Morgan nodded: 'Yes, I can understand that, too much has happened and you have lost so much. The past never really goes away, does it? It's been horrid for you. I think New York would be good for you for a while and give you a chance to come to terms with what has happened and build a future. I might also be in New York for a year with work so we could see each other.'

'That would be great, a friend immediately that I can rely on,' said Sophie.

Cameron said: 'What made you decide Morgan?'

'I think I was just a bit bored at work here and they offered me the chance to go and support their expansion in North America. It's a great opportunity, and I get to spend time with Sophie as well.'

Cameron said: 'Your boyfriend is there as well.'

Morgan decided not to answer and turned to Malik.

'What do you think of all this then Malik?' He laughed and said: 'I'm delighted and I've told Sophie she can have any visitors to stay. That's one reason we wanted to see Dave tonight, to reassure him that Sophie is just going for a year to study and he is always welcome. Of course, Morgan, I've also asked Cameron to come out to New York for an initial year to make sure Sophie is safe.'

Before anyone could discuss anything else, Inspector Driver appeared at the table. He seemed in a hurry.

'Dave Campbell's not here then,' he stated to the table in general.

Morgan said: 'We were just waiting for him. Has something happened?'

'He seems to be missing,' said the Inspector. 'Cameron, can I have a word outside?'

They left the room, leaving everyone looking shaken.

Sophie said: 'What does he mean, missing?'

'It sounds mysterious. We'll just have to wait see what the police say but think we just let them get on with it. We should order and get some food.' Morgan called over the waitress.

Outside Cameron and the Inspector found a quiet corner in the bar.

'What's happened?'

'He's missing apparently. Disappeared. He's not at his flat in Glasgow, neither is his wife Amanda,' said the Inspector.

'What, do you mean missing?' said Cameron. 'Why are you looking for him so urgently? What's happened?'

Chief Inspector Driver: 'We have Sergeant Ford to thank. We're looking for him with some questions about the death of his sister all those years ago. I was told they couldn't find any DNA on those nasty letters but the Sergeant sent them down south and guess what?'

Cameron gave a rueful laugh: 'Don't tell me it's the brother?'

'Yeah, seems he didn't like his sister very much. It seems he was trying to knock her confidence in everything.'

Cameron said: 'Remember the family lawyer saying Dave was adopted and was "over familiar" with the teenage Lizzie. She also seems to have been a bit nervous about him. Perhaps when she didn't return his affections, he turned against her. You don't think he had anything to do with her accident and death, do you?'

Chief Inspector Driver laughed: 'I need to find him first to ask him a few questions. We found his wife and she's left him and staying with her sister in Bearsden. I managed to speak to her before I left and someone is on their way to get further details but she told me Dave Campbell was becoming obsessed with Sophie and had pictures of her in a room. She said she couldn't live with him any more as he was staying at home and not running his business. Sounds like a guy with a lot on his mind.'

The inspector hesitated and then said: 'There's something else worrying.'

'What now?' said Cameron.

'Well, you know that woman at the music school who was friends with Lizzie Campbell, you and Morgan went to see and Sophie's been as well. Well, she's turned up at the police station in Edinburgh crying and demanding to see you. It seems she was having an affair with Dave Campbell when Lizzie was at the music school. For what I can gather she feels she may be responsible for Lizzie dying. I've asked them to bring her down to Stranraer so we can interview her as part of the investigation. She's agreed and should be here tomorrow. It's all coming out now. It seems Dave Campbell was already married to his wife when he was seeing Rosie Murray.'

Cameron said: 'It sounds like we've disturbed a hornet's nest. Sophie and her dad are due to meet the relatives from Skye tomorrow morning about 11 am at the farm for a final look before it's sold. Morgan is going too and I plan to go. Do you think Sophie is in any danger?'

The Inspector shook his head. 'I'm not sure but I'm glad you'll be there. I've asked Sergeant Ford to take a few men and watch the farm and the surrounding area for any signs of both Trimble and Uncle Dave. We've had one sighting of Trimble back in the Portpatrick area and one witness said they saw him talking to a man in suit. I'm wondering if that was Dave Campbell? Perhaps he knows more about Trimble than he's told us. I'm going back to the station now to see what's happening. I'll speak to you in the morning before you leave for Portpatrick.'

Cameron nodded: 'I'll go back and have dinner with

everyone and tell them that I don't think Uncle Dave is coming.'

Morgan was first to speak: 'What did the Chief Inspector want Cameron? Is Dave Campbell not coming?'

He explained that Dave Campbell was missing and they were trying to find him. They think he is in the Galloway area.

Sophie said: 'Is he all right?'

Cameron said: 'They have no reason to think he's not but I suggest we should enjoy our meal and get a good night's sleep. We have a long day tomorrow, but let me know if he contacts any of you. The police need to talk to him about something they've discovered.'

Morgan gave him a questioning look but he ignored her and started eating his steak and chips.

The group was pretty quiet and everyone decided to turn in early. It was on the way out when Malik walked behind Cameron and said: 'What is it you're not saying Cameron?'

Cameron pulled him to the side and said: 'I think you suspect. They need to talk to him about the horrible letters that were sent to Lizzie in the weeks leading up the fatal crash. We are finding out a lot of unsavoury things that have been hidden for so long. Finding Sophie has opened a can of worms. I wouldn't say anything to Sophie yet but we all need to keep her safe.'

Malik gave a big sigh and said: 'She seems to be losing trust in so many people. Really, it's why I want to get her away from Scotland for a while and learn to live on her own terms with confidence in the future, and get to know me and my family in India.'

Cameron said: 'That sounds eminently sensible Malik. I think we need to get some sleep now and hope we find out more in the morning.'

The next morning Cameron managed to have a word with Morgan and tell her about the suspicions concerning Dave Campbell.

'She was just starting to trust Uncle Dave. What on earth is going on?'

'I'm not sure and I don't think anyone is. It was almost impossible to get DNA from those letters after so long but they managed. They found Dave Campbell's DNA on the envelopes. Lizzie was very wise to keep those safe.'

Morgan said: 'Do you think Lizzie suspected it was her brother?'

Cameron shook his head: 'I think she was a little scared of him. From what the family lawyer said she left home pretty fast when she became a teenager, bit creepy he became very interested in his little sister.'

Just then Sophie came down the stairs, followed by her father. He said: 'I've suggested to Sophie it might not be wise to go to the farm today with all the police activity but she is determined to go and meet with her relatives.'

Morgan noticed Sophie playing with a gold necklace around her neck. Thinking it was the necklace she had bought her in New York, but she noticed some words in gold and asked: 'That's a lovely necklace Sophie.'

Sophie said: 'I love the necklace you gave me Morgan but this is the necklace the lawyer gave me the other day. He presented me with a box and said it was instructions from my grandparents that it was to be given when I was found. I am still so gobsmacked so didn't want to say anything about it. It was like something being handed from another world. Apparently, it was designed by my grandparents and made by a jeweller in Ayr, all those years ago, and they asked the lawyers to keep it until I was found. It spells out "hope" at the front and at the back it says "never lose." They must have been so confident I would be found.

‘It has given me the strength to go back to the farm, look at it one last time and close the door on that part of my life, so I can just look ahead. I also want to see my relatives from the Highlands. Then I am going to follow the message from my grandparents and never lose hope that life will get better.’

Morgan said: ‘That’s such a sweet present and so poignant. It sums up the hope your whole family had that you would be found after the sad loss of your mum. I think we all understand that you want to see the farm, one last time, and move on with your life.’

Morgan, thinking everyone looked deflated, thought she should lighten the atmosphere and keep everyone busy: ‘Let’s get breakfast. Are you and your dad ok to come in my car and Cameron will bring his?’

Cameron said: ‘I think the Inspector wants one of his team to follow us down so Sergeant Ford will probably come here and we can all leave together. We’ll make sure you can visit and see your relatives safely.’

They sat in silence tucking into full Scottish breakfasts. Only Malik declined and asked for plain yoghurt and fresh fruit. The waitress looked bemused.

Malik laughed and said: ‘I forget I’m not in New York now. In New York no one I ever have breakfast with eats anything fattening. It’s usually trends like all white omelettes or plain yoghurt.’

Morgan said: ‘If I’m going to live and work in New York for a year starting pretty soon so I’ll be trying out all the food and seeing you two when I get there.’

Sophie smiled for the first time that morning and said: ‘That’s brilliant. When do you move?’

Morgan said: ‘My firm has asked me go out and help set up a new office to cover north America. They are moving into that area. I was a bit bored with my current job and was talking of leaving, but they offered me this, a job and flat for a year and I thought it would be good for me. It also helps that Sophie will be in New York and we can settle in together.'

Morgan added: 'I want away from Edinburgh for a while. Anyway, that's enough about me. I think we should all go upstairs and get ready to leave.'

As they came out of the lift on the ground floor, they met Sergeant Ford, who pulled Cameron into another room.

'Hi Peter,' said Cameron. 'We're just leaving. Are you going to follow us in your car?'

'Yes, and the Inspector will meet us there. I don't want to say too much to everyone else but we've had a sighting of Trimble in the area so the Chief's bringing out a team to scour the area. We haven't had any sightings of the uncle and his phone is turned off. But at least the weather is better this time for your visit.'

The sergeant looked a bit shy but summed up courage to ask: 'I've enjoyed working with you Mr Steel. Are you going to re-join the police, if you don't mind me asking?'

'No, I don't mind at all Sergeant. I've enjoyed being back in the fray but I don't think I want my future, at the moment, to be in the police. I don't want to go back to London – too many bad memories. I need to do something else. Who knows what I might do in the future, but we need to focus on today – everyone in agreement?'

Just then Cameron's phone pinged. He looked up and said quietly to Morgan and Malik.

'That's the chief. He says they've done a sweep of the farm and surrounding fields and it looks clear. He says he thinks Sophie's relatives have arrived so best we leave if we don't want to keep them waiting.'

Malik said: 'I'm so glad you're here Cameron. I know Sophie's happier with you all here and I'm grateful as well.

'Coming back has made me realise something was not right about Lizzie's so called accident. I feel so sad that I wasn't here for her when she was getting all these letters. She must have been so scared and I don't want Sophie to grow scared. I want her to feel safe. She feels safe with Morgan and yourself which has been such a blessing to me. Thankyou both.'

Morgan said: 'It's been my pleasure and I am sure I speak for Cameron when I say we both were happy to be there for Sophie. She has been through so much and we are friends for life. Now let's get in the car and get this show on the road.'

The drive was less than ten miles and Malik and Sophie were quiet as they turned off the main road and drove along the coast until they came to the entrance to the farm. They could see the old farmhouse nestled among the sloping green fields.

'This is it dad,' said Sophie.

'What's that old castle, Sophie?' said Malik staring out across the sea.

'I will take you down there to see it if you want after we have finished at the farm. It might be my last look around it. It's got a great view of the Irish Sea and the entrance to Belfast Loch and you can sometimes see the Isle of Man. It has something to do with the history of the village but it's a ruin now and a good walk from the village for any visitors.'

As they drove down the country road to the farm Morgan hardly recognised it. When she had last been there it was surrounded by huge mounds of snow and the farm had looked almost romantic. Now in the clear light of day with the sun shining she realised it was pretty shabby. The roof looked like it was about to fall down, paint was peeling off the windows and there was an air of abandonment. She could see two cars parked in the farm yard and the Inspector talking to a couple.

'There's my aunt and uncle,' said Sophie.

Morgan and Cameron stood back with the Inspector as Sophie was hugged by the couple. Sophie turned and introduced her aunt Jean and uncle Neil from Skye, and said they were going for a look round the farmhouse.

Inspector Driver turned to Morgan and Cameron and said: 'Seem like a nice couple. They said they had no idea the girl they knew as Rebecca was not Christine and Artemis' child. It was a bit strange talking to them as they kept saying Christine was not a bad person and loved the child. I suspect they're still a bit shocked at what has happened. They certainly don't want to lose touch with Sophie.'

Malik went to follow them into the farm but turned to the chief saying: 'I'm sure Sophie will keep in contact with them. I don't want her to lose touch with her roots here but I want her to find out about her family in India. I've explained this to her Uncle Dave and he seemed all right with it. I think people will understand that with everything that has happened here she needs breathing space to find out what she wants to do. She says it's music but who knows.'

He turned and followed the family into the farmhouse.

Inside Sophie was wandering about the rooms and showing her aunt the basement room where she had to stay when visitors came.

Jean said: 'My God Sophie. You mean they made you go down there.'

'Yeah, it wasn't too bad really. I had a bed and a toilet and they gave me a flask of tea. I could play my music but the acoustics weren't good. I was never down there for too long, just when visitors came, like the doctor or Uncle Quintas' friends. They didn't want me to be seen.'

Jean said: 'I understand that now. You don't really look like Christine or the Rev so perhaps they were scared someone would ask about you.'

Sophie laughed: 'People did but Christine laughed it off and the Rev got angry at them. I preferred to stay out of the way as much as possible. The aunts were actually very kind to me and sometimes asked me to go my bedroom upstairs or go downstairs if Quintas was in a strange mood. He was always looking at me and it gave me the creeps. The sisters thought he was wonderful though and the three of them used to go out for the day to the shops in Dumfries and markets and leave me at home, locked downstairs.'

'That's barbaric,' said Jean.

'I agree,' said Malik coming into the room. 'Thank goodness that's over and you never have to see this farm again. What's happening to it?'

Jean turned and smiled at Sophie and Malik following behind. 'Well, most of the agricultural land has been sold to a local farmer, a Mr Farrell, who says he knows Cameron and Morgan. He's just going to incorporate it into his farm. The lawyers sold the farmhouse with ten acres and it's been bought by a young family from Northern Ireland who plan to renovate the farmhouse and make a family home and small holding, keeping some sheep, I think. They take possession of the house in a week's time so this is last time to see it.'

Sophie shook her head: 'I'm not bothered about seeing it ever again. I'd forgotten how dark it is in here with these small windows. It doesn't feel like a home now. Will the aunts get some of the money?'

Jean said: 'Yes but I'm not sure what will be left. There were debts on the farm. There will be enough to make sure they are looked after in the home in Dumfries and happy and the rest will come to my family. Is that ok with you Sophie?'

'Yes, I don't need it and I'm not sure I should get any. I'm not family, although they did all look after me, as you did Auntie Jean.'

Morgan could feel the atmosphere get emotional and said in a bright voice: 'Why don't we all go to the village and get a coffee? Its freezing in here.'

Sophie said: 'I want to take my dad down to the castle to see the view of the Irish Sea. It's where I used to go and sit and think when I could get away from the farm. There's a bit of land in front of the old castle.'

Cameron said: 'If you are going there Sophie I'll be coming as well as the Sergeant and Morgan just to make sure you are all right.'

Jean said: 'I think we'll pass. We'll be in the village having coffee if you want to join us later. But keep in touch Sophie and let us know what you are doing. It's been nice to meet your dad and I'm so sorry for what happened to your mum.'

When they got out in the farmyard they waved as Jean and her husband left in their car.

Just as they were about to set off across the fields to the castle the inspector beckoned Cameron over.

'I'm going back to Stranraer but I wanted to let you know that we have some news on uncle Dave. His wife contacted my team to say she could not get any money out of any of their joint accounts. And yes, they've all been emptied. It looks like shy of £3 million has been transferred. We're trying to find out where it has been sent, looking at the Cayman Islands and anywhere else the financial people can think of.'

Cameron said: 'What do you think is going on?'

'I have no idea but my gut is telling me Uncle Dave is not as innocent as he seems. I need to find out how close he's been to Trimble. They must have met him and perhaps got to know him when he was protecting Malik at the university. I might know more when I get back to Stranraer. I'm also seeing that old music college friend of Lizzie and see what she knows about the past. She seems to feel guilty about something that's eating away at her.

'I've got people looking at all the old communications to see if there was any between Trimble and Uncle Dave. When you get finished at the old castle and get Sophie safely back to Stranraer come to the station and we can have a chat. I feel this guy Dave Campbell had a heart of ice, doing what he did to the sister he was brought up with.'

Cameron ran to catch up with Sophie, her dad and Morgan. He could see Sergeant Ford and another officer walking about 100 yards away.

He hadn't been to the old castle for about 20 years. It used to be favourite walk of his parents across the cliffs from Portpatrick. The wind had got up and he could see the waves picking up out at sea, the sky closing in with grey clouds scurrying across.

'I don't think we should hang around too long. The weather's closing in,' he said to the group.

They were inside one of the big rooms at the castle when he heard Morgan, who was behind him, gasp out, 'look' she said, pointing to a large rucksack hidden in a recess of the room. As she moved towards it, he shouted: 'Don't touch it.' She backed off and Cameron signalled for the sergeant to have a look inside.

He put on gloves and gingerly opened the rucksack zip.

'It's mostly clothes and an old sleeping bag.' He opened the other zip and stepped back.

'I think this is Charlie Trimble's rucksack. There are old videos and a large notebook inside. I'm not going to take them out as we need to get them to forensics and let the chief know.'

Looking around Cameron said: 'Do you think Trimble's here?'

Malik was standing next to Cameron and Morgan. They realised Sophie was at the window looking out to the sea. He hadn't heard anything because of the noise of the sea but suddenly she turned and he saw a look of horror on her face. She couldn't speak but pointed out the window. Cameron was first there and it took him a few minutes scanning the sea and horizon before he saw a body bobbing up and down in the waves.

'What the hell!' he exclaimed. 'Sergeant, I think there's a body in the sea. It could be Trimble in there.' They all watched mesmerised as the body was smashed against the rocks again and again.

Malik pulled Sophie away from the window and hugged her close. Morgan forced herself to look away.

Cameron said: 'Sergeant can you get a phone signal? If you can, call the Chief and let him know. I think we need to get Sophie and her dad back to the farm for safety. I'll go with them and take them down to Portpatrick to be with people and have a coffee. Morgan, can you stay with the Sergeant until the police can get here? I'll be back as soon as I can.'

Sergeant Ford said: 'I can't get a signal in here, too thick walls. I'm going outside at the front and see if I can pick one up.'

When he came back inside only Morgan was there, looking white and scared.

He said: 'Are you ok? I got the office so the chief and his team will be here soon. We'll be all right till then.'

Morgan nodded and said: 'Can we go outside? I'm feeling claustrophobic in here.' They walked outside and Morgan made to move closer to the sea.

'I would stay here. I went down there and there's some

disturbance and some items left on the cliff. It looks like a crime scene, best we don't disturb it.'

Morgan stepped back: 'Do you think he jumped from here?' as she pointed to the cliff edge.

'I don't know,' said the Sergeant. He took off his jacket and draped it around Morgan's shoulders.

'You're shivering. When Cameron gets back, we'll get you down to the village for a coffee and get you warmed up. I don't want you going back to the farm by yourself yet. We don't know who's around.'

Morgan laughed: 'Don't worry I'm not going anywhere just now. I'm fine but seeing that body in the sea was a bit of a shock.'

'Yeah, not what we expected. Strange it's there just when we come here?' They stood huddled together chatting about their jobs. It seemed just a few minutes when they heard sirens. 'Ah the cavalry,' said Sergeant Ford.

Within minutes Morgan saw the Inspector and a team of officers and men and women in white gear coming over the field.

The chief and his sergeant looked at the body floating in the sea. Then the sergeant took the chief down to the cliff edge and they stood there for several minutes.

When he came back, he said: 'Morgan are you ok?' I'll get two of my men to escort you back to the farm, then get in your car and go down to the village to meet Sophie and her dad. Cameron's on his way back. Are you ok to drive?'

Morgan nodded and turned to leave with the officers. As she left the Inspector turned to Sergeant Ford and said: 'I've contacted the lifeboat team at Portpatrick and asked them to come and try and get the body out of the water. Some of the forensic team will go out on the boat.'

Sergeant Ford said: 'Is Tam Mitchell coming out? It looks

like his brother.' Inspector Driver said: 'I spoke to him and told him it could be him – he says he wants to come and help. I can't stop him as he is the lifeboat coxswain. I'm more interested in this rucksack. It's on its way to Stranraer but my first impression is that he left that to be found deliberately. Whatever is in there might answer a few questions. Now what do you think happened on that cliff face?'

Sergeant Ford said: 'It looks like there might have been a struggle there. I don't think Trimble was alone. There's a phone and a wallet lying on a rock and it doesn't look like it belonged to Trimble. It needs thoroughly examined to find who was there on the cliff edge. The guys think three people might have been on the cliff edge.'

The chief said: 'Do you think there's another body in the sea?' Just then Cameron arrived back.

'What the hell has been going on here do you think?' he said.

'Are Sophie and her dad ok?'

Cameron nodded and said: 'Safe in a coffee shop and I passed Morgan on the way down. They'll be fine. I think they should all get back to town as soon as possible.'

Chief inspector Driver said: 'I hope you're staying in Stranraer for a wee while? We need to have a good look at this rucksack. Trimble left it for a reason. Once the teams are finished here, we can get back. I brought coffee with me so help yourself.'

They stood in the windy, freezing castle drinking coffee and feeling the cold seep into their feet. They'd only been there for about 30 minutes when one of the forensic team came up to speak to the chief. He left after a few minutes.

'Well, that's interesting. The phone and wallet you saw on a rock belong to Dave Campbell. It looks like he, and perhaps another person, were on that cliff with Trimble and there was fight. The question is, did both of them go into the sea? It's looking like it. There are scuff marks on the edge of the cliff, apparently, and they think it was made by possibly two men or three. If there was fight then how many of them have gone into the sea? When the tide's high, they would go straight in. There's no way out.

'I've asked the lifeboat to have a look around and I called Edinburgh to get another search and rescue boat at the site. The helicopter is going up as well. If the lifeboat can get Trimble, then I think we are still looking for another body. No-one could survive long in that. I'm just going to wait to see if the lifeboat can get the body and then back to the office.'

It took the lifeboat crew, backed by a search and rescue crew, almost an hour to get the lifeless body out of the sea. The Inspector and Cameron watched as Tam Mitchell covered his brother's body and then waved at them before the lifeboat turned for home. The inspector said a vehicle would be waiting at the harbour to take the body to Dumfries and a post mortem. There's no doubt it was Trimble. Meanwhile the search and rescue boat remained to search for any other bodies.

Inspector Driver said: 'Let's get back to Stranraer and warmed up. There's nothing more we can do here.'

As he was walking back to his car Cameron called Morgan. 'Everything ok?'

'Yes, we're all fine. I'm thinking of getting back to Edinburgh with Sophie and Malik. What are you doing? I think Sophie just wants away from here, she seems in a state of shock and Malik's worried about her. What are you doing?'

'I'm staying down for a couple of days. Don't say anything to Malik or Sophie but we think Dave Campbell may have gone in the sea, possibly after a fight with Trimble. While they are still looking for him our priority is what's in the backpack. I should be back in Edinburgh in the next few days and the chief has promised he will brief them then once we know what we are dealing with.'

Morgan said: 'I understand. I think we are just going to have something to eat in the hotel here, have a good sleep and leave for Edinburgh early tomorrow. I think what Sophie needs is normality for a few weeks.'

Cameron said: 'No wonder. It's not often you look at the sea and see a body floating. She'll be fine with her dad and you keeping her company. See you soon.'

He rang off and sat in the back seat of the police car with the Chief as they drove back into Stranraer.

Two hours later they were sitting in a room at the police station with the rucksack contents spread in front of them.

Inspector Driver said: 'We've found five old videos which are going to be converted so that we can watch them. But we can tell what they are. Two are videos of concerts where Lizzie Campbell played. The other three are videos of someone following her as she had coffee and went to classes. I can only assume that Trimble was the cameraman.

'The other thing we need to examine is the notebook. Rather it is a confession. It looks like Trimble was the person who tampered with Lizzie's car in Inverness and caused it to crash. It sounds like he didn't want her to die but merely have an accident so that he could rescue her and the baby. He was obviously in love with Lizzie. It seems to have intensified when Malik went back to India. I am getting the whole text transcribed as we can both look at it.'

An hour later they had the statement transcribed and easy to read. They sat in silence as they read the words of Charlie Trimble. There was a foreword to what amounted to a confession from Trimble. It read. 'I am leaving this record to explain what has happened. Dave Campbell has asked to meet me to discuss payment for my work finding

Sophie. He suggested we meet at the old castle esplanade. I have written this note and left it in case anything should happen to me. I have always taken orders from Mr Campbell but do not feel he wishes me well.'

There was silence in the room as the chief finished. He looked at them and said: 'Ready for the rest?'

He wrote: 'I loved Lizzie Campbell but she never looked at me. I was invisible. Then when her boyfriend left her pregnant, I decided to try and make her like me. I sent her letters and flowers. Her brother knew how I felt and encouraged me. He said to keep trying to get her attention, that she would notice me one day. Then when he found out she was going north for a few days he suggested I followed her and gave me his car.

He suggested I punctured her tyre so she would have to stop and I could come to her rescue. He said I would be her knight in shining armour.

But she didn't break down, she crashed into a tree. I saw it through my binoculars and I didn't understand how she crashed like that. I only did something to her tyre and she shouldn't have crashed.

I went to help her but before I could get there this caravan sort of thing stopped and a woman got out. She never checked on Lizzie. She just took the baby and left. I never forgot that van.

I called the emergency services but Lizzie was dead. I was heartbroken. It had all gone wrong.

I knew I had to leave and I drove home to my mother's house in Glasgow.

I don't remember much but my mother started nagging me about not working and I snapped. I broke her neck.

I was in a hospital, a sort of prison for many years. In all that time, I knew I had to find the baby. It became my reason for living. She was Lizzie's girl.

When I was released, I moved to Galloway. Dave Campbell gave me money to survive and asked me to find Sophie. So, I started my search for the baby Sophie.

In the two years I've here I started to see the family with the camper van. I never saw the child. Then this Spring I was walking on the cliffs when I saw the family with the girl at the farm. I knew it was the same baby. The age was right and the van was the one I remembered and photographed.

I watched the farm. The brother was a bad man. He was selling pictures of children. He deserved to die. I don't regret killing the Rev and his wife. They stole Lizzie's baby and never told anyone. It was cruel. When I met them on the road outside their farm the father was rude to me and told me to move. I killed him and his wife, just like my mother. The brother tried to run away and I shot him.

I don't want to go back to prison or hospital. I've been living in the woods since then. I think I was ill after I left the army. I didn't mean to kill my mum.

I never meant any harm to Lizzie, I loved her, Please forgive me.'

Charles Trimble.

They both sat in silence, stunned by what they had read.

Inspector Driver was the first to speak. 'I'm not sure the brother has committed a crime but morally he's guilty of encouraging Charlie Trimble to do certain things. I suspect that Trimble, having been in the army, was used to taking orders and I think Campbell knew how to press the right buttons to get Trimble to do what he wanted.'

Cameron nodded in agreement. 'Do you seriously think he's in the sea as well?'

'I just don't know. There was obviously a fight on that cliff top and it looks like it was Trimble and uncle Dave, and possibly one more. We should know more once forensics are finished up there and thawed out. The rucksack also had Trimble's gun which we've just matched to the death of the brother Quintas. He's definitely our killer but I don't think we can put Lizzie's death on him, that just looks like a plan gone wrong.

'Search and rescue will be out for next few days to see what they can find. I've had to tell his wife, Amanda, that he's missing -she didn't seem that bothered.

'Another thing that I don't want to go further than this room but the family lawyer, the older version, contacted me to say he had been talking to an old friend of the Campbell parents. This old friend said that Mr Campbell told him on the golf course that they were worried about their son, David.

'I understand he had unnatural feelings for her, his own sister.' said Cameron.

'Adopted brother, remember,' said the chief. 'He was sent away to university soon after and the father bought him the flat in Glasgow. I don't think the relationship between Lizzie and her brother ever recovered. He was obviously jealous of her. Men seem to have become obsessed with this young musician and it cost her the ultimate price- her life.'

Cameron sighed: 'What a strange family, no wonder Sophie wants to get away from here to America. I won't mention this to anyone. Do you reckon, if Dave Campbell was supporting Trimble with financial support after he left prison, then he must have let him know that he had found Sophie in Portpatrick? Remember it was the first time the girl had stayed in the bed and breakfast as a treat, and Dave Campbell came to hear her play the violin.'

Inspector Driver said: 'Yes, I think that's probably right. I'm sure Dave Campbell has been looking for her. Morgan said Sophie, or Rebecca as she was known, was also on social media playing her music and thousands of people saw that. If Morgan had seen it then Trimble and Campbell could have seen her and put two and two together.'

The inspector continued: 'I can't prove it but if Dave Campbell engineered Trimble to tamper with Lizzie's car how could he be sure that the baby would survive any crash? It was just by luck she survived and was taken by the MacNeill couple. I'm beginning to wonder if he didn't care about either of them being involved in a car accident.'

Just then an officer interrupted them and said: 'The woman Rosie Murray has arrived and is in one of the conference rooms.'

They found the music teacher sitting in the room with swollen eyes from crying.

She looked up at the Inspector and Cameron and started crying again saying: 'I think I'm responsible for Lizzie dying,' giving another gasp.

Inspector Driver asked for coffee to be brought and said: 'Rosie, perhaps tell us what you want to say. I know yesterday you told our officers that you were seeing Dave Campbell when Lizzie was at college with you.'

She nodded: 'Yes, I met him when he came to see Lizzie and he asked for my number. He was charming, good looking and older and he seemed sophisticated to me. I went out with him for about a year. When I met Cameron and Morgan, it brought it all back to me and I heard about the accident for the first time. I realised I might have been partly responsible.'

'In what way?' said Cameron.

'Dave always wanted to know what Lizzie was doing. I was young and naive in those days, totally infatuated with him, I told him everything. Then when Lizzie had the baby, he became even more insistent. He's been finding out about his birth family and had made contact with some of his half brothers. One of them ran a garage, he was a sort of rough chap and Dave started bringing him with him when we met. It was at one of these meeting I told them Lizzie was going north to get away from Edinburgh for a few days and see friends. They seemed very interested and Dave persuaded me to give him the itinerary Lizzie had left with me, detailing where she would be staying. I never thought about it at the time or since but when Cameron came to say that her car been tampered with, I realised it must have been that mechanic who came with Dave. He would know what to do to make it crash. I'm so very sorry. I feel so awful that I helped them find Lizzie and do something to her car.'

Inspector Driver said: 'That's very useful. Do you remember the name of Dave's half brother?'

Rosie said: 'I've been trying to remember but all I can think of it started with a T, Tommy or Tim, but I can't be sure.'

The inspector said: 'We're still trying to find out about Lizzie's accident. Whatever this guy did, Uncle Dave was having Lizzie followed anyway. I'm going to ask you to write a statement and then get you back to Edinburgh. Thank you for your honesty. I don't think you should blame yourself for anything. If someone meant Lizzie Campbell harm, then they would have found a way, with or without your help.'

They left Rosie Murray sitting alone, waiting for the officer to come and take her statement.

The inspector waited till they were in his office and said: 'Blow me, this puts a new perspective on things. So, Dave is in contact with his birth family and they have been helping him. I wonder if they were using Trimble as the fall guy, getting him the blame for Lizzie's accident, when he had a mechanic doing his dirty work? So, it sounds like two people tampered with Lizzie Campbell's car. Trimble made sure the tyre deflated in the hope she would have to stop and he could help. The serious guy, the mechanic, tampered with the brakes ensuring it crashed, neither the mechanic or Uncle Dave could be sure the baby would be all right. Nasty.'

Cameron nodded: 'There's something very cruel and calculating about all this. It sounds like Uncle Dave had a very cold heart.'

He added: 'Morgan and Sophie and Malik are all going back to Edinburgh tomorrow morning. I'll go back to Edinburgh in the next couple of days. Meanwhile, how's is the search going?'

The chief shrugged his shoulders: 'It's still going, that's about it. We'll keep looking but not holding out much hope. It's very cold and there are bad rocks all along the coast-we might never find his body. We're still looking for his money, and have more hope of tracing that. They've got the lifeboat out today, although Tam Mitchell isn't on it as he's still a bit upset after recovering the body of his brother. There's a helicopter out as well but we're not holding our breaths. There are lots of currents around.'

Just then the Inspector took a call. He finished and said: 'That was forensics. They think three people were on the cliff that day. The pathologist's initial examination says Trimble was struck on the back of the head before being thrown over the cliff. I'm starting to think he met Trimble on the cliff as arranged and was talking to him when a third party smacked him over the head. I think it would take two to throw him off that steep cliff. Trimble was still quite a powerful guy.'

'We're still looking for another body at sea but I'm starting to think this was all planned and Uncle Dave and his accomplice have fled, for now. They've got rid of Trimble and anything they think he can tell us. They probably don't know he's left some evidence, his truth, as they say. How much of it is true I will wait for the evidence to inform me.'

CHAPTER TWENTY-TWO

Two days later Morgan was making dinner for Sophie and Malik. They were sitting in the lounge chatting and waiting for Cameron to arrive with the inspector, aware that he'd something to show them. Morgan had the white wine chilling in the fridge.

Sophie had been quiet on the drive up from Stranraer. Even her father had little to say, both keeping their thoughts to themselves. But tonight, they seemed to be chatting and planning their return to America. Morgan could hear Sophie ask her dad what he did every day. Did he go out at night? Fatherhood might be a bit strange with a young woman needing a lot of answers, she thought.

Cameron and the chief arrived together, the Inspector carrying a brief case with him. He asked Morgan if he could speak to Sophie and Malik by himself. She left them in the lounge and took Cameron into the kitchen for a glass of wine.

The moment the chief put the new disc in the player and switched on the film of Lizzie Campbell performing on stage, Sophie and her dad started crying. He knew it would touch their emotions as it had touched his and his team when they first saw them. It was a talent and beauty cut too short. He wondered what this young woman, Lizzie, could have achieved in her life both as a musician and a mother.

They sat in silence as he played both videos.

It was Malik who spoke first: 'Can we keep these?' The chief nodded. Sophie said: 'Thank you so much for bringing them. It makes it all so real and so sad. Where have they been, who filmed them?'

The chief said: 'They seem to have been filmed by this man Trimble who looks to be the same person as the security man hired to look after your dad when he was in Edinburgh. We can only surmise that he became infatuated with your mother and was following her. We don't know if the idea of filming her was his or your uncle – we might never know. The films themselves don't answer a lot of questions but I hope they give you and your father some comfort.'

Malik nodded and said: 'Just now it's heart breaking to watch but I know, in time, they will give us both some happiness and comfort. It's so lovely to see Lizzie so full of life and happiness. It's how I remember her.'

The chief excused himself and left them sitting close together on the couch, comforting each other.

In the kitchen Morgan and Cameron were sipping a glass of wine as Cameron told her he was going to take the job with Malik in New York on an initial six-month contract to help Sophie settle into life in America.

He said: 'I hope we can see each other when you get to New York. I hope I can take you out for dinner once in a while, that is if your old boyfriend doesn't mind?'

Quickly Morgan said: 'He's not my boyfriend. We were living together but Max has moved on and has a new life in America. I actually met him earlier today, he's back to meet the procurator fiscal about a court case in which he may have to be a witness. It was good to see him, he has a new girlfriend, a colleague from the museum who comes from Taiwan. He seems happy.'

Cameron said: 'Did that bother you that he moved on so quickly?'

She shrugged her shoulders: 'I thought it might but it didn't. It seems I have moved on too. In fact, I think I was in a bit of rut, both relationship and work wise. It seems strange to say but this drama in Galloway has actually helped me see a new life ahead. I plan to get to New York in a month. Max and I are going to sell this flat. I still have my old flat which is rented out so I can move in there when I get back. I'll have a rent free flat in Greenwich village for a year. It's a no brainer really.'

Cameron said: 'You look great, if I am allowed to say that. I think you have changed having Sophie to look after and the house full of people. You seem to enjoy it.'

Morgan nodded: 'I do and that's why I think we should go in and see the other two and check they are ok. I heard the chief leave so they might be needing a glass of wine and something to eat.'

When they entered the lounge Sophie and her father were still sitting close together and it looked like they were studying the violin. Sophie looked up: 'It was so strange seeing my mother play this violin.'

Malik said: 'It brought back to me why I fell in love with Lizzie all those years ago. I just wish things could have been different. I let her down. I'm not going to let our daughter down now.'

Morgan smiled at them both: 'This must have been so difficult for you both. I think we need to have a break and eat and drink something. That's what Lizzie would have wanted, you all round a table enjoying each other's company.'

Sophie had tears in her eyes when she said: 'Morgan, I don't trust many people and most of them are in this room just now. I have a favour to ask – can my father stay here tonight? I want us to be together.'

'Of course, your dad can stay. I will make up a bed on the couch for him. If that's ok?'

Malik nodded and smiled. 'I think Sophie is just worried that her uncle Dave will come calling. She is finding all this stuff about him very scary.'

Sophie said: 'I just don't understand how he hated my mother so much. She had to cope with him writing nasty letters and the other man idolising her. No wonder she needed to get away.'

Cameron said: 'I don't think you need to worry about Uncle Dave, Sophie. The police are looking for him and he won't get far.'

Malik said: 'Thanks Cameron. I'm hoping when we get to New York Sophie can put all this behind her and start a new life. We're planning to go Delhi to meet my family. I can't forgive that man Trimble. He was employed by my father to be my security when I was a student. So, when he called to tell my father that Lizzie had been killed in an accident, he must have told my dad that the baby had died as well. That lie lived with me for 17 years. If not, I would have come back to Scotland to search for Sophie. It's history now and I must think to the future. I have my daughter, Sophie back.' The matter was closed, Cameron thought.

He left about an hour later, promising to come over in the morning.

The next morning Cameron arrived early. He sat with Malik and Sophie and planned their trip to New York the following week. Cameron was going to live in a one-bedroom flat Malik owned on the same floor as his apartment, a three-bedroom flat in the upper west side where he would live with Sophie. Cameron confirmed he would leave a week after Malik and Sophie.

He left the father and daughter to have a coffee with

Morgan who was working on her laptop in the kitchen, taking a call from the chief.

When he went into the kitchen Morgan looked up smiling: 'Hi Cameron, I'm just finishing some work and getting organised for the move to New York. I think I'll be there in the next two months. I have some work to finish in the office here. Any news on the search in Galloway?'

'Well, they have the post mortem results on Trimble. I think they've found he didn't fall in by accident. He suffered a sharp blow to the back of his head before he went in the water. There was no water in his lungs, so was dead before he fell.'

'My God. Do they think it was Dave Campbell?'

'Him or the third person. The inspector is still trying to work out what happened. This is the end of a very long story since Lizzie Campbell had the unfortunate interaction with her adopted brother and a sad former soldier who was infatuated with her. It seems to me she never had a chance.'

In Stranraer the chief and his sergeant were having a catch up. The search for the body of Dave Campbell had been going on for a week and the chief was about to scale it down.

'We're asking locals to keep searching the bays along the coast from the Castle and the lifeboat is keeping an eye out. I don't think we're going to find anything, a bit like his money. Several million pounds missing and his wife penniless. She's having to stay with friends as even their flat has been re-mortgaged. I get the feeling that Mr Campbell was a lawyer in Glasgow for many years and met up with some unsavoury people who might owe him a favour.

'On top of that we've established that Campbell has been back in touch with his birth family. He'd been searching for them, bit rough from Glasgow's east end, one of his brothers has a record for robbery. We are starting to think there might have been two people with Trimble on that cliff and I wonder if one of them could be one of the brothers, helping out.'

Sergeant Ford said: 'How can we prove all this? Any chance we can find out if Campbell was paying Trimble?'

Inspector Driver said: 'I'm not sure we can ever prove anything about this whole sorry saga. We can't find any trace, yet, of the money Trimble says he was given by Campbell when he came out of prison but Campbell could have had access to cash we don't know about yet.

'More worrying are these videos. The two of Lizzie playing at concerts are fine and have provided some comfort to Sophie. The other ones are more intimate and seem to be of Lizzie in her flat walking about. Through the prism of today's world, it would be classed as stalking but really, it's just creepy. What on earth made Trimble think he stood a chance with a lovely, talented young woman like Lizzie? I get the feeling that when Lizzie died, he became obsessed with finding the baby, probably egged on by Lizzie's brother. Let's hope we can now put Lizzie's crash into perspective. If Trimble was alive, he would face some serious charges. I just hope that Sophie can put all this behind her and start a new life with her father.'

Sergeant Ford said: 'Why did Malik not come back when Lizzie died? I didn't like to ask him.'

'I did,' said the Chief. 'Apparently Trimble called his father in Delhi after the accident and told him that both Lizzie and the baby had died in an accident. Malik was dealing with the death of his mother and coping with his own and father's grief. It seems they went away to their summer place to be alone together. When Lizzie's parents tried to get in touch with him, the messages were never passed on by the staff. Malik never even knew they were calling. He says he was too young and didn't want to bother Lizzie's family. Anyway, he had just lost his mother, and according to information his father received, Lizzie and his daughter had died.'

'How sad, all that confusion and mischief by her brother, and of course his lackey, Trimble, it seems,' said the Sergeant.

The chief said: 'We'll get to the bottom of it. Thankfully it looks like the girl is going to live in New York for a while, best thing in my opinion. It strikes me that Campbell was obsessed with Lizzie his sister and was starting to become obsessed with her daughter. I'm going to Edinburgh tomorrow to tie up the reports and get the post mortem on Trimble.

'I'm asking if the team in Glasgow can focus on finding Mr Campbell's birth family and our financial teams are still searching for the money. I'm asking for resources to make sure the search for Dave Campbell is intensified. He has some very serious questions to answer.'

Sergeant Ford added: 'He certainly has but when you look at all the allegations going round it might be difficult to make anything stick. The only thing is the nasty letters we know came from him but it was a long time ago. We have no evidence that he actually had anything to do with his sister's car crash, only the words of Trimble and he could argue that Trimble was ill and a fantasist, and that he caused the crash all by himself. And we don't know what happened on that cliff, if there was someone else or what. There are no witnesses, the fact he's disappeared with all his money isn't really against the law, although very unfair to his wife.'

Inspector Driver nodded: 'I absolutely agree. I'm calling off the search for any more bodies off the coastline although they are going to keep an eye out on the beaches but I tend to think he got away. If that's the case then I'm sure he'll pop up sooner or later. The important thing is that he doesn't go near Sophie, until we know what his intentions are. I'm going up to Edinburgh later today to meet with her and Malik just to keep them up to date. I'm sure Malik is making sure his daughter is safe.'

Sergeant Ford said: 'Are you going to speak to the music teacher about what happened before Lizzie's accident?'

'Yes, I've arranged for her to come back in to the Edinburgh station. I'm not sure if she can add anything but I still think it's worth chatting to her to see if she remembers anything else, like the name of Campbell's brother. I'll call you tomorrow once I'm settled in. Will you just keep an eye on things here and check up on Tam Mitchell and give him any information about Trimble's death.'

He called Cameron to tell him he would back in Edinburgh that night and planned to come round to Morgan's flat and see Malik and Sophie. Cameron said he would make sure they were in.

When the Inspector arrived in Edinburgh the light was starting to fade as he drew up at the flat in the west end, looking up to see lights in Morgan's flat. He parked and grabbed his briefcase before making his way to the front door. He moved to ring the doorbell when he saw a letter lying at the side of the front door. He peered at the front and read 'For the attention of Sophie Campbell.'

He stepped back and immediately called Cameron. He answered on the first ring: 'Where are you, boss?' he joked.

'I'm outside the flat. I need you to come downstairs and say nothing to Sophie or her dad.'

All Cameron said was: 'Ok.' A moment later he was opening the front door. He saw the chief standing at the bottom of the steps pointing to small letter lying close to the front door.

'It's addressed to Sophie.'

Cameron said: 'What on earth. Who's writing to Sophie, and at this address? What are you going to do?'

The chief said angrily: 'I've had enough of all these letters. I thought about calling the bomb disposal but it's a small letter and I'm hoping you keep an eye on it while I go and get gloves from the car and an evidence bag to put it in. I'm going to take it to the station, not mention it to anyone, and you and I open it. If you let Morgan know what we are doing we can be back at the flat in about half an hour. Morgan can keep everyone else in the lounge. I want to see what it says and then we can see who sent it, if we can find out.'

Cameron disappeared for a few minutes and when he came back, he nodded at the inspector and got in his car.

Within minutes they were back in the police station, neither of them talking until Cameron said: 'Sorry, I'm just a bit shell shocked. I thought this was almost all over. Trimble is dead, we sort of know what has gone on and Uncle Dave is missing, presumed dead or whatever. I know you still have work to do to find the money and the real reason for the crash of Sophie's mum but for Sophie I thought this was all over and she could get on with her life.'

Chief Inspector Driver nodded: 'I know the feeling. But let's see what this says.' With this he took a sharp knife and slid open the envelope. A single sheet of paper fell out, clearly showing a typed message.

He read out: 'Sophie, you never need to worry about your Uncle Dave again. He won't be back.'

They both stared at the paper, trying to work out what it meant.

'We'll send this to forensics but, not sure it will reveal anything, and what the hell does it mean?'

Cameron said: 'I hope you agree but I don't want to say anything to Sophie or her dad till we know who sent this and what's behind it. She seems pretty shaken up by everything and I think she just wants away from Scotland for a while.'

Inspector Driver nodded: 'I agree. I'm going to stay at the office for a while. Can you get a taxi back to the flat?'

Cameron said he would meet the Chief the following morning at the police station to discuss the latest letter. Cameron had only been gone for a few minutes and the chief was sitting staring at the letter when his mobile rang. It was his Sergeant in Stranraer.

'Sergeant Ford, what's wrong at this time of the day?'

'You're not going to believe this boss but we've found Dave Campbell, he's dead and it looks suspicious.'

'My God, where's he been found? Who found him?' He kept firing questions and heard his Sergeant tapping his fingers on the table, listening to the questions.

'Ok,' said the chief. 'I'll let you explain.'

The Sergeant started. 'We'd searched the area on both sides of where Trimble went into the sea and the old castle, including that small cave. Campbell has been found propped up in the same cave wearing a wet suit and with a hole in the suit almost where his heart would be. On first examination they think he's been dead for some time but not killed there, looks like he was moved, and placed there after we searched it. The body is on its way to the pathologist in Edinburgh, they're not even taking the wet suit off. I'm going to interview some people who live near the bay and then join you in Edinburgh.'

'Sergeant, what the hell's going on here? I'm in Edinburgh because we were at Morgan's flat thinking all this was over for that young girl and found a letter lying on the doorstep addressed to Sophie Campbell. I didn't like the fact that someone knew where she was and the message inside is strange. It basically said she didn't need to worry about old Uncle Dave. I was confused and thinking we were still looking for him when you called to say he was dead. The question I have is, was he killed not long after Trimble died?'

'It looks that way, chief, the preliminary examination makes us think he was killed after he got out of the sea, after the fight with Trimble. It's only a couple of bays south of the castle. It looks like he went into the water, swam around the rocks and got out at this bay, and was then killed by person or persons unknown. Someone must have been waiting for him.'

Chief said: 'Get up to Edinburgh as soon as you can and we can discuss all this. We were thinking there were two people on the cliff with Trimble, Uncle Dave and one other. I'm sure it was one his half-brothers from Glasgow helping him out. Perhaps there was more than one. I'm going to tell Sophie and her dad about this new development and the death of her uncle. I'm not sure she'll be very upset. Like her mother I think she was a bit scared of him. I'll see you at the station tomorrow first thing and we should have something from the pathologist by then.'

The chief then called Cameron and told him what had happened.

'Good God, what now?' said Cameron. I've left the flat but I can go back and meet you there if you want to speak to Sophie and her dad. They're all still there chatting about New York and their plans.'

The chief said: 'Yes, let's all go there. I think we should let them know as soon as possible. The letter is with the experts to see if there are any fingerprints but I've taken a copy. I don't know whether to show them or not.

'I need to be here tomorrow morning to see the music teacher who is coming in for a chat. I need to find out if she remembers anything about Dave Campbell's brother from Glasgow. I have a feeling his birth family are involved in this somehow. I'll be round in ten minutes.'

The chief arrived to find Cameron already there and sitting quietly with Morgan and the clearly traumatised young lady and her worried looking father.

'What's happened?' said Malik. 'Cameron wouldn't tell us but we know something has happened. We're getting used to bad news.'

As Morgan handed him a coffee he started to explain. 'When I arrived here tonight, I saw an envelope, addressed to you Sophie, that basically said you did not need to worry about your uncle as he would be not be bothering you again.

'Cameron and I took this to the police station and while it was being examined, I got a call from Sergeant Ford in Stranraer to say a body, believed to be that of your uncle, has been found in a cave on a bay close to the castle.'

Sophie looked shaken and said: 'What on earth is going on? Who hates my family so much with all this killing?'

Chief inspector Driver looked at Cameron and nodded: 'Sophie, I can tell you what I think just now but our investigation is still ongoing. I'll start with your mother's crash which is where all this started. We know your uncle resented or was a bit obsessed by your mother. He befriended Trimble, the security man, and I think because Uncle Dave had been in the army, he was able to make Trimble do things or suggest things he wanted him to do.

'Therefore, I think, or I know, it was your uncle who suggested to Trimble to follow your mother and to cause an incident pretending that he could go to her rescue. What Trimble did not know and never questioned was how the uncle knew where Lizzie Campbell would be, and that he had arranged for someone else to tamper with Lizzie's car to ensure that it crashed with the dreadful consequences it had. Dave Campbell, I believe, was behind it all.

'Now, move forward to the Rev and his wife. We now think it was Dave again paying Trimble to find you and, whether he had anything to do with the deaths or not, we don't know. It could just have been Trimble.

'But we do now suspect it was Dave Campbell, and another, who killed Trimble on the cliff that day. They probably didn't want him to talk but they didn't know he'd left evidence that shows the link between him and Dave Campbell.

'It now looks like Dave Campbell got into a wet suit after Trimble was pushed and swam round to another bay. He must have planned to get away but something went wrong and he was killed. My bet is that he fell out with his birth family, probably over money as he must have been paying them to help. We suspect it was one of his brothers on the cliff with him when Trimble was disposed of. That's where we are now but I want you to know I don't think you are in any danger. To be on the safe side keep staying here and a policeman will be at the front door all night.'

Malik said: 'I'm staying here tonight as well. I'm not leaving Sophie. Is that ok Morgan?'

They could all see the tears slowly running down Sophie's face as she sat on the couch. Her voice was shaky as she said: 'So much hate, when will it stop?'

Malik said: 'It will stop Sophie. I hope that when we get to America you can look forward and come to terms with the past.'

'I know that dad but I feel I have lost touch with the people who could have explained to me what happened and why they did things, like finding out why uncle Dave disliked my mum so much, asking the Rev and my other mum why they didn't call an ambulance when they found me in the crashed car. I believe if they had been good people the first thing they would have done is get help for my mother and not just take me and leave. It sounds too cruel.'

The chief nodded: 'We might never know what drove them to take these actions but jealousy from the brother of Lizzie and an overwhelming desire to have a child drove what were on the surface respectable and godly people to take a baby.'

He looked at Cameron and nodded at him to leave the room. They both got up and signalled to Morgan to follow them.

'I didn't want to go into details as I think the girl is upset enough but Dave Campbell's body is in the city. Tomorrow morning his wife is coming in to formally identify him. I'm going to have to explain to her that we haven't found the missing money but we won't give up. Then the music lecturer, Lizzie's old friend, is coming in. Sergeant Ford will sit in on the interview but I'd like you there as well Cameron. She knows you.

'Morgan, appreciate you keeping an eye on Sophie and her dad, and providing them with somewhere they feel safe. Just in case, a police presence will be outside your flat for the next few days until we work out who was at your house delivering notes that proved only too true. It all seemed too planned and I need to get to the bottom of it.'

Morgan said: 'Of course, but who do you think it could be? If, Trimble is dead and now Dave Campbell, there must have been other people involved. I think that's what's scaring Sophie and her father. I think they want to get away from here as soon as possible. He's worried about her, not unsurprisingly.'

Cameron said: 'Yes, he's very determined to get her to

New York and allow her to concentrate on her music and studies, and not suffer the hounding like her mother. He really wants her to have people around her that care and for that reason I've agreed to go out. She's hoping Morgan is going to be there as well.'

'It looks like I will be, probably in about a month or so, if all goes to plan. I think Max and I will be selling this place as it looks like he's not coming back to live in Edinburgh.'

Inspector Driver said: 'I hope we can all move forward. I just want to get the bottom of all this and I'm hoping the music lady tomorrow can fill in the holes. We have the post mortem from Trimble and the finding reinforces my belief that there were three people on the cliff that day, Trimble and his two killers. They think he was talking to Dave Campbell when someone hit on the back of the head. It would take two strong men to throw him over the cliff.'

'Any news on Dave Campbell's post mortem?' said Cameron.

'Not yet, but pretty obvious he was shot through the heart. It looks like he got out of the sea, met someone, someone he had probably arranged to meet, and things went wrong and he was shot. Who then dropped the letter off here telling Sophie not to worry about Uncle Dave again? They knew something we didn't.'

Cameron stood up and said: 'I'm just going to see Sophie and Malik. In light of what is happening is there any problem with them getting flights booked to New York?'

The inspector nodded and said: 'Actually I would be happier if they were away now. I'm worried that someone knows where Sophie is staying and I want to find out who it is. With Trimble and Uncle Dave out of the picture my priority is to find who else is involved. Obviously, I have my suspicions that it's to do with Uncle Dave's birth family in Glasgow and a major falling out.'

Cameron said: 'I agree. It's worrying. I plan to leave a week after Malik and Sophie but I am always available to keep you up to date with what's happening in New York. You don't seriously think other people are interested in Sophie, do you?'

'No, but I'm not taking any chances. I'm hoping this music teacher can give me some background on Dave Campbell in the morning. I've also asked his wife to come in later for a chat after she has formally identified her husband.'

Cameron and Morgan left the chief in the kitchen as they went back to see Sophie and her dad.

As they entered the lounge Malik looked up and said: 'I think we will make flight arrangements tomorrow morning, if that is all right with everyone. There is nothing to keep us here and I need to get back to work. Sophie needs to get away from all this for a while, concentrate on her music and studies, and getting to know me and her heritage. I'm hoping you, Cameron, will be able to join us next week. I know Sophie will be glad if you're there and she's also hoping that Morgan will be too.'

The chief popped his head round the door to say he was away to his hotel. He asked Cameron if he would meet him at the police station about 8a.m in the morning. Cameron nodded.

The next morning when music teacher Rosie Murray, old friend of Lizzie Campbell, was shown into the interview room at the police station, both the chief inspector and Cameron were shocked at the change in her. She looked haunted and had obviously been crying a lot with swollen and red eyes.

The chief spoke first: 'Thank you so much for coming

in to speak to us. Really, it's just to clear up a few things. Do you want to explain to me what you said to my sergeant?

'I want to say first that I always loved Lizzie and would never have done anything to hurt her. When she was found dead, I was just so upset and missed her so much but I never imagined that I might have been partly responsible for her death. It was only when Cameron and Morgan came to see me about her daughter being found, and then you told me that you were investigating how Lizzie's killer knew where she was. It was then I realised I might have told Dave Campbell. It all came back to me, him asking where she was going and where she was staying. I was so infatuated by him that I told him, despite Lizzie asking me not to say anything to anyone. I never thought she meant her own brother, but I was obviously wrong.'

The chief said: 'I'm not sure you can take all this on your shoulders. Her brother was intent, with the help of the hapless Trimble, to do his sister harm. If it hadn't been that accident up north, I'm sure he would have found another way. Do you remember the circumstances of you telling him?'

She nodded: 'Better than that I kept a diary in those days. But I remember it well. Our affair had been going on for several months, when he arrived to take me out for the day on Loch Lomond, to ply me with champagne and tell me he was getting married. I was devastated as I thought I was in love with him. I was young and foolish. I remember when we were having lunch overlooking the loch a man joined us. Dave introduced him as his brother from Glasgow that he had just met again since childhood. This man joined us and if I remember correctly, he was there when Dave asked me where Lizzie was going that week.'

Cameron said: 'So this brother knew where Lizzie was going. You don't remember his name, do you?'

She nodded: 'Yes, I do and I have evidence of that meeting all those years ago. I kept a diary when I was a child up to the age of 25. I searched my attic for several days and found the one with the note about the meeting. I brought it here today. His name was Tim or Timmy Torbet and he came from Glasgow's east end and owned a garage. I hope this can to make up for what I inadvertently did to my friend.'

The chief looked more animated than Cameron had ever seen him: 'Did you bring the diary today?'

Rosie Murray pulled a tattered book out of her bag and laid it on the desk. The date matched the year Lizzie was killed.

'Thanks. Could you leave this with us for a few days? You have been very helpful and may I say, you don't need to feel guilty. The people who did Lizzie harm are Trimble and her brother and perhaps another person. It was not you.'

When Rosie left the chief immediately opened the diary at March. He read in silence for a few minutes and then looked up and said: 'Listen to this Cameron.'

He read: David is taking me for lunch at Loch Lomond. So excited, he said to dress up and champagne to celebrate our six month anniversary. He loves me, I know he does, he must.'

The chief stopped and said: 'The next entry is better.'

He started reading: 'David booked a room at the hotel and we made love all night, he's so romantic. The next morning at breakfast his brother arrived to join us. I didn't really like him, Tim Torbet, Dave called him just TT, and he kept asking questions. He kept asking about me, about music school and about Lizzie and where she was. Dave then started asking me about her trip and I told them where she was staying in Inverness. I'm sure she won't mind, it's her brother.'

The chief stopped speaking and looked at Cameron: 'Bloody hell, no wonder that girl is feeling guilty. She must feel she betrayed her best friend now she knows that whoever knew where Lizzie's car was parked in Inverness meant her harm.'

Cameron nodded: 'But she was young and infatuated, if not in love with Dave Campbell, who by my reckoning was due to get married to Amanda the following month. He was a nice piece of work, wasn't he? More importantly there is something about this brother's name that is going round and round in my brain thinking back to my memories of my Met days. Something about those initials rings a bell. I'm going to get a coffee and go for a walk to think.'

The chief looked distracted, and waved him away: 'Whatever. I'm going to ask my counterparts in Glasgow to start looking into this Torbet family. We need their DNA to confirm if they are related to Dave Campbell.'

As Cameron left the room the chief reached for the file containing the report on Lizzie Campbell's accident, lying on his desk.

An hour later when Cameron returned the chief was still poring over the reports. He looked up and said: 'I think two people tampered with the car outside the bed and breakfast. One was Trimble, and as the report says one of the tyres was interfered with, which would probably have resulted in a flat tyre and a need for Lizzie to come to a halt, Trimble to ride to the rescue and change the tyre. But someone else, and my money is on the car mechanic from Glasgow, tampered with the brakes so the car would always move to the left. They cannot confirm exactly what was done but they firmly believe it caused Lizzie to crash.

'I think Dave Campbell manipulated Trimble to such an extent he believed everything he said. He actually believed he could come to the rescue of Lizzie and win her affection. Deluded or what? Sad bastard.'

Cameron nodded: 'Listen I'm going back to Morgan's flat to see Malik and Sophie as they called to say they are leaving for New York early tomorrow morning. Malik indicated he just wanted Sophie away from all this sadness. Morgan thinks she will be following them in about a month and I plan to go in a week.

'I think you are spot on with your interpretation of everything. I phoned a couple of mates in London to see if they remember anything about this Tim Torbet? They do but they called him just TT from Glasgow. It seems the family own a garage in Kirkintilloch, suspicions that it has been used for moving money around. There are three brothers involved, probably all related to Campbell but its TT, the youngest, who has the reputation of a "fixer", a man you go to when you have a problem that needs fixed, and that could involve violence.'

The chief said: 'I've asked our Glasgow team to have a look for Mr Torbet so we can have a word with him. They plan to visit the garage tomorrow morning so I'll let you know what transpires. Away now and see Malik and Sophie and wish them a safe journey. Tell them I'll keep them updated. I've Campbell's wife Amanda coming in later for a chat so I'll you know what she says.'

When Cameron got back to the flat Malik had gone and Sophie and Morgan were in the lounge.

Cameron said: 'How are things going?'

Sophie said: 'Dad's at his hotel making arrangements. We're leaving tomorrow morning for London and then onto New York. He's not wanting people to know how we are travelling. Do you know now who killed my mum?'

Cameron nodded and said: 'I'm sure the Inspector will be here later today but we know Trimble was involved in the accident that killed your mother, but we also think that a relative of your uncle was involved as well and tampered with the car causing it to crash.'

Sophie said: 'My poor Mum, she seems to have had people obsessed with her and yet she only loved Dad and me. She didn't stand a chance. Uncle Dave must have hated her to be involved in her death. I've been so scared. I just want away for a while to concentrate on my music and come to terms with all we have found out.'

Morgan said: 'Your mum was a very beautiful and talented woman, Sophie, and they can often attract people with problems. Trimble obviously harboured something for her and it led to him being manipulated to do something he regretted.'

Cameron said: 'Let's not forget he tampered with her car, killed his own mother and killed the Rev and his wife and the Rev's brother. He was a deeply troubled man but dangerous as well. He never forgot seeing the Rev and his wife taking you from that crash Sophie and when he met them on that cliff, he dealt his own justice.'

Sophie said: 'I understand all that but I know Uncle Dave was behind it a lot of it, a much more malevolent presence in my mother's life.'

Cameron said: 'We're still finding out about him. But I suspect your grandparents came to understand there was something wrong. When they adopted him, they knew little of his background, only that his mother could not look after him, but they came to understand there was a darkness about him.'

Sophie said: 'I'm glad he's dead, although he was only person who could tell me what my mother was like, growing up. I feel I'm chasing a shadow and I need away to find my own path in life.'

Back at the station the chief was waiting for Campbell's

widow Amanda to arrive. She was coming straight from the mortuary after identifying her husband.

When she was shown in the chief hardly recognised her. Gone was the frumpy woman with mousy brown hair, and a sallow complexion. This was a glamorous, blonde confident woman holding out her hand to introduce herself.

'You look shocked, Inspector,' said Amanda Campbell.

Chief Inspector Driver shuffled his papers to give him time to come up with an answer.

He said: 'I assume everything was ok at the morgue?'

'Yes, it was a relief to see him there. I didn't believe he was dead until I saw him. Before you ask, I don't feel anything. In fact, I'm relieved he's dead. He wasn't a very nice man.'

The Chief said: 'Tell me Mrs Campbell, what was it like?'

She waited until a cup of coffee was placed in front of her and said: 'He was always very controlling and constantly criticising me, and pretty mean. I had no idea he had all that money until it went missing. He never discussed money with me and I never even knew his parents left him several million.'

The chief said: 'What was it like when you got married?'

Mrs Campbell laughed: 'It was pretty low key. I knew he was seeing other women before we got married but whenever I raised it, he just said I was being paranoid, he was always right and spent his time making me feel useless. He was a good looking, charming man but hid a dark side.

'Did you get on with your sister-in-law, Lizzie?'

'She was lovely and sweet but she didn't come to our flat very much. She never talked about her life in Edinburgh.

'It took me a while but I came to realise that Dave was obsessed with Lizzie. He wanted to know everything about her, and what she was doing. He had a basement in our last house and I was never allowed in there. Now I've seen inside it was full of pictures of Lizzie and of Sophie. I knew he was becoming obsessed with her as well. I think he was sick.'

The chief said: 'Did any of his business friends or family visit at your home?'

'In the early days his parents, the people who brought him up, used to come for Sunday lunch and we went there. In fact, it was mainly at their home in Ayrshire that I saw Lizzie.

'I once went to his legal office in Glasgow and met that man Trimble there. It seemed like he went there quite a lot. I also met his birth family at the office. He never invited them to our home. Dave said he didn't want them to see he'd money. They looked a bit rough to me but they were polite and, I think, ran a business. They treated Dave as a bit of an outsider.'

The chief said: 'That's useful Mrs Campbell. Now our teams are still trying to trace your husband's money but I assume you are staying with friends?'

'No,' she said, 'I'm back in our house. The strangest thing happened, the day I heard that Dave's body had been found. A million pounds was put back into my bank account and the bank think it's part of the original stolen money. He also made sure the house would be left to me, if he died, so I have something to be grateful to him for. He must have had some conscience. I will be comfortable and intend to enjoy life. I have his funeral and then I leave for a cruise.'

The chief said: 'You sound like you have everything sorted. Because of the news about the return of some of the money then I need you give us a statement and talk to one of our financial experts. We need to establish who returned the money to you.'

She laughed: 'I hope you don't mind but I simply don't care. It's my money now. I don't think Dave ever loved me and the marriage wasn't happy. I intend to be happy now.'

The chief smiled and said: 'I'm happy for you Mrs Campbell but our teams will still need to chat to you. We're still looking for the bulk of the money and who has taken it. Someone will be in touch.'

When she left the chief sat quietly thinking over the last few days. Then he put in the calls to his teams in Glasgow looking for the Torbet family.

An hour later he had Cameron and his Sergeant sitting in his office.

'Well guys I thought I would update you. It seems that Tim Torbet or TT, as he is known, has left the country. The garage was closed down in the last few days and the family, still living in Glasgow, won't say where their brother has gone. We've obviously put an alert out for Torbet as a person of interest in a murder inquiry.

'Our financial people are also still trying to find the rest of money. We know from his widow that a million pounds has been returned. My thinking is there was a falling out between Campbell and his birth family. Perhaps he didn't want to pay his brother for the help he got in dealing with Trimble and they killed him and stole his money. Why they returned some of it to the widow, we might never know, some sense of doing her right after her husband stole all of it.'

Cameron said: 'I think you're right. Sophie and her dad are leaving early tomorrow. Do you think she's safe?'

Sergeant Ford said: 'She must be. Anyone who wished her mother or Sophie harm is dead.'

The chief shook his head: 'With this family I would not be too sure. I'm pleased you are going to be with them in New York for a while as I can keep in touch with you about the elusive Mr Torbet and the missing money.'

Cameron looked at both of the police officers and said: 'I agree a bit with both of you. I'm not sure what Campbell's family would want with a young girl. Surely, they have Campbell's money and have washed their hands of Trimble and Campbell and what happened all those years ago on that quiet road in the Highlands. Malik thinks Sophie is having nightmares about it all but won't talk about it. He hasn't told her yet but when they get to New York and spend a quiet week settling her into the flat and he can check in with work, he has booked two weeks in Mauritius and I'm going to fly there straight from London to join them. He wants her to relax and spend time with him. It seems she's finding all this a bit too much to handle and doesn't even want to play her violin.'

The chief nodded: 'She's lost so much and yet found something that will sustain her in the future. We must always remember, that while we have criticism of the Rev and his wife for taking that child and not calling for help for the mother, they did raise her as their daughter with some values and love. She is also grieving the mother she never knew but inherited her talent for music. Now she has found her father I hope she can come to terms with all she has been through and build a relationship with her father and his family. She also has both you and Morgan as friends. Now you, I understand why you don't want to become a police officer again or work in Stranraer. I slightly envy you a break in the sunshine but, really, I just want to get back to Stranraer, to my wife and family.'

Cameron smiled and said: 'Very funny chief. I'm not turning my back on my future with the police but I just need a break. I've actually enjoyed being part of this investigation. I feel I want to stay with Sophie and make sure she's all right. I'm going to the airport tomorrow to see them off on their flight to London. I fly out a week later so can still help out here if needed. It might be nice if you came to the airport too. She trusts you and is very grateful for all the help.'

The chief said: 'Malik actually contacted me earlier to say he would like if I would come so I said yes. I'll see you all at the airport at 8a.m. Now I think we all need some sleep. After they leave tomorrow, I'm going back to lovely Galloway to get my life back and have a holiday. Then I will be back in the thick of things and this investigation is not over.'

The next morning there was no sense of excitement about an impending flight. They looked a sombre crew as Cameron, Morgan and the inspector stood in the lounge with Sophie and her dad.

Sophie hugged both Morgan and Cameron, tears in her eyes, as she turned to the chief inspector and said: 'Promise me, you will find the man who really murdered my mother.'

The chief inspector looked tearful himself and could not bring himself to speak. He just nodded.

They both waved as they went through the gate to a new life for the girl who was first Rebecca and is now rightly Sophie.

Ends

ACKNOWLEDGEMENTS

There are so many people I want to thank who have encouraged me to return to my first love of creative writing.

To my husband Bruce whose love has been my constant for more than 30 years.

To my sister Rosie who, like our parents, supported me throughout my life.

To Brenda and Ian for their support.

To my friends, firstly Anna Smith, journalist and veteran crime writer, who has always encouraged me. Thank you.

o all my girlfriends, Babs, Jan, Louise, Carole, Annie, Donna, Pauline, Lucy, and top journalist Patricia.

laine and Ken for all their support and help

My thanks to editor Sally Orson-Jones, based in lovely righton who helped me find my voice.

nd to designer Heather Macpherson who worked her magic to help me publish.

Helen Murray McKain

A journalist for more than 30 years I have worked in the north of England, covering major stories before moving to Glasgow to work on the Glasgow Evening Times and the Herald in Edinburgh.

I then spent more than ten years in corporate communications.

From the age of 16 I knew I wanted to be a journalist and tell the stories of people, who often have no voice.

Printed in Great Britain
by Amazon

36810546R00169